The author was born in Bradford and now lives in East Yorkshire with her husband and their two married children living nearby.

Qualified as a graduate teacher she has worked from Bank clerk to college Lecturer and finally a Television Extra.

In 1996 she took up writing full time and has had various articles published in a variety of magazines. Her first novel in print is Eleanor.

DREAMS OR REALITY

Laura, a teenager in the 1960s, thought she knew it all in the permissive society. Married very young, she is soon disillusioned, she has three children in quick sucession and suffers physical abuse in the marriage. She develops into a person in her own right and believes that material possessions are now the most important thing in her life in order for her to attain happiness. Although she achieves the possessions, her world still collapses around her, so she must finally make the important decision as to where her loyalties lie. Whatever she decides will have a tremendous impact on her future.

SUSAN SHAW

DREAMS
OR
REALITY

Complete and Unabridged

ULVERSCROFT
Leicester

First published in Great Britain in 2004 by
Authors Online Limited
Hertford

First Large Print Edition
published 2005

British Library CIP Data

Shaw, Susan
Dreams or reality.—Large print ed.—
Ulverscroft large print series: general fiction
1. Marriage—Fiction 2. Acquisitiveness—Fiction
3. Large type books
I. Title
823.9′2 [F]

LP

ISBN 1–84617–097–4

Published by
F. A. Thorpe (Publishing)
Anstey, Leicestershire
Set by Words & Graphics Ltd.
Anstey, Leicestershire
Printed and bound in Great Britain by
T. J. International Ltd., Padstow, Cornwall

This book is printed on acid-free paper

To my husband who encouraged
me to continue.

I would also like to express my gratitude
to my friend Carol Hancock who gave
me her time and help.

1

It slowly dawned on Laura that she'd arrived. Where had the journey gone? She'd been so pre-occupied with her own thoughts that she'd never noticed the miles ticking away. She was glad to see the building appeared just the same from the outside.

Taking a deep sigh she braced herself to go in. She gave a slight jump of shock as she saw how different it was when she entered the building. A young man came up to her. 'Can I help you?'

Once more taken aback as this wasn't the person she was expecting she stammered, 'Er, yes I've a room booked.'

'What name please?'

'Oh, Mrs. Watson.'

'Fine, this way please and I'll show you your room.'

Laura carried on looking around as she went. This wasn't what she'd imagined at all. She'd thought the pace of life was so slow here that everything would be just the same as it was all those years ago, hoping some familiarity would help with the decisions she had to make.

'Here we are then,' said the voice again. 'Is this all right for you?'

'Oh, fine thanks.'

'Okay, I'll leave you then. Don't hesitate to ring down if there's anything you need. Breakfast is between seven thirty and ten.'

'There is just one thing. Can I have a packed lunch tomorrow?'

'No problem, I'll organize that for you. Just pick it up at breakfast.'

'Thanks.'

Laura quickly unpacked the few things she'd brought with her, then she sat in a chair looking out of the window. Her thoughts quickly retraced back to those distant years ago when it had all begun.

Now she thought back ruefully over the many mistakes she'd made with her life. How in the sixties and as a young teenager she had imagined she knew so much. It was supposed to be the start of the permissive age, but how naive they all really had been. She knew she needed to think back and learn from these mistakes, if she was to make the right decision now, to move forward for any possible future.

Laura had been one of the lucky ones and passed her eleven plus and gone on to Grammar School. People who didn't go there thought you were posh if you did. Of course, that was not true at all. Her parents were just working class people. They lived in a terraced house, but both her mum and dad had to work hard to get the things they wanted. Like most people of their generation they didn't even have a car.

Some of the girls in her year did come from better off families, but that made no difference to what class you went into at the school. If you were really bright and could do well with languages, you were in the top group and were allowed to study German and French. All the other three classes in the year were supposed to be of equal ability. When Laura looked down at the school picture she'd brought with her, she realized what an odd assortment they must have looked. In those days each thought they were trendy even though a strict school uniform had to be worn. By trying to just do something different they thought they were getting away from the uniformity. What a laugh! Now when Laura looked at the picture they all looked little innocents. Far different to what they felt and thought they were.

There was Anne, the tiny one who looked rather like a dwarf. Katherine next, the prim one, yet according to recent accounts she'd gone on to be a real family person. Then Eileen, who looked so out of place towering above the others, although as a teenager today she would not be such an unusual sight. How tall they all seemed to grow now. Many of those faces looked so pure, yet within their innocence they'd tried to be grown up.

The lack of knowledge regarding sex made them try things that many of today's teenagers wouldn't dream of needing to do because they were informed of the consequences. If Laura had thought her own daughters had got up to what her and her friends had, she would have been incensed, yet it seemed acceptable when she did it.

Every morning at school each would ask the other, 'What did you get up to last night?' It became a challenge for each one to try to beat the other in what they replied.

At fifteen Laura knew she wasn't that much to look at. She was small but rather big busted like her mother, top heavy for her age. Maybe this was what attracted the boys. She seemed to have more boyfriends than some of the, what she considered were, more attractive girls. The others in her class were rather envious of her mature boyfriend, because he was nineteen. So the game continued, the more they questioned each other the more Laura liked to say what she had got up to with Peter.

Her mother and father were quite openly affectionate with each other so this gave her ideas what to say. One particular incident had always stayed in her mind, because it had created the most impact, as she knew it would. Her mother had been in the bath the night before. Her father had teased her mother and asked, 'Is the bath big enough for two? I think I'll join you.' Then with a twinkle in his eye he had gone on to say, 'We can have some fun and games.'

Seeing the children standing there with mouths wide open listening in amazement her mother had quickly replied, 'I hardly think so.' Her father had just burst into fits of laughter at all the expressions on their faces.

But this had given Laura the idea when once again the question was asked, 'Did you go any further with your boyfriend last night or did you do it?'

There seemed to be some shame in answering, 'I didn't do it.' To admit to being a virgin was a disgrace. What fools they all were. Now Laura was sure many girls, like herself, did make things up just to keep in with the crowd. Probably in truth all of them or at least most of them were still virgins, but had the sense not to admit it in case of ridicule from the others. The ones who admitted to being virgins were shunned or laughed at as some kind of freak.

Laura always did have a vivid imagination so she liked to make it sound as good as she could. Therefore after hearing her father on about the bath it set her mind in motion. When the question was asked she was quick to jump in with, 'We had fun and games last night.'

A chorus of voices quickly exclaimed and asked, 'Oh! What did you get up to then?'

Smiling as much as to say 'I know it all now,' Laura looked around at them and simply said, 'We had a bath together.'

Various voices chirped up excitedly, 'A bath together?'

'That's what I said.'

Eager to hear more now their appetites had been whetted they begged, 'Come on tell more, you can't say that much without going into full details.'

One excited voice asked, 'But where were your parents whilst this went on?'

'They were out with my brother visiting our Grandma. They thought I was around at Pete's house, but I have a key so we sneaked back.'

That part of the story was true. They had gone back together to Laura's house, but they had only watched telly with an odd kiss sneaked in-between.

Still wanting to hear more another voice piped up. 'Come on, get on with the story, otherwise it will be time to go into class before you've told it. I can't wait until break to hear more.'

Imagination running riot Laura carried on. 'Well it was like this you see - I said I didn't want Pete to leave too late as I wanted to get a bath. He said why wait, I could have my bath whilst he was there. At first I didn't cotton on to what he meant. Once I'd said he might be bored waiting for me, I saw the gleam in his eyes when he said he wouldn't mind in the least. I knew what he meant then. I must admit at first I said, 'Dare we?' but once he had given me a passionate kiss or two I soon lost any fear. It was great. We touched each other's body and rubbed soap up and down.' In a sensual voice she added, 'Oh yes! I can still feel his hands.'

A few voices clamoured together to ask, 'But did you?'

Laura knew what they meant but felt she had given them enough excitement for one day.

'No, that was enough, but we were close I can tell you. We were worried my parents would come back early so it only went as far as that.'

Laura had just finished her tale as the bell

rang for first class so there was no more time for anybody else to question her further. She was rather relieved at that. It was alright telling the tale but she didn't like too much questioning and probing into the details.

Now to Laura it seemed strange what one's mind held in the memory. Even more so when she remembered them all clubbing together to give one of the girl's boyfriends money so he would take them for a ride on his motorbike. They would take it in turns to have a ride around the block with him, in their lunch break. How exciting they all found it. Yet now when Laura thought about it she realized how dangerous it had been. You didn't have to wear a crash helmet in those days, and each one would egg him on to go as fast as he could with the words. 'Come on. Is this the fastest the bike will go?'

'No, hang on tight,' and he would accelerate away.

Maturity made Laura understand how as one got to know people better one's attitude to them could change. This now brought her thoughts to Sally. When they had first started the Grammar School, most of the girls in her class had thought Sally rather a snob. She did come from a slightly better off family and her father had a Rover car. As an only child she tended to get most things she wanted. Laura now understood that the thing she had really sought was companionship. She realized belatedly that Sally bragging she owned possessions was not snobbery at all but trying to seek the attention of the other girls in order to win friendship. Laura gave a shudder as she thought back to how cruel they had been to her at times. They used to mock what she said. 'What's your Father bought you this week then?'

'Oh, a tape recorder.'

Because she hadn't many friends she didn't go out so often. Every once in a while they relented and took her with them. That was how Sally met her future husband. It's funny how things had worked out. She was the one who'd stayed happily married. They'd no need to mock her after all - she was most probably the sensible one.

They were all quite envious of Darren, Sally's new boyfriend. He was older and had a car. Not that they let Sally know they were envious. They didn't want her to think she had something special. How mean they all were. Yet they were all more than willing to accept a lift with them when the opportunity arose. Laura gave a chuckle to herself as she thought of the lunch times they used to sit in his car for a chat. As many of them as could would squeeze in. The only problem was it misted the windows up. One day they were all laughing and chatting away when a sudden tap at the car window could be heard and a sharp voice asked, 'What are you up to in there? Wipe those windows so I can see in.'

Laura could remember it was she who cleared a tiny spot to see who it was. 'It's Miss Shields,' she said quickly. With no more ado Darren started the car engine and moved the car leaving the teacher standing where she was, with mouth wide open, looking after them in bewilderment. They all knew Miss Shields. They thought she was not quite right in the head. She was the biology teacher, so maybe it was something to do with that, or maybe it was as rumour would have it she had been let down at the altar twice. Whatever, none of them wanted to get into an argument with her. Again, Laura laughed to herself as she thought back and wondered what she had really imagined could have been going on in the car with so many bodies in it.

Now she thought about all of the girls different looks. There were some who looked as if they would develop into pretty young ladies. The problem was, as was the fashion at that time, a lot of them had long hair in a rather shaggy hang dog style, covering most of their faces. This did not go down well at school. Laura remembered the day the Head

Mistress had tried to embarrass them all. Being the high spirited girls they were it didn't work out that way. At that age it was easy to turn things around into a joke. A few girls were picked to set an example to the rest of the school. For some reason, Laura had to admit to herself, she always seemed to be one of those girls. They had to tie their hair into pigtails and sit on the hall floor for all to see. All they did the whole time was giggle. The staff were not well pleased with the attitude taken to the reprimand. Maybe it was at that time the teachers decided to write her off as an education failure.

2

Laura awoke feeling amazingly refreshed and ready for the day she'd planned. As soon as she went into the dining room for breakfast a friendly young woman came up to her. 'Do you want to sit at this table by the window for your breakfast?'

'Yes, fine thanks. Oh! I've got a packed lunch ordered.'

'I'll get it for you after you've eaten your breakfast. I hope you had a good night.'

'I did and I feel full of energy now for a day's walking.'

'Do you know where you plan to go?'

'Oh yes, I've done the walk before. Mind you, that was a number of years ago now. We stayed here then, but I think it was different people running this place.'

'Most probably, my Mum and Dad only took it over a couple of years ago.'

'It would be then.'

'Help yourself to starters and I'll just go and get your drink. What do you want, tea or coffee?'

'Tea please.'

After stoking herself up with a typical

English breakfast Laura prepared herself for the day's walk. She'd a lot of thinking to do and didn't want anything to distract her. Once she was on her way on the path that still looked familiar after all these years, she let her mind wander back to the past once again.

When it had become time for the all important exams, Laura could at last now admit to herself, that she put no effort whatsoever into them. At sixteen she had asked herself what was the point and there hadn't seemed to be any. Her parents tried to push her to stay in and revise and if anything that had made her worse. Her father would say to her, 'What do you want to do with your life?'

The only thing she could answer was, 'Leave school as quickly as possible.'

Her father would try to impress on her, 'Yes, but if you pass your exams you then have the pick of what you want to do.'

None of this made any impression on Laura. Boys were far more important than exams. She remembered it must have been about that time she met Keith. Now it seemed alien to her nature to think she was attracted to a boy younger than herself. When she said to herself he was fifteen and only just at that, it now sounded as if she was going out with a child. At the time she didn't think so. He seemed so mature for his age. For someone so young he had seemed knowledgeable on sexual matters.

She could remember one way or another she used to manage to go out every night. Her father would say to her, 'I think you should stay in tonight to do some revision,' but Laura would quickly answer with tongue in cheek, 'Oh, I did some at school, we have plenty of time to revise.'

In honesty she could remember they had been allowed time to revise but as she recalled she didn't think many books were actually opened and any studying done. Revision time meant chat time.

Not all the girls were like that. There was one she could remember, Sharon, who was a real swot. She never went out. As soon as she arrived home from school, out the books would come and revision would start. She had never had a boyfriend and was very frumpish in her appearance. She had long hair which she usually wore in a single plait down her back. By now they had all heard of the word Lesbian and its implications. Because of Sharon's lack of interest in boys it seemed a good idea to label her one. Laura remembered how very adept they became at making sly remarks if she came too close to them. Now Laura could only think how cruel they had been and she now had a great deal of sympathy with her for what they must have made her life like. She never did see her again after leaving school but she did hear, that she had indeed succeeded and passed to go to university and also that she had a boyfriend. Laura suddenly thought how interesting it would be to know where she had got to in life and whether she had actually achieved anything. For all the mockery of her, whilst they were at school, maybe she had been the sensible one and really knew what life had in store for them.

As Laura had told her parents all along she was going to leave school and get a job in a bank. So the applications went in and the interviews had to be endured. To give her parents credit Laura had to admit they did help her with this. She could still remember clearly one of the interviews was in a large city branch some distance from where she lived. Her father went with her to give her moral support. In the sixties jobs were easy to get. She had four interviews and was offered all four jobs and that was even before they knew the exam results, despite there being supposedly a minimum requirement of qualification.

It was decision time, which job to accept. It was really a case of sticking a pin in the names and saying she would work for that bank. As far as Laura could tell, with her limited knowledge, there wasn't anything to chose between them.

Then the all important exam time came. This did give Laura a few qualms when she knew she had barely picked a book up to revise. To her, when the results came out they were not as disappointing as they could have been. She had passed what she needed for the bank, despite the fact they had offered her the job without the results. She had been pleased but now she remembered her parents had been very disappointed in her.

Her father's comments still stuck in her mind. 'If you passed those without any effort, imagine what you could have passed had you done any real work and revision.'

Maybe she could have but the time wasn't right then for her to do it. Anyway, she had achieved something, she had got a job in a bank, that was surely a decent enough job.

The last day at school was still fresh in Laura's mind despite the passing of the years. Of course, a lot of the girls were moving on to the sixth form, but by some fate hers seemed to be the class where most of the girls were leaving. Great, to be leaving. Out into that world where they were allowed to meet boys. Although the boys' Grammar School was part of their building, there was a locked door that kept them separate. The playground was split in two by a high stone wall. Of course this hadn't deterred them from talking to each other over the top of it. Laura couldn't help but laugh out aloud when she thought about the trips to the art class. They had to go through the boys' school. Not alone, of course, but as a whole class chaperoned by the teacher. Still, it was the highlight of the week, as they cast their eyes one way and another in a then vain hope of seeing a male person. Funny, but they had allowed male teachers in the female school. But there again none of them could have been younger than fifty.

But the last day at school offered freedom from this. No more navy tunic and white socks because it was not until you were in the sixth form that you were allowed to wear nylon stockings. This didn't stop them wearing them under the white socks and removing the offending socks as soon as they were away from school. Oh, yes! They had it all down to a fine art how to keep within the school uniform rules yet alter their appearance as soon as they were away from the school. Laura shuddered as she thought about those horrible cherry coloured berets they were supposed to wear. For some reason since school she had always had a hatred for navy or deep pink clothing. It must have been a legacy from her school days.

Then they had realized — no more homework or the pretence of doing it once they had left school. Seven evenings a week free to do what they wanted! Not only that but the money to do it with. She would be earning proper money.

Laura's mind went back to her work life. She now appreciated how easy it had been to find a Saturday job when she was in her teens. She had been lucky and found a job at a local drapers, so she hadn't even the expense of bus fares out of her wages. It had been quite a laugh there. Much of Laura's grown up attitudes had been learnt from watching the behaviour of what she considered the mature young ladies working there at that time. Once she started work in the bank she had to leave her part time job, as she was required to work most Saturday mornings at a sub-branch.

But that final day of leaving school was all cheers and laughter for Laura. Many of the girls were in tears at leaving, some hugging each other in sympathy. The more Laura saw this the more her heart soared and she laughed. It was like a huge weight had been lifted from her, the thought of this new found freedom. Never again in her life did she feel so elated. She didn't know why or what she was moving forward to. It didn't matter, she was free from school. As she went through the school gates she let out a loud cry, 'I'm free, at last I'm really free.'

She couldn't help but smile to herself now at the thought of this naivety. How silly she'd been. The time she'd really been free was when she was at school, not once she'd left it.

She came back to the present with the sudden realization that her little smiles and giggles to herself were getting some strange looks from other hikers passing her by. She'd better keep her musings to herself otherwise they'd think a mad woman had been let loose in the Dales.

3

One of Laura's pet hates was smoking. Maybe it was something to do with the fact that she'd been a passive smoker so much of her life. She thought of this with disgust even now. Both her mum and dad had smoked, but despite this, for some reason Laura had always been against it. Most of her friends were smokers but she had not even wanted to try a cigarette. Once when they were all out as a gang, one evening, they had tried to get her to have a drag. That was the nearest she even got to trying, because as soon as the cigarette end came near her lips she felt sick. All their protests had no effect on her whatsoever. She showed a great will of determination and refused.

This caused a lot of mocking comments. 'Ah, are we too much of a baby to try, we thought you were the experienced one.'

Laura had felt cross at these words. 'It's not a case of being the experienced one, I just don't see any point in smoking. You might as well roll a ten shilling note up and smoke that.'

She knew it cost them most of their

spending money to buy their cigarettes. She liked to spend her money on other things. In those days there were not the same warnings that smoking could harm your health. Even without the warnings, for some reason unknown to Laura, her dad suddenly decided to give up smoking. He found himself an empty dimple whisky bottle and each week, instead of buying cigarettes, he went to the bank and had the money he would have spent on them changed into sixpences. These he then put into the bottle. 'When it's full there'll be forty pounds in it,' he said to them proudly. 'Then when I've saved enough I'll be able to book a holiday abroad for us all.'

'Great, Dad.' Laura and her brother, Mark, said, but inside herself Laura couldn't see him stopping smoking long enough to achieve this. But he did, he never had another cigarette from that day on.

It just worked out he had his money saved for them to have the holiday before Laura started work. But how was she to bear two weeks away from Keith her latest boyfriend. 'Mum, ask Dad to let Keith come with us,' begged Laura. 'I'm sure his Mum will pay for him.'

To her amazement her mum was as adamant on this topic as her dad; he couldn't come. For some reason they both disliked him. It wasn't as if he came from a different background to them. He was never rude to her parents, overly polite if anything, but still they didn't like him. She should have been so excited, but this was all taken away from her by the thought of leaving Keith. In another way, she was also eager to start her new job. She was having to delay the start by two weeks.

Yet there was a curiosity to see a new country and experience flying for the first time. What a performance it was to get them all packed up. Anybody would have thought they had never been on holiday before. Her mother seemed in a constant panic in case they had forgotten anything.

Her father kept saying, 'Come on, Marjorie, stop this. They do have shops there. If we have forgotten anything we will buy it.' But still this didn't seem to calm her mother. Her brother and herself just looked at each other, shrugged their shoulders and carried on as they were.

The thought of flying — now that was a different thing. They were going to a small Spanish island called Menorca. First of all they would fly to Majorca on a large plane, then a smaller one from there to the island. Neither were jet planes but still to Laura they were large enough to be frightening. As Laura approached the plane to get on it she couldn't believe it would ever get up in the sky. Looking quickly at her dad she asked, 'Are you sure this thing is safe?'

Laughing he answered, 'Of course it is — it's one of the safest forms of travel.'

Knuckles white, she clung on to the arms of her seat until they were up in the air. That part wasn't too bad after all. It was the rest of the journey. The plane seemed to have a movement all of its own, something she had never experienced before. But her stomach didn't like that feeling. She felt sick all the journey. When they came down to land the final jostling movement did cause her to heave into one of the paper bags supplied for the purpose. Her father was furious, as if she had done it on purpose. 'Trust you to show us up.'

She couldn't help it, but still felt as if she must apologize. 'Sorry, Dad.'

From then on she always took travel pills to stop it happening again. But when they arrived, after what seemed a never ending journey, it was worth it. It was like nothing she had ever seen before, and the heat, that was something else. As the coach transferred them from the airport to the hotel Laura looked out of the window mesmerized. It was fantastic, well worth that horrible feeling during the flight. Although in actual fact Laura had enjoyed being in the small plane that had taken them from the larger island Majorca to Menorca. That didn't upset her, it seemed to be her parents who didn't like that. Her father questioned, 'Why you're happy on this plane I don't know. Particularly when it's so small, flies so low and creaks all the time as if it is falling to pieces.' Laura decided it must have had something to do with the altitude, because her stomach seemed to stay where it was during that flight.

Anyway that had passed and they were nearly at the hotel. Laura looked eagerly out of the coach window to see if she could see it. All that she could see was a totally blue sky making the white of the many low buildings they passed reflect even brighter. A voice interrupted her thoughts to say, 'Ladies and gentlemen, over to your right is your hotel.' Already they had dropped people off at two other hotels which had been high rise blocks. The only thing Laura could see when she looked in the distance was a group of low white buildings clustered together. This looked interesting. She was glad they were not going to be in one of those tall buildings. The coach stopped and everyone rushed off to see who could get to their cases first. As each passed the courier she stated, 'Will one member of each party go with your passports to reception in order to check in.' Her dad and brother were seeing to the cases, so Laura turned to her mother. 'Come on Mum, we will go and get that done. The men are busy looking after the luggage. The quicker we do it the quicker we will know which is our room.'

In fact it wasn't a room they were allocated but a small bungalow, the only thing it lacked was cooking facilities. This was far better than anything Laura had expected. In the middle of all the buildings was a swimming pool which looked so temptingly inviting. Laura quickly asked, 'Can I go for a swim please, Mum?'

'Don't be so impatient, you have a fortnight in which to do lots of swimming. Help get unpacked first and let's find our way around,' her mother replied trying to keep her own impatience out of her voice at the thought of going in the pool herself. Whilst her mother had dealt with the formalities at the reception Laura had noticed that part of the hotel also housed the dining room. She wondered what the meals would be like. She wasn't so keen on the thought of it being foreign food.

Whilst in this trance-like state of amazement Laura watched the people around the swimming pool. Her attention was caught by some young males. With more interest now Laura looked at them properly. She couldn't help but think to herself they were dishy. There appeared to be three of them. With a guilty start, Laura suddenly realized she hadn't thought about Keith for hours. This fantastic place she had seen had knocked him totally from her mind. Now she felt sad wishing he were here to see all this himself. Surely he would be as mesmerized by all the beauty as she was. Her mother's voice broke into her thoughts. 'We're going for a short walk to see what the beach is like and if there are any shops around. We just have time before we need to get ready for dinner. Are you coming with us?'

'You bet. I don't want to miss anything, it is fantastic. Oh Dad, I'm so pleased you brought us here.' With this Laura flung her arms around her father and gave him a great big kiss. She was rewarded by a look of delight on his face.

Mark interrupted them. 'Come on you two — don't be so soppy.'

Laura couldn't stop herself breaking into her childhood habit of sticking her tongue out at him when he said something she didn't like. But she soon forgot her annoyance at her brother as they came out of the hotel gate.

Straight opposite and as far as she could see was a beach like she had never known before. It was exactly as picture postcards depicted. The beach was of fine yellow sand, gently sloping to lapping waves leading out to a bright, clear, blue sea. It looked so inviting Laura exclaimed, 'I don't know which to swim in first, the pool or the sea. They both look so perfect. Which do you think will be the warmest, Dad?'

'I wouldn't be surprised if it is the sea. Mind you, we had better check at the hotel reception that the sea is safe to swim in. I can't say I have heard adverse reports, but it is better to be safe than sorry. What do you say, Mum?'

'I agree entirely. Although I must confess myself I can't wait to get into that water. It doesn't look as if it could be harmful, that gentle blue colour and those waves so calm. But I know the sea can be deceiving. Still, I'm sure they will know, as you say Dad, at the hotel. Come on let's move on and see what else we can find. I want to see if there are any shops.'

'Already wanting to spend your money are you, Marjorie?' laughed Frank good heartedly.

'No. But you never know, there might just be something different.'

'I thought we had come on holiday, not to look at shops,' moaned Mark.

'Oh shut up, don't be such a spoilsport. It is a different country so we want to see all there is to see,' chastised Laura to her brother.

Majorie just looked at Frank and sighed. She was well used to them arguing like cat and dog. They had done this ever since they could first talk and they didn't seem to improve with age, like she had hoped they would.

'Oh! That looks like some shops. Let's go up that street,' said Marjorie trying to keep the peace.

Laura felt all interest go from her, suddenly it was Keith she was thinking about. The fun they could have had swimming in that sea. The amount of passion could have set them both on fire but with her parents there that would have been too dangerous for them to see. These thoughts sent a feeling of warmth through her body to parts she didn't want to be so aware of. She didn't know what was happening to her but when she heard her mother's voice ask, 'What are you looking so pleased about Laura?' She answered with panic in her voice, hoping her mother couldn't read her real thoughts. 'Only the pleasure of being on holiday here, that's all.'

'Good, I'm glad you're enjoying it. Your Dad is so happy he could do this for us.'

'I know and I do appreciate it.'

'Um, I didn't think so at the time it was suggested. You seemed real awkward about coming.'

'Well to be truthful, Mum, I am a bit sorry Keith isn't here. He would have enjoyed all this.'

'Yes, well I would rather not talk about that topic, thank you very much. Look here is a gift shop, do you want to come in with me to have a look?'

'Okay, but I'm not going to get anything yet until we have seen what else there is. I don't want to spend all my money in the first few days.'

'Come on, then. Leave your Dad and Mark looking at the knives in that window. They'll not be interested in this. Mind you, I'm not too keen to look at those knives, they look too sharp for my liking. Those blades send shivers down my back just looking at them. I can't stand sharp knives, they set me all on edge.'

Somehow Laura had lost some of her interest. She would rather be back at the hotel but she didn't want to upset her mum. They would have to go back soon enough, to be in time to get ready for dinner.

When they entered the dining room

Laura's flagging interest in the holiday was revived as she saw the three gorgeous young men at one table. She felt her arm pulled as Mark tried to get her attention. 'Come on Laura, the waiter is pointing that we have to go and sit over there.' Then with a smirk on his face he added, 'I saw you looking at those fellas. Thought you were sweet on Keith. I can't wait to tell him about this when we get back home.'

'You horrible brat. Just you wait 'til you do something wrong, I'll tell Mum. I won't have to wait long because you're always into some mischief.'

Back held straight Mark marched away from Laura trying to look as if he didn't care, but she knew he did. He was always getting caught out for doing something he shouldn't and he didn't like having to stay in for an evening as punishment.

Each of them was handed a slip of paper which was the menu. 'Thank goodness it's in English,' Laura sighed then she added, 'Not a lot of choice is there?' She'd quickly noticed there was only a choice of two dishes for the main course.

'Doesn't sound bad though, Laura. Green beans and ham to start should be okay. Then what do you fancy for the main course? I think I'll have the chicken,' said her father, who was already wetting his lips in anticipation of the food.

A wine waiter appeared and asked if they wanted to have something to drink. All the tables seemed to have a bottle of wine on them, so their father ordered wine.

'Are you going to let Mark and me have some as well?' enquired Laura.

'I don't see why not. The other youngsters seem to be drinking it. A taste will do you no harm,' quickly responded their mother.

Laura thought maybe they were beginning to see her as growing up, this could be a sign of more freedom. All the time they were waiting for their food, Laura kept trying to sneak a look at the attractive young men she had seen previously. As she was looking once at them, whilst she was trying to give the pretence of looking around the dining room, one of them saw her and gave a wink. She was sure she must have turned bright red, but none of the family commented, maybe they just thought it was a touch of sun.

She tried to look interested in the meal as the waiter put the plates down. All of them let out an exclamation together. 'Goodness, what is this? I thought I ordered ham and green beans.'

Each quickly picked their forks up and started prodding amongst the beans. Laura was first to ask, 'But where is the ham? This is only a plate of beans. I don't even like these — I only ordered it really for the ham.'

'Never mind, dear. Just try to eat what you can. Remember we are not in England now and they will have their own way of cooking.'

'Oh, well at least it looks as if I am going to go home thinner than when I came, if the meals carry on like this.'

'Now come on Laura, don't be like that. This is only the very first meal you have eaten here,' cajoled her father. 'I'm sure they can only get better.'

'Yes, I'm sure your Father is right. Anyway, if they don't we can soon treat ourselves to an ice-cream dish at one of those cafés I saw. I haven't let you starve yet so I'm not about to now.'

'Well I think I'll just give the beans a miss and wait for the chicken,' stated Laura.

'I'm going to eat mine,' sneered Mark at her.

Their mother just sighed; would they ever stop goading each other.

At least when the next course came it didn't look too bad apart from the lack of quantity. Laura looked down at the chicken, on the plate, accompanied with a few stick-like things, which she thought were supposed to be chips. 'Where are the vegetables Mum?

Do you think they will bring them in a minute?'

'I don't think so love, I think that is it. I haven't seen anybody else get any.'

'Cor, where have you brought us, to a concentration camp,' grumbled Mark.

'Don't be so cheeky, young man,' his mother and father said sharply to him in unison.

Laura just picked up her knife and fork thinking that everything else seemed to be perfect and the food was really the only thing she could fault.

It was still so warm outside when they left the dining room, it was amazing. A lot of the guests were just sitting around the pool chatting. 'Can we sit here a while Mum, everyone else seems to be,' asked Laura hopefully.

'I don't see why not. Mind you, I'm rather tired so I don't want to be too late to bed tonight, then we can get a full day tomorrow and enjoy it.'

Laura was hoping to get to know people better if they were going to have to be amongst them for the next fortnight. She wasn't disappointed. It wasn't long before a middle-aged woman came over and introduced herself. She was called Marion and was obviously well versed on who was who and what was going on. She pointed to a young couple in deep conversation and said they were on their honeymoon. Their names were Susan and Tim. Without asking, Laura found out who the three young men were. They came from London and were police-men. Well, at least a bit of respectability there. Even if she was in love with Keith there was no harm in being friends for a fortnight. She had to occupy herself somehow or other she decided, after all she was only young once.

Marion's voice broke into her thoughts. 'Do you swim, Laura?'

'Oh, yes I do, actually,' stuttered Laura feeling rather guilty now at her thoughts.

'Good. I like swimming but haven't found a companion yet, my husband isn't keen. Do you want to come and have a swim in the sea with me tomorrow? It's lovely and warm, warmer than the pool actually.'

'Oh, yes please. That's all right isn't it, Mum?'

'Of course. I'm not a swimmer myself Marion, but I might come and dip my feet in the edge, you never know,' replied Majorie, in very good humour now they had made friends.

Laura tried to stifle a yawn as the many events of the day started to overtake her. Majorie saw her daughter yawn and realized herself how tired she felt. 'Come on, all of you, I think we have had a long enough day. Let's get a good night's sleep then we'll feel refreshed to enjoy ourselves tomorrow.'

She was quite amazed when nobody protested. They all stood up and quickly moved to the bungalow.

4

As she sat on the rock, in the Dales, eating her lunch and looking up at the sun she remembered the first morning of that holiday abroad.

She'd opened her eyes to a ray of sunshine sneaking through a gap in the curtains. Realizing where she was she'd sprung out of bed and peeped out. For as far as she could see it was blue sky. Looking at her clock she saw it was eight-thirty, a decent enough time to wake up the rest of them. Running out of her bedroom she shouted, 'Come on, you sleepy heads, time to get up. The sun is already out.'

She heard a moan from Mark and her mother mumbled, 'Must you make all that noise Laura? Let me wake up in my own time.'

Now she was up she had to get dressed, there was no time to waste. She opened the door to have a look at the world outside. It was beyond belief, all so exciting. She suddenly felt like the teenage girl she really was instead of the young woman she wanted to be. The rest of the family must have felt some of the same excitement because it seemed no time before they were at her side.

'Come on then. I thought you were impatient to have breakfast then get on with the day,' stated her dad.

'Well, I expect it will be a continental breakfast, not a full English breakfast. I can't say I mind if it is, I don't feel much like a lot of food. They do say the heat makes you feel less hungry,' said her mum in a matter of fact voice. Marjorie had been correct in her assumption of the kind of breakfast they would be presented with, but none of them cared. The sun was far more important now.

After breakfast, not sure if Marion would want to keep her promise of a swim, Laura was uncertain how to make the first approach. Maybe if she lounged around the pool she would see her and come and talk again. Already the sun's rays were hot on her body. With eyes shut she was surprised to hear a male voice speak to her. 'You want to be careful on your first few days here. Even when you are not fair skinned, it is easy to burn in the sun. Take the advice of one who has already done it. It's painful until it settles down. By the way my name's Barry, what's yours?'

She could barely answer as she realized she was looking at one of the three young men she had seen the evening before. 'Laura. Have you been here long?'

'We came last Saturday so we've already had a week of our holiday. Those two approaching are my friends, the fair, tall one is Peter and the other Trevor or to their friends Trev and Pete. There don't seem to be any other single young people here unfortunately.'

'No, I thought I hadn't seen any more people of my age around. I only have my younger brother for company and he can be a real pain. An older lady called Marion has asked me to go swimming with her in the sea.'

'We've hired some scooters. There is room for a pillion so ask your Mum if you can come with us.' With this Barry turned to his friends who had just joined them. 'This is Laura. I was just saying to her if it was okay with her Mum and Dad she could come for a ride with us to one of the other beaches.'

In unison the pair let out an enthusiastic, 'Great.'

Laura felt as if she was really wanted but on the other hand she was sure her parents would refuse to let her go with them. Anyway, when the time came, if they really meant the offer she would have to see what happened. She was really flattered that three, what she would call sophisticated young men, could be interested in her. She had never thought of herself as glamorous, but thinking about it she knew she must be a little bit attractive for them to have taken notice of her. The only thing in her favour was she knew she looked older than she was. She was sure the lads were in their early twenties, so if they knew she was only sixteen she was certain they wouldn't be interested. She peeked a glance over at them where they lay on their sunbeds and felt really proud that they had asked her. She told herself there was no harm in being attracted to other men. That wasn't disloyal to Keith, it would only be so if she let it develop to more than friendship. With three of them to her one, she thought that all they meant her to be was simply a female companion for them.

She gave a start as she heard a voice at the other side of her. 'Good morning Laura, are you ready to go for that swim in the sea we mentioned?'

Realizing how hot she'd suddenly become she was rather relieved by this suggestion. 'You bet. I think I'm just about to melt in this heat.' Now the rest of her family had joined her she quickly turned to her mum, 'You said yesterday it was all right to go swimming in the sea with Marion. That still stands doesn't it?'

'Of course. Off you go and enjoy yourself.'

'Do you want to come with us and dip your feet in Mum?'

'No thanks. I think I will give that a miss today but just one word of warning — make sure you have plenty of suncream on. It is easy to burn when you have been in the sea because of the salt you get on your body.'

'Don't worry, I've had plenty of advice on that issue already.'

'Oh yes, who from?'

'Just three rather dishy young men.' Laura answered cheekily as she ran after Marion.

The sea was no disappointment to her, as soon as she dipped her toes in, she realized it was actually warm. When people had told her it could be warm she had not really believed it, but it was beautiful. Marion suggested they swam a little way out and turned to swim along to follow the coastline. 'When you don't know the waters too well I think it is better to be safe than sorry. Even though I am a strong swimmer I don't like to go too far out. You never know, an attack of cramp if you're on your own and that could be it.'

Laura thought her rather a fusspot, but at least she was company. The sea was brilliant, the gentle warm waves rippling over her body as she swam were rather erotic. Sensual shivers went up her spine as if fingers were gently caressing her. She gave a low moan with the pleasure.

'Are you all right, Laura?' asked an anxious voice.

'Yes. This is fantastic, absolutely fantastic.'

'Good, I'm glad you can get the pleasure I do from it. When you look around it is surprising the number of people who don't bother coming for a swim in the sea. They don't know what they're missing.'

'I can come again with you, can't I?'

'Of course, it's lovely to have a companion. Let's turn now and swim back, it can be more tiring than you think at first.'

'Um, my arms are beginning to ache, but thanks for sharing the experience.'

'Think nothing of it, as soon as I saw you I somehow felt a kindred spirit. I've always wished I had a daughter. At least it is nice every so often to have the pleasure of the company of somebody else's daughter,' Marion said ruefully.

Feeling rather sorry for her Laura asked, 'Have you no children then?'

'No, just one of those things, but never mind we make the best of it. We have some good times but sometimes like this, I feel the regret. Come on we're back, I'll get you a drink at the bar. I bet you're thirsty now?'

'Sure thing, now you mention it. I will definitely come again with you. Thanks for inviting me.'

'Great. But I also saw those three London lads eyeing you up. If you get the chance to go out with them, do. After all, you're only young once.'

'Mm, but I do have a boyfriend at home and we're serious about each other.'

'Oh, you're far too young for that, enjoy yourself whilst you can. Anyway what's the harm in a little fun. What the eye doesn't see the heart can't grieve over.'

Laura was amazed that this frumpish woman could speak like this. She gave a laugh. There was no answer to that, but in her mind if she was honest she did fancy having a good time.

Her mum didn't let her stay much longer in the sun, as she said she had been out long enough for her first day. But Laura wasn't worried, tomorrow was another day.

On waking the next day Laura had to run to the window again to make sure the sun hadn't vanished. But it was as before, a perfect blue sky with not a cloud in sight. She just couldn't believe it, that you could wake up each morning to this perfect weather. But Susan and Tim, the honeymoon couple they'd chatted to who had been there a week already, had assured her it had been like that every day that they were there. Maybe then today the lads would ask her to go with them. She decided not to go out as early to sunbathe, then she could stay out till later, giving her more opportunity to see them.

But then this didn't seem to make her mum happy as she pointed out. 'You know the sun is hotter mid-day, you shouldn't really sunbathe then.'

'All right, I'll just have a short while out this morning. Anyway, we're in at lunch when it is the warmest, then I can go out again later this afternoon.'

As she expected once she was sunbathing the voice was soon at her side. 'Well, are you game for a ride on the scooters after lunch?'

'Of course, that's if my Mum and Dad will let me.'

Laura looked across to her mum on her sunbed. 'Is it all right to go for a ride on the scooters, after lunch?'

Much to Laura's amazement she received a positive reply. 'I don't see why not. Just make sure you have plenty of suncream on.'

'Well you heard Barry, so I will get my towel and things ready after lunch and meet you here. Is that okay?'

'Fine, see you then. Have a good sunbathe,'

shouted Barry as he moved away to join his friends.

Now Laura could no longer settle as she was so excited. To no-one in particular she said, 'I think I'll go inside to read a while, it'll give me chance to cool down.'

A female voice mumbled, 'Good idea,' but she wasn't quite sure who replied.

Being an avid reader she was soon lost in her book and before she knew where she was her brother's voice was whining at her side. 'Come on, time to go for lunch. Hurry up I'm starving. We're all waiting for you. We thought you'd have come and joined us when it was time to go in.'

'All right natter can. Just let me get something on my feet then I'm ready.'

The family was getting used to the meals. They weren't over filling but they had at least found a reasonable system of how to cope with what they didn't like. At the worst they could resort to a tuna salad, if there was nothing on the menu to whet their appetites. Her mum had been right, with the heat she was nowhere near as hungry as she usually was.

'I've finished,' she said after what seemed only a few minutes in the dining room. 'I'll go and get my things ready for the trip out this afternoon.'

'What's all the rush. Look the lads are nowhere near finished with their meal. Just sit a few minutes otherwise you'll get indigestion,' stated her mother abruptly.

But she could scarcely contain herself a moment. Giving up her mother said, 'Be off with you. Go and get ready. I'll be up to the bungalow before you go, no doubt. Now remember take care and behave yourself this afternoon.'

'Don't I always.'

'I'm not sure about that.'

This gave Laura a few moments thought about what exactly her mother did know. But she soon forgot the comment as it was time to go and she joined the lads and scooters at the hotel entrance. Each quickly rushed forward to greet her and vied for her attention. In unison they said, 'You can come on my scooter.'

Laughing Laura tried to resolve the situation fairly. 'I'll take it in turns whose scooter I go on, if that is all right with you. As Barry asked me to go on his scooter first I will start with his. Does that suit you all?'

With a rather hang dog expression the others replied, 'Yes.'

It was brilliant on the back of the scooter, the warm air blowing on her as they sped along. This was nothing like the motorbike rides she had been given in the school lunch hour. All too soon the journey ended and they were at the beach. It was totally isolated; all that could be seen was yellow sand and blue water. Laura exclaimed, 'How on earth did you find this place?'

'Just a little bit of exploring that's all. We've ridden down various small lanes and you'd be amazed at the number of beautiful spots we've found,' Trev quickly replied.

Jumping in so Laura had his attention, Peter said, 'We'll show you some of the other places we've found before we go home.'

Barry had to say to her, so he wasn't left unnoticed, 'Take your pick madam where you want to put your towel to sunbathe. But be warned it's hot, very hot, it won't be long before you're in the sea to cool down.'

Laura felt she'd like to walk a little way to put her towel down as the feel of the warm sand on her feet was something else. Not wanting to appear to be spoiling their routine she came to a sudden stop. 'Here will do nicely,' but she couldn't stop herself saying with a touch of sarcasm. 'I think there'll be room enough for all.'

'Just, I like a lot of space,' bantered Peter back.

Laura decided this was the most enjoyable afternoon she had ever spent. It set the pattern for most of the holiday until the lads went home.

Many an afternoon she would go out with them, sometimes her brother Mark would come along. Her mum and dad had even allowed that. Laura decided her mother was cunning enough to be trying to take her mind off Keith, no doubt in the hope when she went home she would break her friendship off with him. She could read her mum's mind. Laura knew she thought if she had a good time with other young men then she would want to do that when she arrived home. What her mother didn't realize was that she loved Keith. The friendship with these lads was platonic. Still, she might as well have a good time whilst she could. But it was a bit of a drag to have Mark along. She much preferred their undivided attention herself because all of them were so attractive. She even said as much. 'Oh Mum, must he come along, he's only a kid.'

'Yes, he must young lady. He's as much right as you to have a good time on this holiday.'

Laura had to give in, she knew it was pointless arguing further.

She still had the odd swim in the sea with Marion. She was too soft hearted to disappoint her when she had promised she would go again with her after the first enjoyable morning. After they'd been a few times Marion asked, 'Still as good?'

'You bet,' replied Laura enjoying every minute.

The lads went home before Laura and her family were due to leave and suddenly the holiday seemed to fall flat. Now Laura wanted it to end so she could go on to the next stage of her life. That was to start work and most importantly to go back to Keith.

On the last evening, as her parents had made a few friends, they decided that after dinner they would invite them back to their bungalow for a small party. Laura, herself, thought that a good idea. That was until the party started. Suddenly it made her feel very sad. She felt lonely because each one of them had a partner, but she was on her own. Now she had an intense feeling that she wished Keith was by her side. She quickly brushed away the tears of sadness that were forming before they were seen by the others. Somehow she managed to respond when spoken to, even laugh but it all happened as if she was functioning on automatic pilot. Deep inside she felt sad and lonely. Here she was a woman, but not recognized by her parents as that, they still thought of her as a child. But she had all the womanly feelings and they were very present now. All she could wait for was this party to finish, the packing to be completed and she being on the plane on her way back to Keith. The only problem to surmount there was the illness she would probably feel on the aeroplane. But still when she was back in Keith's arms it would all be worth it.

'Come on Laura, wake up, people are saying good-bye to you,' said her mother giving her a nudge.

'Oh! Yes, sorry. I was just thinking back over the holiday,' she said with a sweet smile.

'Aye, that's true. We'll all have memories to keep with us for ever, come what may,' said her mother part in a dream-like state herself.

Those last few hours flew by and it seemed no time before they were all scrambling to get on the coach to take them to the airport. The friends they had made, who were not leaving yet, were there to wave them off on their journey.

Even the flight didn't seem so bad. Maybe it was because Laura was thinking of so many things, the holiday that had been and the future that was to come.

5

It was very late on Saturday evening by the time they arrived home. Laura hadn't realized how tiring travelling was. There was a quick check around the house, a glance at the post and they all decided it was time to fall into their beds before they dropped where they stood. Her mother was quite adamant that she was to stay in most of Sunday. But as soon as Laura woke she was on the phone to Keith. 'It's me, we're back,' she said with delight as soon as she heard his voice on the other end of the phone.

They planned to see each other for a few hours in the afternoon. Her mum said she had to have all her unpacking and jobs done before she went out and in the evening prepare all her clothes and things for her first day at work the next morning. Then she insisted she needed to be in bed early.

As Laura went to meet Keith she had butterflies in her stomach as if they were meeting for their first date. Unfortunately all the parents were at home so they were meeting in the park for a quick walk around. As soon as they saw each other they ran to meet. Keith nearly ate her up, his kisses were so affectionate. All he could say between each kiss was, 'Thank goodness you're back. I have missed you so much.' Laura was amazed. Much of the time she thought the more intense feelings of caring were from her side only.

'Come on, let's walk,' he said grabbing her hand. As they walked along Keith saw a park pavilion in a quiet corner and pulled her quickly into it. No sooner were they inside than the kisses came fast and furious and he was getting quite carried away.

'Be careful what you are doing. This is a public place and in daylight at that,' Laura had to say as she managed to pull herself away from him.

But he ignored this warning and quickly grabbed hold of her again as he couldn't seem to get enough of her. He was kissing her furiously whilst hands roamed all over her body.

Finally pulling herself away again Laura asked him, 'Well, aren't you going to ask me about my holiday, if I enjoyed it.'

'I'm more interested in you.'

'I'm going to tell you anyway. It was fantastic. One day we are going to have a holiday like that together. All the while I dreamt about you, that you were by my side doing the things I did. Anyway what did you get up to whilst I was away?'

Looking a bit startled at this question he asked sharply, 'What do you mean by that?'

'Nothing. I'm just asking did you go out with your friends or anything?'

'Ah, just an odd night. I used the time to catch up with my school work.'

Laura looked at him. 'Now I know you are teasing me.'

Wanting to change the subject before she asked any more questions he took a sudden interest in her holiday. 'Come on then, your turn. You tell me about your holiday.'

Laura's eyes glazed over as she thought of all that blue sky, sea and golden sand. 'It was perfect, just perfect. You can't imagine the heat, it isn't anything like we get here. Nearly all the buildings are white and the sun seems to reflect off them. The sky is so blue, it is hard to imagine. I don't think we saw a cloud the whole fortnight. The sea is the deepest blue you have ever seen. I don't know if the blue of the sky reflects to make the sea a deeper colour. It is so tempting for having a swim in, which I did with an older lady called Marion.'

Laura went on to describe her and then came to her first experience of walking on the sand. 'It was so warm. It was quite sensual as it ran through my toes so I just wanted to keep on walking and walking.'

Keith interrupted with a cheeky grin. 'Oh yes, I bet you did.'

Laura described the hotel, the pool, their apartment and finally, with not as much enthusiasm, the food provided in the dining room, particularly the green beans and ham.

'So you would recommend it, would you?' Keith queried.

'I've told you, I already plan one day we'll go there ourselves. Then you can experience it all for yourself.'

'Come here now, enough about that. Let's have another kiss,' conjoled Keith.

'No, I really will have to go now. I don't want to get on the wrong side of Mum, particularly as it is my first day at work tomorrow. I feel stressed up enough as it is at the thought,' replied Laura pulling away from Keith.

'All right, but we are seeing each other tomorrow night aren't we? My Mum and Dad are going out so we can go to my house.'

'Presuming I'm out of work on time. Remember when I got the job they did warn me that the time I left work could vary depending whether they balanced the books straight away or not. Don't meet me. I'll say

I'll come anytime after seven o'clock. Is that all right?'

Looking rather sulky now he'd reluctantly to agree to that. 'It'll have to be, but make sure you do come. We have got a lot of catching up to do. Come on then, I'll walk you back.'

Laura went home rather disappointed that he had not bothered to wish her luck for the next day. Being her usual rather generous self, she excused him on the basis that he hadn't started work yet himself so he didn't know the feeling.

Laura asked herself what was that feeling. She supposed in one way she was excited, yet on the other hand she was nervous. What if she couldn't do the work? Then there was the thought of meeting all those new people. It was like a whole new life beginning for her.

All night long she dreamt she was at work. But rather than being the pleasant experience she imagined, first of all she missed her bus, then when she arrived the door was locked against her. Finally after attracting attention to get in, all the staff were laughing at her. It was horrible. She woke up in a sweat and then couldn't settle back to sleep. She'd no need to set her alarm, she was awake in plenty of time. In fact her mother jumped with fright when she went down for her breakfast. 'Good gracious! What's wrong with you up so early? I was just going to come into your room and expected to have to give you a good shake to wake you up.'

'I couldn't sleep very well. The thought of starting work ended up more of a nightmare than a pleasure.'

'Don't worry, it was only a dream. You'll be all right,' said her mother in a sympathetic voice. 'You must eat something then you'll feel better.'

'I don't think I could eat a thing, my stomach is all butterflies.'

'You must have something to eat otherwise later on you'll feel hungry. Just have this slice of toast - it'll settle you.' Laughing she added, 'You don't want your tummy to rumble.'

'I'll try to eat some toast then.' Laughing back Laura stated, 'I'd better not embarrass myself with my stomach rumbling with hunger on my first day.'

Sensing Laura was already feeling better her mother smiled to herself and turned to get her toast.

An enquiring voice asked behind her, 'Were you nervous, Mum, on your first day at work?'

'Of course love. I think everybody is. It wouldn't be natural not to be. You'll find as you go through life that many events make you feel like this. Don't think because you get older you don't feel nervous at strange situations. I still feel the same if I'm going somewhere new.'

'Do you really?' said Laura seeing her mother in a different light.

'Of course. Probably experience just makes me a bit better at hiding it.'

She'd not realized she'd eaten her toast whilst the discussion had been going on. Suddenly looking at the clock Laura jumped up. 'I'd better finish getting ready now.'

'Don't panic. You've plenty of time left.'

'I know, but I'd rather it be that way.'

'Remember not too much make-up,' her mother warned her.

'I know, I know, I'm not that stupid.'

At last she was ready. Her mother, of course, had to give a final tweak to her hair, then she handed her a packet and some money.

'What's this?' asked Laura looking at the things she had been given.

'Some sandwiches in case you can't buy anything for your lunch and some money for the fares and lunch in case you've the chance to go for lunch with some others from the bank.'

Laura quickly thought to herself, that she knew all the fussing got on her nerves but her mother really did care. Feeling her mother deserved it for being so considerate, she gave her a big hug. 'Thanks, Mum.'

'Now mind you take care and good luck.'

Going on the trolley bus was no novelty to Laura. She caught the same bus as she'd done for the last five years in order to get to school. The only difference to-day was she'd stay on it longer, all the way into the town centre. Getting excited again her steps quickened as she moved to the bus stop to make sure she was on time.

When the bus arrived at the school stop Laura suddenly felt very grown up not having to get off there. Here she was amongst all other workers. At the terminal everybody got off the bus and rushed to their work place. She had to walk all the way through town, up a hill to the very edge of the city centre to where the branch was that she was going to work at. With each step she felt as if they were saying, 'Look at me, I'm on my way to work.'

Finally she arrived at the bank, but then panic set in as she wondered if she was at the door she had been told to go to. Deciding it was better to be safe than sorry she moved quickly around the building to see if there were any other side doors. No! Thank goodness for that. Gathering her confidence she put her finger on the bell and rang it.

Before she had time to get all her thoughts together it was pulled open sharply and Laura had to stop herself letting out a scream. She felt as if she had been transported to some sort of weird movie. The figure facing her looked as if he was from one of the latest feature films. He was so tall, with all his features large to match this height. Laura expected when he opened his mouth to see a row of metal teeth and either he would grunt at her with no real language or a big voice would bellow out. She was so shocked when neither happened that her fear nearly turned into giggles. He had a kind, gentle voice and simply said, 'I bet you are Laura. I have been waiting for you to come. This way, Miss. Follow me and I will show you where to go.'

Laura could only stammer, 'Yes,' in shocked surprise.

They walked into the bank behind the counter and across to some stairs that seemed to lead to a cellar. 'Down there, Miss.'

Laura muttered, 'Down there?' She was quickly thinking he was leading her to her doom.

'Aye, the cloakroom is down there. Some of the other young ladies are already there. They will direct you from there on.'

Much relieved Laura turned to look at him fully and thanked him. But then the butterflies returned. What if she didn't get on with the others? Then she realized she was being silly. Why shouldn't she?

Laura felt a funny feeling going down the stone stairs to a cloakroom. But when she got lower down she could hear a buzz of voices. At least she knew she hadn't been tricked into going somewhere she shouldn't, so they could all have a good laugh at her expense. Her mum had warned her about the possibility of practical jokes on her first day. She had said that most people new at work had to go through some leg pulling. She couldn't believe it when she turned the corner as directed because one of the girls was Sally, who had been in her form at school. She hadn't even known she had got a job with this bank.

Seeing her Sally shouted, 'Hi, surprise! Surprised at seeing me here I bet. I only started last week, but at least I can show you the ropes.' Turning to the other two girls who were there, 'Let me introduce you. This is Laura, my friend from school. Laura this is Jane and Jane. Don't worry Laura you'll be even more confused, there are three Jane's who work here.'

Laura was thankful that Sally was making it appear that they were the best of friends at school yet in reality they were more like acquaintances. Still, it was nice to see one familiar face. Trying to break the ice and appear friendly Laura smiled and said, 'It seemed a very funny place to come down here to hang my coat up. I wondered where the security guard was sending me.'

All the girls laughed in chorus and one of the Janes chipped in, 'I bet you thought he was having you on, pulling your leg as a lark. We all did the first time we were sent down here. You'll get used it. Not only do you hang your coat here but the toilets are over there. One of your first duties will be to go in the strong room over there to sort out all the daily standing orders to be paid.'

By now the other girls had put on their navy blue three quarter length nylon overalls. Panic set in as she wondered if she was supposed to have brought one with her. Nobody had told her, so she asked Sally quietly. 'Should I have an overall like yours?'

'No, the manager, Mr. Batty will want to see you soon. He'll give you some money to go and get two overalls. He'll tell you where because you can see they're all identical. We all have to get the same style and colour. Then he'll send you to have your photograph taken.'

'Photograph taken, why?' Laura asked in a puzzled voice.

'I don't rightly know. Nobody explained but I should imagine it's for security reasons. You'll have a lot of papers to sign regarding confidentiality of information and security. Most of your morning will be taken up with all that. But I'll try to organize it so you can have your break at the same time as me, then I'll show you where to go. I must go now to make tea.'

'To make tea!' Laura repeated like a parrot.

Laughing Sally turned to Laura. 'Don't worry, it'll be your turn tomorrow. Last in is the tea maker, that's you now. Frank, the security guard, usually helps. The cashiers all like a cup of tea before they get on working at their tills.'

Laura was rather taken aback at all this information as she had come to learn banking not make tea. Anyway they would soon want somebody else to make it, she could never make a decent cup of tea.

It was as Sally said, before long she was called in to see the manager and sent on her way for her photo and overall. She felt really important going out on her own for these tasks, already as if some bank duty had been delegated to her. By the time she had done this and back at work she wasn't quite sure what to do next, as the manager had a customer in with him. But he had said she had to see him when she got back. Stood looking around her, taking in everything she felt a tug at her sleeve. 'Come on, time to go for our break. I'll show you where. Just follow me.' Laura turned to see one of the Jane's standing by her.

'Oh thanks, I was wondering what to do until I could see Mr. Batty again.'

Laughing Jane looked at her. 'Not that you deserve a break. You haven't done any real work yet.'

Not sure how to take this Laura stayed where she was as Jane moved away and called after her, 'Do you think I would be better staying here?'

Turning back Jane caught hold of her arm. 'Come on, silly. Mr. Batty told me to take you for a break when I went. Of course you can have one, we all do.'

Not sure where they were going Laura quickly followed Jane this time. Up some stairs they went into a rather bare, uninviting room, with a table tennis table in the middle. A few easy chairs were spread about. As she moved her gaze around she noticed a dart board on one wall.

'Don't even think about playing any of the games. You never get the chance. All the men are on them at lunch time and they won't let us girls near.'

'Oh!' said Laura with disappointment. 'I like to play table tennis.'

'Come on, we don't have long. If you want a drink the heater has hot water in it and there is a spare cup in the cupboard. I don't suppose you brought your own?'

'No, I didn't think to.'

'It doesn't matter. There are always some spare mugs, but try to remember eventually to bring your own.'

'Yes, thanks I will but I don't bother too much about a drink during the day. Some of them do drink a lot of tea around here don't they?'

'I suppose so. I have never thought about it. I quite enjoy a drink myself at break time.'

Not sure what to say next, Laura thought she had better get lunch time sorted out. 'Do I come up here for my lunch?'

'You can do if you want, but I don't like to. As I said before all the male staff come up here, and surprisingly they get quite noisy. Also they seem to like to make fun of us young girls. I go out each day for my lunch. It doesn't cost much. If you like I'll try to get us on the same lunch then you can come with me. Sometimes I've to go on my own, other days one or two more girls go with me. Monday, Tuesday and Wednesday lunch I just go for a cheap snack but Thursday there are usually a few of us as we go for a fish and chip lunch. It is only two and sixpence for fish, chips, tea, bread and butter. Friday, once a month, I call it treat day. I go for a business man's lunch. That's three and sixpence for a three course meal.'

'That sounds great. Thanks very much, I'd like to come.'

Already Laura felt as if she were being accepted. She would have so much to tell her family and Keith tonight. Really the rest of the day passed in a haze as she was shown one job and another that she would eventually become involved in. Some of the men who worked there seemed a bit odd; they did seem to like to make snide remarks. But then when she watched them they seemed to be like that with everybody so it wasn't just her as the newcomer they were getting at. It was rather amusing watching them chat to each other as they seemed to discuss so much about their personal lives. More than the women did. Laura decided that, if she was one of their wives she wouldn't be pleased to know they were talking at work about so much of what went on at home. They shouldn't be telling some of the things because they were private matters.

There were no glass partitions around the cashiers, so the people at the back of the bank could hear the conversations between cashier and customers. It was all so fascinating. In fact, at times she became transfixed listening to the conversations then she would feel a gentle tap on her arm reminding her where she was.

During the day Laura had a conversation with a young man who had worked there two weeks. So counting herself, there were three newcomers. It had transpired he lived on the same bus route as herself. She did have to admit he certainly wasn't her type. He couldn't help it she knew, but he was on the short side with bright carrot coloured hair. Still, he seemed friendly enough and had suggested when they finished work, if she wanted, they could walk to the bus stop together. Laura decided it would be nice to have company for that trip as she could imagine that it would get lonely and boring doing that walk each day. She could chat to him and learn more about other characters at the bank.

All too soon she saw the security guard go to the main bank doors and shut them to keep any more customers out. She couldn't believe how fast the time seemed to have gone. Instead of everything slowing down when these doors were closed, it suddenly became a hive of activity. The cashiers started rushing around and going to help each other. The assistant manager emerged from his office and went to help.

Laura quickly asked Jane, 'What's happening? Why are they all rushing around?'

'They're trying to balance. The quicker they do that the sooner we all go home.'

'Oh!' said Laura still not fully understanding what was going on.

Slowly each cashier gave a thumbs up sign and started to move their tills away from the counter. Money was bagged and then they all started carrying it towards that cellar staircase.

'What are they doing now?' Laura asked Tony the new lad.

'The vaults where the money is kept overnight are down there. Once they are balanced, all the money goes into them for safety. When Mr. Batty is happy everything is done and balanced he'll announce we can go.'

'That won't be a while yet, will it? It's still early to finish work.'

'If it's all done whether it's early or not he'll let us go.'

'That sounds good.'

'It is — not all branches are as efficient as this I can tell you. Come on, we might as well get everything tidied up here.'

By the time they'd finished their tidying up

behind the scenes, all the cashiers seemed to have vanished and Mr. Batty was surveying the bank. The assistant manager had just finished totalling up some figures.

Mr. Batty turned to him. 'Well do you balance?'

'Exactly, not a penny out.'

'Good, well done. If everything is finished and put away as it should be, you can go.'

Laura turned to Jane. 'What if it had been out a penny?'

'Then we'd have had to find it.'

'Now I know you are really having me on,' laughed Laura.

'Actually I'm not, we do have to balance to the penny,' Then in a serious voice Jane added, 'After all, they don't call us the Penny Bank for no reason.'

Laura just looked at her and said, 'Oh, not really quite sure how to take all this and didn't want to ask any more in case she made a fool of herself.

'Come on, time to go,' Jane reminded her as Laura gave one last look around for the day. She thought that at least she'd survived the first day and hoped that the next day they'd let her have a go at more jobs so it should be even more interesting.

6

As she opened the door Laura called out. 'Hello Mum, I'm home.'

Her mother rushed agitatedly into the hall. 'Good gracious me! What has happened? You're home early. I didn't expect you for a while yet.'

'Nothing's wrong. In fact, everything's great. I'm at a really good branch which is so efficient that it balanced straight away. Provided everything has been done when they balance we are allowed to go. I've so much to tell you. I've had a really great day.'

'Come on, then,' said her mother, all ears by now. 'I've a few minutes to spare before I start getting tea ready. We might as well go into the lounge and sit down whilst you tell me all.'

Her mum gave the odd laugh or two as Laura recounted the days events. All in all, Laura was pleased with how her first day's work had gone and she felt a true adult now. After she had told her mum all she had to, she suddenly had an impatience to be with Keith. It was him she wanted to be telling. To her, once pay day came she would be able to help save towards their future. Not that he had said they had one in so many words, but to care so deeply for each other must mean they could look forward to a lifetime together. Next summer Keith would leave school, so they could really start to plan.

'Will tea be long, Mum?'

'Now give me chance. Haven't you kept me busy telling me all about your day?' questioned her mother.

'I suppose so, but I don't want to be late getting ready.'

'I'm going to get on with it now, don't worry. You go and get yourself changed whilst I do that, then you can get out when you've finished your tea.'

'It's all right, I'm not in that much of a rush. I just want to have time to tell Dad how I went on.'

'He'll want to know, I'm sure,' replied her mother as she moved into the kitchen to get on with the meal.

By the time Laura had told her father about the day's events she was feeling she knew it word perfect. Her dad did seem really pleased how it had gone for her. His initial reaction of disappointment that she had left school and had not continued with her studies to go on to university seemed to have gone. He appeared quite proud of her as a bank clerk.

Laura wasn't quite sure what their reaction would be when she announced she was going out for the evening when they still wanted to talk about her first day and all the events. Quite surprisingly, her mother automatically presumed she was going out with friends as well as Keith.

'I suppose you'll have a lot to tell your friends tonight?' asked her mum. 'Have any of them started work yet?'

'No, I'm the first. Some wanted a longer holiday before they started.' Quickly trying to think who was starting work and where so her mother's curiosity would be satisfied. 'Maureen starts work in a Building Society next week.'

'Oh good! You can give her some tips for her first day at work.'

'Yes, I suppose so.'

'The only thing I want to remind you, I don't want to appear to be nattering but remember you've to be up early for work, so don't be late in. You'll no doubt find your first few weeks at work a lot more tiring than school until you get used to the routine. It's taking in so many different things that does it and even if you left work early today you might not do that every day. Work hours are longer than school hours you know.'

'Don't worry Mum there is no chance I'll forget it's work tomorrow. I'm still excited about all I have to learn, more so now I've seen what goes on. See you later then. Bye.'

Laura knew she was rather earlier than she said she would be at Keith's. She wasn't sure if he would have told his parents she was coming to their house whilst they were out. Maybe not, because she had a feeling they wouldn't be too keen. It was obvious they thought Keith too young to have a steady girlfriend.

As she approached the corner to turn around to go into the street where Keith's house was, she went round it very slowly. She hoped nobody was watching her otherwise they would wonder what on earth she was up to. Slowly she peered around the corner and quickly sprang back as she saw Keith's mum and dad leaving the house. Not quite sure which direction they would take she quickly retraced her steps and up a side street until she was certain she was well out of sight. She would give them five minutes then, whichever way they went, the coast should be clear.

When the time was up, she moved very cautiously from where she had kept herself hidden. She just hoped she had given herself enough time for them to have gone. Imagine

71

if she had gone to all this trouble and she still bumped into them as she turned the corner. Her heart was hammering loud in her chest as she turned the last bend. So far so good. She couldn't help but let out a sigh of relief as she could see Keith's house in view but no parents. Then she had another panic, what if they hadn't gone out at all yet, but had forgotten something then gone back to the house. Shaking herself mentally she told herself she was getting paranoid, after all, if they were still in she could always say she was calling for Keith so they could go a walk and she could tell him about her first day at work. That was it, all sorted out now whatever happened. With this thought in mind she placed her finger on the bell.

The door quickly opened with Keith peering around it. 'You're early! Mum and Dad have only just gone out. You didn't see them did you?'

'I saw them.' Seeing the panic on his face she quickly added, 'But they didn't see me. I went back and out of sight until they were gone.'

'Thank goodness for that. Anyway come in quickly before the nosy neighbours see you and tell Mum afterward.'

Laura had only been in the house once before. His parents had been out that time as well. Making a quick grab for her as soon as she was in, Keith started to give her a kiss. Feeling a bit put out that he hadn't bothered to ask about her day at work she said, 'Stop that, give me chance to catch my breath.'

'Come on, we have a lot of time to catch up on and we are on our own now.'

'But aren't you interested in my day. It's special. I feel as if I've moved forward to adult life.'

'If that's the case, then let's do some adult things. I've got prepared.'

'What do you mean?' asked Laura now totally lost where the conversation was going.

'Don't play stupid with me,' said Keith getting quite impatient and frustrated. 'What do adults do?'

'You mean have sex?'

'If you want to put it like that, but I was going to say make love. Come on, admit it, Laura, you do love me.'

'You know I do, have I ever said otherwise. But you're too young.'

Keith sneered at her. 'Age doesn't come into it. If I can do it, does it matter how old I am?'

'Don't get upset, I didn't mean it like that. I just didn't want to cause any trouble for us. Anyway what about the possibility of me getting pregnant? I certainly don't want that.'

'I told you I've got prepared; I bought some rubbers today. A friend at school told me of a bike shop that sells them. Seems a funny place, but he didn't know me. It was only a wooden hut. But it doesn't matter where they come from as long as they do the job. Two and sixpence they cost me for a packet of three.'

'But I thought the idea of me coming here tonight, when we could be on our own, was to tell you all about my new job,' said Laura feeling rather let down that he didn't seem interested in that.

'Of course I want to know but you can tell me afterwards. Come here let's have some petting to get you in the mood. We don't want to do it too late in case my parents come home. We know we're safe at the moment. We can talk later then if they do come in and find us together talking it will all look innocent.'

'I don't know,' said Laura still not certain she wanted to go that far. It was all right to have talked about it at school and pretended but to actually do it was a different matter. Then she didn't like his attitude towards her. This wasn't how she'd imagined the first time would be like, at all.

'Come here, silly. I won't make you do anything you don't want, but a few kisses and

74

petting and you'll be begging me to carry on.'

Laura saw no harm in the kissing - she was sure she could control herself further than that.

'Promise I can talk to you later though,' she said as Keith pulled her onto the settee.

'Now what did I say earlier. Just be quiet now and concentrate on this,' murmured Keith as he pulled her down onto him.

Laura felt a panic in her, wondering if what she was doing was right. The more he kissed and touched her the less she felt it was wrong and the more she understood Keith's reaction. His hand started to move up her dress and touch her where it gave her real delight. She felt there was no stopping now, they had to carry on. Only moving slightly Keith said, 'Come on Laura, take your briefs off.'

Without question she did as she was told and at the same time carried on what she was doing. Keith then freed one hand to undo his trousers and took them off. This done he pulled back from her. 'We'll just have to pause a moment whilst I put this on,' he said producing a small packet.

Laura watched with fascination, never having seen one before. 'Are you sure they're safe?'

'Of course, trust me. I wouldn't have gone

to all the trouble of getting them if they weren't.'

With this he moved to lay on top of her on the settee. Laura could feel a lot of fumbling but nothing seemed to be happening.

'Try to relax, you seem a bit tight. Maybe we should move on the floor where there is more room,' said Keith with frustration in his voice. Agreeing to anything that would make it work Laura edged herself off the settee on to the floor and somehow Keith landed on top.

Finally she felt a piercing pain as he entered her and it took away the pleasure she was expecting to feel. Keith bucked and cavorted like a horse with a thorn under the saddle. My word thought Laura, there's nothing erotic about this. She felt more as if she were being steamrollered by a bus.

Abruptly Keith stopped. 'That was marvellous,' he said. 'Did you enjoy it Laura?'

'Of course,' she felt she had to reply. 'You were wonderful Keith.'

He turned to look at her and could tell she was only trying not to hurt his feelings. 'It's that silly rubber thing I had to wear. Flesh together would be far better. We'll have to try it without, then you can get some real pleasure like me.'

'But that wouldn't be safe!' Laura exclaimed

with panic in her voice at the thought of the possible consequences.

'It would be if it was the right time of the month, trust me.'

'M'm,' said Laura deep in thought, deciding this all seemed to be getting way out of hand. She realized what she had done tonight was only because she had been carried along by the euphoria of the day's events. Once she wasn't as elated by her first day at work she was sure she would easily be able to say no to him in future.

'You did promise you would let me tell you about work. I have kept my part of the bargain, are you going to keep yours?'

'Come on then, sit next to me here and tell me all about it if you must. It isn't fair you being at work when I have to still go to school.' Laura could hear a slight hint of jealousy here and realized she would have to be careful how much she talked about work. Maybe she was growing up if she could appreciate this. So she went on to recount the days events trying to make it lighthearted and she did get him laughing when she described the men, making them appear like old women gossiping rather than bank cashiers. He didn't seem too pleased at the mention that she had been out at lunch time but as she pointed out it was better surely to go out with a female friend than be closeted in a miserable room with a lot of rather sarcastic men. All the while she was recounting the tale he kept trying to nibble her ear and get the odd caress in, but Laura felt enough was enough and kept edging away from him.

Suddenly it struck her that if his parents came home she wouldn't be able to look them in the face. She was sure they would see evidence of what had been going on. 'Are you sure you have got rid of that thing and the packet?' Laura suddenly asked.

'What thing?' laughed Keith.

'You know — the protection'

'Of course, you don't take me for a fool? Like you, I don't want my parents to find out. Don't worry so, all is taken care of. We don't want to spoil things. We want plenty more opportunities to be on our own here, now don't we?' He gave her a knowing look.

'Yes. Well, I think it would be best if I go now before they come in.'

'Oh, they will be ages yet, no panic, come on stay a while. Let's have some more snogging.'

'Don't say that, it sounds horrible,' said Laura feeling rather annoyed at his couldn't care less attitude. 'Anyway, I promised Mum I wouldn't be late in tonight. After all it has been my first day at work and as she said it has tired me more than I thought.'

'What after one day?'

'Yes, after one day. It's not just the work but the first day it is all the tension as well, being amongst strangers and the different environment. Just you wait till it is your turn and you'll soon find out.'

'All right, if that's the way you feel go home. I can see you'll just keep on until you do.'

Laura thought that was rather an unfair comment, she didn't think she went on. Seeing the look on her face Keith decided he might have gone a bit far in what he had said so quickly added, 'We're seeing each other tomorrow aren't we?'

'Of course, but where?'

'Well my Mum and Dad won't be going out. It's Mum's favourite programmes on the telly tomorrow.'

'Mine don't go out on a Tuesday either, usually only at weekends. Oh well, it looks as if we'll just have to go for a walk.'

'Come on then, now that's settled I'll walk you home if you like.'

'No need, it's still light.'

'Might as well, I've nothing else to do. In any case it'll pass some time.'

Laura felt put out by this attitude, particularly after what she'd just done with him. 'I hope that isn't the only reason. I trust you do really want to walk me home?'

Realizing he seemed to be making rather a mess of things tonight after all she'd done for him, he became contrite. 'Course I do. Anyway are you all right after what we did? Not sore or anything?'

'No, fine. Don't worry, as long as you're sure it was safe.'

'It was believe me. Do you think I'd be that much of a fool.'

By the time she arrived home Laura felt happier with herself again. She just hoped there was no way her mum could tell what had gone on that night, by maybe a mother's instinct. She gave herself a mental shake as she decided she was getting really silly now about things.

The only slight worry she felt was that she had been carried along with the dream-like state she had been in all day and this had made her do things she otherwise wouldn't have done. Oh! Well it was too late now. What was done was done. With this Laura gave a quiet giggle to herself thinking how much had happened to her in just one day.

7

Each day there seemed to be a little more excitement in the bank as Laura learnt new tasks. The very next day, because she wasn't out of the bank as on the previous day she was allowed to go with Jane on the local clearing system. Off they both went to another bank. There they were shown in a room with very unusually high slopping desks. Most of them had another young person standing in front of the desk. Jane and Laura found an empty one. Laura whispered, 'What's going on here?'

'Watch and you will see,' responded Jane.

Soon an older man came in to supervise, did a quick head count and asked, 'All here?'

A chorus of 'Yes' went up.

'Then let's get on with it.' With a quick chuckle he added, 'I'm sure you all have plenty of other work to do when you get back to your branch.'

A few grunts of agreement could be heard. Then suddenly it was as if bedlam had begun. All of them started moving around handing each other bundles of cheques.

Laura could only stand rooted to the spot mesmerized.

Finally, when Jane came back to their desk she had to ask, 'What was that all about?'

Jane then showed her the cheques she'd been given; all were ones written by customers from their branch. Jane went on to explain, 'These are now taken back by us and debited from the appropriate accounts. That is why we call this local clearing because we hand cheques that have come into our branch back to the branch that issued them then they can all be posted to that customers account.'

Laura queried, 'Why posted when they take them back?'

Jane laughed. 'I don't mean posted as in a letter box. It means when the amount of the cheque is debited from the account. If we didn't get the cheques back, how else would we know to deduct the money? There are also credit slips or paying in slips if that makes it easier for you to understand in the bundles. These are credited to the customers' accounts. We only do this here for the branches in town. All other cheques and credit slips go through a central clearing, then are sent on to the branch to which they belong.' Seeing Laura's face still looking puzzled, 'Don't worry, you will come with me for a few days to do it, then once you have understood what we are doing it will become your task. It's quite good because it gets you out for a little walk. Anyway, come on they will be waiting for these back at the branch to get on with the rest of the work that's to be done on them.'

Before Laura could reply Jane turned tail and was rushing back out of the branch. Laura did a quick trot to follow as she wasn't quite sure of her way around the maze of corridors to find her way out.

Once they arrived back at their own bank, Jane set to showing Laura how to check the signatures on the cheques. Once satisfied they were correct she had to put her own initials through it. Then she had to check the date wasn't more than six months old and the word and figures for the amount said the same thing. To Laura it seemed to take her for ever to look at one cheque. Jane had already done a small pile by the time she finished her first one. Puzzled at the speed Jane did the task, she couldn't stop herself commenting, 'How come it's taking me so long to do this? It would take me all day to get through all of these, for you it only seems a few minutes job.'

Jane laughed. 'Well, you have heard the saying practice makes perfect. That's all it is, getting used to doing the job. You will soon know a lot of the signatures then you won't need to refer back to the cards to check each one is correct also your eyes just get quicker at looking with practice.'

'All right I'll take your word for it.' With this Laura moved on to the next cheque.

It was funny, even though she had started newly here with Sally, it was Jane she seemed to be getting to know better. Both her and Sally were being shown different duties so they did not have a lot of direct contact.

In the evenings, Keith was still being his very passionate self. Despite her resolve not to, she had let him have his way and they had made love again. It still wasn't as Laura had imagined it to be but all Keith could say was, 'I'll tell you when it's safe then I'll show you how much better it can be, trust me.'

To Laura it had become an obsession with Keith, as if he was trying to prove himself. All Laura could say to him was, 'Don't worry so much, it's fine for me, honestly.' Even so this did not seem to satisfy him, he just kept on and on until he was wearing her resolve down. Slowly it began to dawn on Laura that all this trying to prove himself as an adult in her eyes had started when she began work. It was obviously some form of jealousy. Yet she did love him and there was plenty of time for them to be together and grow up. It wasn't as if they were planning marriage yet or had even talked about it.

Meanwhile at work everything was still new and exciting to her. She soon found out that the hours weren't as easy as they first had seemed. She had to work Friday evenings, only getting one in three off, and Saturday mornings with only one in four off. But that wasn't as bad as it sounded as she had been taken by one of the older women, Pat, to help at a sub-branch on Friday evenings and Saturday mornings. The only person at that branch was a cashier so they had to do all the rest of the work. It was all go but it seemed so different at a small branch rather than a main one. She was told once she was trained she would be on the rota for going there as relief. This made her feel really important.

Try as she would at times she couldn't stop herself bragging to Keith about what was happening at work. He would usually answer with a sneer, 'All I hear from you is about your work. You aren't asking what I'm doing new at school.'

Laura quickly tried to reassure him. 'But I know really. Remember it's not so long since I was at school. I know what lessons are like and the homework. I do feel sorry for you having to go through all that work for the exams, but I've been there myself. I should know, look at me - I was one of the worst for bothering to get on with the work and revise. My dad always said one day I'd wish I'd tried harder. Already I'm beginning to see what he meant, although I was lucky. At least I got enough results for the job I wanted. I don't regret not staying on at school, I've to admit that. It's far better at work.'

What was even better was Laura soon had her first pay day. She did wish they were paid once a week not once a month, it seemed such a long time in between. Because they worked in a bank they'd to open a cheque account and their wages were paid direct into that. It would have been nice to have had the money in her hand and count it. Not that she thought it was going to go very far. Her mum and dad had given her a shock when they announced, 'We'd better discuss your board money.'

Laura could only stutter, 'Board money! What do you mean?'

'Now you're earning you don't think you're going to keep all your wages and out of our pockets we buy your food, clothes, supply your laundry service, catering service and electricity do you?'

'Well no, I suppose I hadn't really thought about it.'

'We have, and it is written down here how

we have calculated it and what we think is a fair cost.'

Laura felt herself go white as she read the figure. It was half the money she was paid each month. Finally, she felt she had to say in rather an annoyed voice, 'That's a lot of money - it's like a small wage in itself.'

'You try and keep yourself so cheaply in lodgings,' her father challenged her.

Little did he know she was already debating in her mind whether she should do that. At least she would have more freedom and not be accountable to them. But then reality taking over she realized she wouldn't like to live on her own, it would be lonely. And she would have to do all her own cooking and washing.

Seeing all the different emotions going on in her face her mother did fall a little bit soft. 'Of course, because it's to cover your food, I'll give you your dinner money back each day and I'll give you your bus fares.'

Deciding this didn't sound quite as bad as at first, she had to relent. 'Okay, I'll get the money out of my account for the first month's money tomorrow.'

She knew she was going to have to re-think how she allocated her money now. She'd planned to save up for driving lessons ready for when she was seventeen and also put some into a saving account so when she'd passed her test she could get a small car. Then she was going to open another account where she would put a small amount each month to save up for hers and Keith's future. As all young people she had planned a few spending sprees on clothes. It certainly wasn't going to go that far now. Maybe she would concentrate on the driving lessons but she hadn't long to save before it was her birthday and she was old enough to drive. Perhaps she could get her mum and dad to pay for one or two lessons as her birthday present. That sounded a good idea.

By the time she went to see Keith, she still had mixed feelings against her parents. She felt rather cross about it all. It was a good job it was going to be an evening on their own, so she could vent her feelings to Keith.

As soon as he opened the door to her knock he could tell she wasn't well pleased about something. 'What's wrong? Have your parents been getting at you again?'

'Not in that way,' she said as she quickly moved down the hall knowing he was referring to them going on at her about going out so often. Then realizing his parents might be in, 'Are we on our own?' she whispered.

'Yes, Mum and Dad have gone out. Go on with what you were saying.'

'It's my board money.'

'Board money!' repeated Keith like a parrot.

'Yes, how much they want from me each month for my food and lodgings.'

'You don't pay your parents like that.'

'Yes you do. I suppose if I'd listened to the others at work I would have realized they all do. It just came as a shock at the amount. They want nearly half of my money and I still have to buy my own clothes out of the rest.'

'Well my parents have no need to think that when I start work I'm going to hand my money over. What do they think they're doing? Do they think they can retire and you keep them?'

'No silly; I don't think the money I give them will do that.'

'Still, when I start work I want plenty of money to do just what I want. I might save up and get a motorbike.'

'You'll have no need to do that. I'm going to save to get a car.'

'Who wants a car? I want some excitement. No, it's a motorbike for me.'

Laura felt the need to ask, 'But what about us?'

'Come here and I'll show you about us.'

'I mean our future. We do have a future don't we?'

'Of course, now come here.'

'But we'll want to save up.' Laura tried to tell him, being practical.

'Save up, for what?'

'For when we are a lot older and want other things out of life.'

'Oh, I'm too young to think about all that. I've a lot of living to do. The time will come for that but let's make the most of our time tonight.'

As usual he was soon carried away with his passion. Laura was usually well in control, the only time she lost that control was when her parents made her really mad. This was one of those occasions. She felt as if she wanted to get him interested in the future, so she had to really show him what was on offer.

For somebody so young, his art of lovemaking was advancing quickly. He could easily get her to the point that she desperately wanted him. Not that once she had him did it give her the thrill she was longing for. Afterwards she always felt let down and wondered what all this lovemaking was about.

Before she knew where she was Keith had her briefs and his trousers off and was ready to enter her. As she did she felt instantly that there was something different. Realizing what it was she tried to push him off. 'Keith, Keith!' she said with panic in her voice.

'You've forgotten something.'

Quite calmly he answered, 'No I haven't. Now come on be quiet and enjoy it.'

'The protection!' she shouted at him.

'No, I want you to feel real pleasure. It'll be safe as you only finished the other day. Anyway, I won't let anything happen in you, trust me.'

With his weight on her Laura couldn't do a lot more than that, but as usual it seemed all too soon before Keith was making groaning noises and shuddering. 'Fantastic, I told you it would be.'

Innocently Laura asked, 'Are you stopping now before it gets too dangerous?'

'Dangerous, what do you mean?'

Laura had no need to answer as she felt a stickiness oozing from her. She pushed Keith off her with all her might and shouted at him, 'What have you done you fool?'

Instantly he looked rather sheepish. 'I'm sorry Laura. I got carried away and forgot I wasn't using anything. Don't look like that I've told you it is safe at this time of the month.'

'My God! It better had be, that's all I can say.'

Rubbing up against her he asked, 'Bet it was good wasn't it? Like I told you it would be.'

Rather reluctantly and not wanting to hurt his feelings she answered, 'Yes, but don't you think you are going to try that again. In future protection or nothing. It only takes once you know. Oh no, what have I said? I hope it hasn't only taken once this time. You fool!'

With this Laura ran out of the room to the bathroom in the hope of washing everything away and making it all right.

When she came back Keith was contrite. 'I'm sorry, Laura. I was only trying to make it good for you.'

'All I can say is, don't bother again. Now if you want me to stay a bit longer switch the telly on. That's all I want to do now.'

Knowing he had made her really angry he thought this was the best thing. It would give her chance to calm down. Trying to make amends he asked, 'Did you learn anything new at work today?'

Being used to his unconcerned attitude and still feeling angry she snapped, 'Why do you care? You're not normally interested.'

'I was only trying to be friendly.'

'Well shut up, I like this programme and I want to watch it.'

With this Keith slumped back in the seat with a sulky expression on his face, thinking his earlier pleasure had rapidly evaporated.

8

Laura didn't give much thought to that night again, that was until she suddenly felt sick in the mornings and couldn't face her breakfast. What if she was really pregnant? No! She couldn't be. It didn't happen just like that. Or did it? She just didn't know. Even her breasts felt tender, but surely it must all be her imagination. Not having a very good head for dates she couldn't remember when she was next due. Frantically she tried to work it out, but she didn't want to ask Keith. That would only set him wondering. No, she decided best wait and see what happened, she was sure it would be all right. It was her imagination working overtime because of what had happened.

Yet what really happened? Maybe it was her body giving her a telling off by frightening her. She just didn't know who to talk to. All her close family were ruled out. Many a lunch time whilst she was out with Jane she nearly blurted out what was worrying her. Jane was a year older than her and might have more knowledge on such topics. Something stopped her. Even though she liked Jane,

93

there was a certain primness about her and somehow Laura felt to broach that subject would bring out the disgust in her. She didn't want to spoil the friendship so as to lose her company at lunch times.

Who could she talk to then? As usually happens, when least thinking about a problem, fate steps in. It was time to go for lunch, not her usual time because she had been asked to change for one day to the later lunch. As she went to collect her coat she saw Sally stood there. Out of kindness, because she still seemed rather a lonely person Laura asked, 'Is it your lunch time as well now?'

'Yes,' replied Sally. 'I don't usually see you at this time.'

'No, they've changed my time just for today. Are you going out for your lunch?'

'I was going to but I wasn't quite sure where to go. I don't really like going to eat on my own.'

'Come with me if you like. I was having to go on my own as well.'

'Great, thanks.'

During lunch both kept up a light banter of chatter about their work. 'Are you glad you came to work in the bank?' asked Sally.

'Yes, I think so. It'll be better when I can be a cashier, but I know that time's a long way off. Do you like working in the bank yourself?'

'Yes, but as you say it's just spoilt by having such a wait to get to what you'd call the real banking jobs.'

It suddenly struck Laura during all this conversation here was the person to talk to, she would just have to wait until the right opening came along. Sure enough, on their way back to work Sally asked if she still had her boyfriend. This gave Laura the chance to start talking about him in general and also in return she questioned Sally on her boyfriend and relationship. As they were approaching the bank Laura suddenly paused in her step. 'Sally, we have a few minutes to spare before we need to be back and I want to talk to you, ask your opinion.'

Not really sure what was going on here Sally looked at her waiting in wonder what was to come.

Knowing there was not a lot of time to spare before they'd to be back at work Laura blurted out, 'I'm not sure but I think I'm pregnant.' In those seconds Laura saw a lot of different emotions flicker over Sally's face.

'I see,' she finally said. 'How do you think I can help you? I have little knowledge about that myself.'

'I know. I didn't mean in that sense, but I

haven't spoken to anybody else at all about my fears and just being able to do that is a help.'

Trying to be more constructive about the situation Sally looked at her, 'Do you feel any different?'

'Yes, I've felt sick, not really just in the morning but at any time of day. I hope nobody has noticed me make a few quick dashes down stairs to the loo.'

'I don't think so — I certainly haven't noticed. Anything else?'

'My breasts feel very tender.'

'M'm, but that could be because you are due but it's late, it's just being more painful this month. Are you very late?'

'I think about two weeks and I'm always on time.'

'I must say it sounds a possibility you could be pregnant, but it's easy to build the symptoms in your mind to fit. Even though you feel sick that could be the nerves from just worrying you're pregnant. Oh! Look at the time, we'll have to go in now.'

Finally when they had taken their coats off and because they were alone in the cloakroom Laura asked, 'Sally, feel my tummy, gently press it. Does it feel any different to yours?'

Having felt both Sally had to admit there

was a difference. 'It feels more spongy somehow. You feel.'

'That's what I think.'

'There's only one way to solve it you know, you'll have to go and see the doctor.'

'I know, but I'm frightened he'll tell my Mum when he sees her. Even if it's a false alarm he'll understand that I've been doing something to give me a chance of being pregnant. Then he might tell Mum and I couldn't face that.'

'He won't, they've to keep everything confidential. Anyway if you are pregnant you'll have to tell your parents yourself.'

'I know, it's just plucking up the courage. I'll have to I know. Thanks for listening, it's been a help, it really has. I'll sort out going to the docs and I'll let you know what he says.'

'Good luck.'

Laura decided, at least with finishing work at varying times, her mother would not query why she was a bit late home one evening. She would give it another week, then if nothing had happened she would go to the doctor's on her way home after work. How she got through that week she didn't know. Her stomach heaved most of the time, but she was sure most of that was due to fear. It hardly bore thinking about what she would do if she were pregnant.

She tried to make as many excuses as she could for not seeing Keith. The way she felt she couldn't bear him to touch her and it was taking most of her control not to blurt out her worst fears. He took it as a sign that all was normal when she wouldn't let him touch her. He thought she had just been a bit later than usual.

Laura knew she was even getting curious looks from her family because she was so short tempered, but she couldn't help herself. The worry was just too much to bear.

After the week was up still nothing had happened. Taking her courage in both hands she realized if they finished work early one evening then that was her cue that she'd to go to see the doctor. She didn't really like the thought of going straight from work because she wouldn't have the chance to give herself a good wash down before she went.

By the time she arrived at the doctor's, the waiting room was packed even though she had finished work really early this Wednesday evening and had thought she was in good time. Laura looked around trying to memorize each face that was there before her. The basis of going into the doctor was simply in turn as each arrived. Laura knew how easy it would be to miss her turn if she forgot who was there. Sometimes she had even seen people deliberately try to get in before their turn, but it was surprising how the other patients usually quickly called out and stopped them.

She counted how many people were in front of her and to her horror it was nine. She settled back in her seat as she realized she was going to be ages waiting here. Why hadn't she thought to bring her book to read she asked herself. As she waited her stomach churned. This wasn't a baby causing it, just pure and simply nerves.

To pass the time she made little games up in her head. The first one was to look around and try to guess what ailment each of the patients had. Of course, she would never know if she was right or wrong in her guess, but at least it passed some time on. After all that looking and thinking only two more patients had gone in to see the doctor. What to do next? Then she thought she would try to guess what job each did or maybe some of the women were mums or housewives. She kept on with games like this, as first one patient then another went in to see the doctor. At last only one before her to go although the waiting room was no more empty than when she had come in as a lot more patients had come after her. Now to try to take her mind off what the doctor would say she tried to think of anything she could, all the while her eyes held on the surgery door. The click of the door opening nearly made her jump as she realized this was it, her turn to go in.

'Hello young lady. I haven't seen you for a long time. Now what can I do for you today?' asked the doctor as he saw who it was.

Laura opened her mouth to explain but somehow the words wouldn't come out, she simply stuttered, 'H'm, well you see it's like this.'

'Come on no need to be shy with me, just tell me clearly what's wrong.'

Taking the bull by the horns she then simply stated, 'I think I'm pregnant.'

Without a flicker of emotion Doctor Peterson looked at her. 'I see, and what symptoms have you to make you think this?'

'I'm feeling sickly most of the time.' Feeling rather embarrassed she added, 'And my breasts are tender.'

'How late are you?'

'Late? Oh! I see what you mean, about three weeks which I never usually am.'

'Have you brought a urine sample?'

'No, should I have done?'

'I don't like to do an internal examination unless it's really necessary to do so. It's easier and safer to send the sample away for testing.

Never mind, take your bottom underwear off and up on the couch.'

Laura had never given a thought to the fact this could be part of her visit. She had just presumed she would tell him how she felt and he would say yes or no to whether she was pregnant. This was far worse than she could have ever imagined. With hands trembling she removed what she had been told and went over to perch on the couch.

'That's no good like that, you'll have to lay down.'

Realizing what he meant she did as bid, with knees knocking together instead of staying apart. This seemed an invasion into her privacy. But in actual fact she hardly felt anything and within a few moments he turned away. 'You're correct, you are pregnant. Get dressed again.'

As she did Laura asked, 'What do I do now?'

Realizing the situation the doctor asked of her, 'I don't suppose your parents know?'

'No, actually nobody does.'

'I see. Well, first of all I'll give you a prescription for some iron tablets. We always put pregnant women on those to keep their strength up. Usually I then sort out the hospital arrangements, get that ready so you're booked in for the birth. Once you're booked in, if you wish you can go and have a look around the maternity hospital. I think the best thing you can do is tell your parents, discuss it thoroughly with them and sort yourself out. Then come back with your mother and we'll do all the hospital booking then. By the way are you going to marry the father?'

Laura hadn't even given this a thought so she only gave a very reluctant, 'No.'

'I see. Is he married?'

Quickly Laura jumped in, 'Oh no. Nothing like that, it's just I haven't told him yet. We certainly hadn't planned anything like getting married for a long time.' All the while Laura was wondering what he would say if he knew the true age of her boyfriend.

The doctor's voice broke into those thoughts. 'That's all we can do today. Don't forget your prescription. Now do as I've said, talk it all through with your parents then come back to see me. Look after yourself, remember there are two of you now.'

'Thanks, bye,' said Laura as she walked out of the surgery in a daze. She wasn't really quite sure how she got home that night. She certainly couldn't remember going home, her legs must have carried her there with a will of their own. In her mind she rehearsed how she would break the news to her parents, but however she said it in her head, it didn't sound right. She could imagine them both nearly passing out with shock when she told them the news. Still, she would have to, there was no way she could keep this hidden. This thought made her have a nervous, silent giggle to herself. She was just aware enough of her surroundings to know that she was getting a few funny looks from passersby as if her face was showing her reactions to her thoughts.

Then it suddenly struck her, there was Keith. The news would have to be broken to him. She didn't know which was going to be worse, telling him or her parents. He might not want anything else to do with her. But then she felt angry. After all it was his fault, he was to blame. He had told her it was totally safe.

Suddenly she realized her hand was on the gate to her home. How had she got here? She paused to try to stop her rapid heartbeat and somehow make herself look as if she had just had just arrived home from a normal day at work. The decision was made, Keith must be told first, after all it was his baby as well as hers. He had responsibility for what had happened as well as herself. Somehow they would have to work out what they were going to do about it all before they broke the news to her parents. That was it, with this Laura put a smile on her face and walked with a positive step into the house.

9

'It can't be true, the doctor must have made a mistake,' repeated Keith once more as he paced up and down.

'Come on, Keith admit it, he hasn't made a mistake. All the evidence is there as well to point to the fact that I'm pregnant.'

'But it doesn't happen at that time of the month and anyway not the first time.'

'I don't know where you get your information from but you're certainly wrong. What more proof do you want than my being pregnant.'

'I still can't believe it. Are you really sure?'

'Yes. How many more times do I have to tell you?'

'Well, can't you do something silly like falling down some steps and causing a miscarriage?'

Laura, nearly in tears at this suggestion, just looked at Keith with contempt.

'All right, all right. I can see that was a stupid idea, but there must be something we can do.'

'I don't know, do I? I've never had any experience of this before and seeing as I

105

haven't told my parents yet I can hardly ask my Mum's advice.' Laura was beginning to feel very upset now by Keith's attitude. He seemed more concerned about the effect on him of her pregnancy, not about her. Whatever happened it was her that had to go through with it all.

In the end, with panic in her voice, she had to say to him. 'Look, we seem to be going around in circles and not coming up with any answers. Let's talk this through sensibly. You might as well accept I'm pregnant. Can we at least agree on that?'

'I suppose so but it's just such a shock. Just wait until I see Trev tomorrow I won't half give him what for, telling me it was safe.'

'You'll tell no one, do you hear, at least not until our parents know and everything's sorted out. At least let's have that little bit of respect for them, let them be the first to hear. As it is, it will be bad enough for them to hear it from us, but it would be horrific if they were to hear it as gossip. Do you understand that? No telling anyone, nor any bragging at school. Remember it isn't long since I was there myself. I know what it's like, everyone wanting to go one better than the next.'

'Okay, okay, what do you take me for? A total fool. I get the picture.'

'So if we both agree I'm pregnant, where

do we go from here?'

'I said before can't you take something or do something to get rid of it.'

Feeling very angry now Laura shouted at him. 'It's not an it, it's a baby, our baby, that we made whether we intended to or not.' Suddenly Laura realized she was being very defensive of this new being they had created. She hadn't really thought of it as an actual living thing herself before this.

Calming down now in a resigned voice she said, 'I don't know what we can do Keith, I really don't. What I do know is I couldn't intentionally harm this baby.' A thought suddenly came to Laura. 'Will we get into trouble because you're under sixteen? I'm not sure whether the same law applies to boys as girls. Oh dear, what have we done? There are so many things to think about. I don't know about your parents but mine will go mad when we tell them.'

'You're not kidding! Mine'll be furious. Anyway who said we're telling them, you might have to tell them on your own. Then again can't you discreetly ask some of the older women at work if there's something you can do to stop being pregnant.'

'For goodness sake stop being so naive. You seemed to know it all when you wanted sex. That's the root of all this problem.'

By now Keith was panicking at what he had done and started shouting at Laura. 'Look, I don't know what to do. I'm too young to have to cope with this. For heavens sake, I'm still at school.'

Laura was frightened by his attitude of not wanting to know. 'Well you weren't too young to have sex, you told me so. If you aren't too young for that, then you aren't too young to cope with the consequences.'

Seeing a bit of sense in what she said Keith calmed down a little bit. 'You've given me a shock. This was the last thing I expected. Just let me sleep on it tonight to think a bit more what to do.'

'Yes, I think that's a good idea. We're getting nowhere like this. I think it would be a good idea if I went now. We're only going to carry on arguing about it.'

'Stay a bit longer. At least we can have a bit of kissing and petting.'

'You must be joking. Being like this that's the last thing I feel like at the moment.'

With a rather sullen voice he said, 'Well at least if we went all the way now it would be safe. You're already pregnant so what's the harm?'

Already grabbing her things Laura turned at the room door. 'I'm going Keith. There's no point in continuing trying to talk to you tonight, you just can't understand how I feel. I'll meet you tomorrow and hopefully you'll talk more sense.'

Before he could reply Laura was already down the hallway and the front door was slammed shut behind her.

Tears poured down her cheeks as she walked up the street. She didn't want to go home yet, there would be the endless questions why was she crying, what was wrong with her. She needed to get control of herself before she faced her family. It wasn't time to tell them the news yet. She wasn't ready to face that. At the thought of Keith's attitude, more tears welled up in her eyes and ran down her cheeks. She had expected him to be more supportive. After all, he was to blame as well as her. More so really because it was him who had convinced her all would be all right. How stupid she'd been to believe him, but dwelling on that didn't help the situation now.

Much to her dismay she suddenly heard a voice behind her. 'Hi sis, wait for me.'

Quickly she rubbed her hand over her face to try to wipe away any trace of tears, whilst not pausing in her step.

'Hang on, Laura. Didn't you hear me call?'

To cover her distress without turning she just shouted back, 'Come on slow coach, you should catch me easily, you've longer legs than me.'

She nearly jumped out of her skin when within what seemed like seconds a hand grasped her shoulder and a voice in her ear said, 'Caught!'

Sense took over and she realized Mark had indeed caught her up quickly. Luckily darkness was falling so all she hoped was he couldn't see her face properly.

'You're early going home, aren't you Laura? I take it that's where you are off to.'

'Of course I'm going home. I'm tired that's all so I felt like an early night.'

Laughing at her. 'Oh, getting old already are you, can't keep up the pace.'

'Don't be cheeky to your elders you young monkey,' she replied trying to act in her usual bantering manner with him.

'So what have you being doing tonight with Keith?' Mark asked with a sarcastic voice.

'That's none of your business. Anyway, what are you doing out at this time? You should have been home before this. Mum and Dad will be worried.'

'No, they won't. I rang them to ask if I could stay a bit longer. We were in the middle of a game of scrabble and we wanted to finish it. They said it was all right as long as it didn't happen too often me asking to stay out longer.'

'Go on I believe you this time.'

Indignantly he challenged her. 'Ask Mum and Dad if you don't believe me.'

'I said I did, didn't I?'

'Oh yes, definitely.'

Both walked the rest of the way home in silence. Laura was glad she had met Mark after all. Without knowing it he had made her feel better and she was now sure her mum and dad wouldn't notice there was anything wrong with her. As they walked in the door their mother was just walking down the hallway with a cup of tea.

'Ha, both of you in together, a rare sight. The kettle has just boiled if you want a drink.'

'I don't think I'll bother tonight,' Laura quickly said.

'Why not, don't you feel well?'

'Yes I'm fine, just a little bit tired. I've come home to get an early night and I'm not thirsty anyway. I'll just pop my head around the door and say goodnight to Dad.'

'Are you sure you're all right? It's not like you to have an early night.'

'Fine, honestly. Anyway you know the saying, there's always a first time.'

'Well goodnight then. I hope you feel better after a good night's sleep.'

'I will, don't worry,' and quickly putting her head around the room door. 'Night Dad, see you in the morning.'

He was so engrossed in the telly she only heard a vague grunt in reply.

She wasn't really tired and once her head did touch the pillow sleep eluded her. All she could think about was what was happening to her and Keith's reaction. She put her hand gently on her stomach but it didn't really feel any different. It was hard to imagine there was a life in there.

But how could she tell her parents. Quietly she sobbed into her pillow, she daren't let any of the family hear her. 'Why, oh why, had this to happen to me?' she kept saying over to herself in her head. But she knew the answer, she should have had the strength of will to say no.

However much she tossed and turned no answer came to her how to solve the problem. All she could think was she would have the baby, then maybe get a part-time job like her mother and between them they would look after the baby. That seemed the only possible solution. After the initial shock her family would support her she was sure. Finally as daybreak was nearly there, Laura fell asleep more settled in her mind.

As she went to work the next day she

hoped she would be able to tell Sally her news. She knew she had told Keith not to tell anybody, but she felt the need to share this knowledge with somebody, particularly after Keith's attitude. Anyway Sally didn't know anybody her parents knew, so there was no way this news could get back to them from her. Even if she couldn't help, she knew she would feel a bit better for the chat. Much to her disappointment when she went into the cloakroom it was full of people chattering. All morning as she worked, she watched for Sally going downstairs to the loo, then when she did she could follow and it would give her chance to have a few minutes alone and talk to her.

Finally when her chance came and Sally walked out of the toilet she saw Laura waiting there. 'Hi, how are things going? Have you been to the doctors yet?'

'Yes and the answer is yes — I'm pregnant.'

Sally looked really sorry for her. 'Oh you poor thing, what a shock. How have your parents taken it?'

'I haven't told them yet, I only went to the doctors' last night. I told my boyfriend Keith, but he isn't too pleased. His attitude really upset me. I don't even know if he is going to support me.'

'Well I suppose it was a shock for him too.'

'Maybe, but it was him who convinced me it was safe. I have certainly learnt a lesson. Last night as I lay awake I decided whatever happens I'll keep the baby. I just hope my Mum supports me then we can look after it together. Anyway we'd better get back upstairs before we both are missed.'

To make matters worse Laura was pulled up by the assistant manager, saying she had made one or two errors in her work and he didn't know what was the matter with her. She nearly made a complete fool of herself by bursting into tears in front of him, but just managed to hold them back and keep some of her self respect. She just gave a murmured, 'Sorry, I'll try harder from now on.'

He looked at her keenly and told her. 'Make sure you do, because you are coming along really well. We're very pleased how you are learning the work.'

This gave a little boost to her spirits and she tried to put other thoughts from her mind and concentrate on the job in hand.

But once she left work and started on her journey home she had time again to worry about how Keith was going to be tonight. It was really his attitude she decided that had upset her more than the news that she was pregnant, because after all he was as much to blame as her.

She had no appetite for her tea with the stress of it all, but was then even more worried her parents, particularly her mother, could sense something was wrong. She just couldn't cope with that, not until she had got herself sorted out with Keith.

Now rather than being anxious at seeing him she had an impatience for it to be time. Surely when he had thought about things during the light of day he would have come to his senses and realized it was his responsibility as well. She knew he was young in age but he appeared older in looks and attitude at times.

Trying to keep some normality she prepared herself in her usual manner to go out. At last it was time, but once again the reluctance to meet him, in case he was just as cross tempered as last night, held her back. But she realized it had to be faced and she quickly shouted to her mum and dad. 'I'm off out now, I don't think I'll be late in, I still feel tired.'

This was a mistake to say that to her mother as she quickly rushed out of the room. 'You're not ill are you?'

'No, of course not. Just settling into work is catching up on me. Don't worry, I'll see you later.'

As she walked out of the door Laura

115

thought ruefully to herself what a laugh that comment was. If only they knew she was certain they would worry.

She approached the spot in the park where she and Keith had agreed to meet. She was pleasantly surprised to see he was already there. Normally he wasn't a very good time keeper and it was often rare for him to be first at their meeting spot. He actually walked up to meet her, if not with an actual smile on his face, at least he looked cheerful. 'How are you — have you been feeling sick again today?'

This question took Laura by total surprise, the fact that he could actually show concern for her. 'No, not too bad, not since I found sucking glucose sweets helps.'

'Good. I've thought about you all day and the situation we're in. I'm sorry I was so selfish last night. I realize now it must be terrible for you. Not only the knowledge that you're actually pregnant but also that it makes you feel so ill. Do you want to go for a walk or sit over there?'

'Whatever you want to do, it doesn't bother me.'

'Let's sit a while, then if you feel chilly we can walk.'

He put his arm around her and held her close as they moved over to the seat. Laura could feel all tension go out of her as she felt more contented how things were going.

As soon as they sat down Keith quickly started to say, 'I'm sorry I was nasty to you last night, I know I said some things I shouldn't have. I just never expected it. I did honestly believe everything would be all right. I didn't know it was possible to get pregnant so easily. Anyway, now I've had time to think about it I do realize I'll have to take some responsibility. I could help you tell your parents and we could sort things out so it can be adopted.'

Before he could say any more Laura shouted at him. 'No! I'll not let it be adopted.'

'Sh, keep your voice down. We don't want other people knowing what we are talking about. You don't know who might overhear what we are saying. I just thought we're both young and if we did that it wouldn't spoil our lives.'

'Spoil our lives! Don't you realize I could never live with myself if I gave my child away.'

Rather sulkily now Keith said, 'My child as well.'

Fair smirking at him Laura snarled, 'Isn't that what I've been saying all along. It's your responsibility as well as mine.'

Realizing he had put his foot in it again he quickly withdrew this statement. 'Sorry, it was only a suggestion. Well, I suppose the only other alternative is when I'm sixteen we could marry. Of course the only trouble is, I would still be at school then, so we might have to wait until I get a job, which you realize would be after you have had the baby.'

'Oh, yes and where would we live?'

'Maybe my Mum and Dad would let us live with them. There's plenty of room now there is only me at home.'

This wasn't Laura's idea at all of how to start married life and if she had to live with anybody's parents she would have preferred her own. She had to admit to him though, 'I suppose my Mum and Dad would offer but they don't have as much room as your parents. It would be nicer to have our own home.'

'Be realistic, Laura. How can we afford that?'

'I know, it was just a dream. There's still the main hurdle to get over. It's all right planning all this but we have to tell our parents. Have you given any thought to how we do that?'

'Not really, have you?'

'No. I've been too upset today to give a lot of thought to telling them. I've been more worried about your attitude last night. I even got in trouble at work today because my mind wasn't on my work.'

'I'm not surprised. I don't think I've heard what was said in one lesson today, worrying about how we could sort it out.'

At last Laura thought he was back on her side. Finally he said, 'I couldn't face going and telling them tonight. Sorting ourselves out is enough for one evening. Do you think it would be best if you had a quiet word on your own with your Mum and told her?'

Here he goes again thought Laura, pulling away from the situation. Everytime she felt he was with her, to support her, suddenly he seemed to back away. Then thinking about it she decided even though she didn't agree, she should tell her mum on her own. At the same time if her mum realized from his attitude that he was rather reluctant in what he offered that would make the situation worse from her parents point of view.

'All right then. If I get in early tomorrow before Dad I'll try to talk to her. I'm dreading it. I know they'll feel I've let them down. They've always drummed it into me to not let this happen and now I have. You see, I've never told you this but they had to get married when they were having me, so to them it will be like history repeating itself. Of course, they were older and engaged so they were going to get married anyway. They had already saved up quite a lot of money for a house. Still, their parents must have listened to them, so I hope they will listen to us.'

'Sounds like a good idea. Just tell her when you two selves are alone.'

'But what about your parents, when are we going to tell them?'

'I think I'll let you tell yours first.'

'Aren't you frightened they'll get straight in touch with yours?'

'I never thought of that. But if I tell mine tomorrow night I won't know definitely if you have told yours, then the reverse might happen — they might ring them. That would be terrible for you.'

Laura was getting exasperated how to sort it all out. 'I don't know, there seems no solution. I'll try my best to tell her tomorrow but I can't control what time I get out of work, nor if she'll be in the right mood. Look, as soon as I've told her I'll give you a quick ring then you know to tell yours. That's the best I can think of.'

'Okay. Let's walk as we talk, I'm cold now.'

They walked and chatted for a while going over the same ground again really. At least when they parted for the night Laura did feel a bit happier that it was on a better footing than on the previous evening. But she still hadn't got over the worst, that was yet to come.

10

Next day at work she did her best to not make any more mistakes as she didn't want to feel the wrath of the management again. The thought of further trouble was more than she could bear. She knew if anybody said anything wrong to her she would burst into tears. It was going to be bad enough when her news broke at work, so she could do without making a fool of herself before then.

It seemed that fate was with her or maybe against her, she couldn't decide, but all the cashiers balanced straight away. She had finished early, her destiny was sealed. Tonight would have to be the night she told her mother the news.

Taking the bull by the horns, as soon as she arrived home and indeed found her mother alone she told her, 'Come and sit down. I want to talk to you, I've something important to tell you.'

She could see by the joyful reaction on her mother's face she thought she was going to tell her some exciting news about work. Inside she felt upset because she knew her mother was going to be so unhappy that it wasn't good news as she expected. 'I'm sorry Mum, but you're not going to like what I've to tell you.'

The expression changed on her face and quickly jumping in her mother asked, 'You haven't been sacked have you?'

Laura had to smile despite what she knew she had to say, and quickly she reassured her on that score. 'No, nothing like that. It's nothing to do with work at all.' As she watched her mother she could see her face slowly change from puzzlement to shock as a new thought struck her. 'You're not pregnant are you?'

Laura couldn't stop the tremor in her voice as she knew how much this was going to hurt her mother. 'I'm sorry Mum, but I am.' Then she couldn't control herself any longer as she just burst into tears.

'Oh no! Not that, tell me it isn't true,' her mother pleaded.

'It is. I've already been to the doctors and he's confirmed it.'

'Whatever will we do?' wailed her mother as she wrung her hands in despair.

'Well, Keith has said he'll marry me when he's old enough.'

'Oh yes sure, and what will you live on? If he does even get a job when he leaves school he certainly won't earn enough to support a wife and child. Come on now, Laura, be realistic.'

'I thought I was being. Why do you think we have worked it all out like this?'

Then another thought struck her mother. 'Oh! What will your father say, he'll be furious. He'd set so much store by you.' Her mother was so cross and confused by now, she just snarled at Laura, 'You fool, you silly young fool.'

Laura's quick reaction was to throw back at her, 'I thought you, of all people, would understand.'

'Why, young lady, what do you mean by that exactly?'

'You had to get married when you were having me.'

'I hardly call that the same thing.'

Rather indignantly Laura challenged this. 'Why not? You were pregnant with me, so surely that was the same.'

Feeling quite cross as well as upset her mother started shouting as she answered her back. 'But we were a lot older. We were engaged and had saved to get married. It was only a matter of bringing the wedding forward a few months. Now do you call that the same thing? Keith isn't even old enough to wed you yet. There's no comparison, no none at all.'

Suddenly realizing the full implication her mother started to pace around in anguish and repeated herself. 'Oh! What will your Father say, whatever will he say. He'll be furious, yes he will, but he'll also be disappointed in you. He had so many high hopes for you in the future. What future have you got now, I ask? What future?' So she continued with this anguish whilst not making one sensible contribution to the situation.

By now tears were streaming down Laura's face and she didn't really know how to deal with this situation. 'Maybe we'd better wait until Dad comes home and talk it over with him.'

Her mother was at a total loss how to deal with it further. 'You've wasted enough of my time. You'd best help me get tea. You know it always puts your Dad in a bad humour if his meal isn't ready on the table when he comes home. That's the last thing we want tonight. Come on, help me.'

Wiping her eyes Laura followed her mother into the kitchen knowing better than to say more than, 'Yes, mum.'

It amazed Laura, that when her father came in her mother responded to him as though nothing was the matter. In fact they were both in rather a jovial mood over tea. But once finished her mother took on a more serious note. 'When I've cleared away Frank, we'd better sit down. Laura has something to tell us.'

Just like the look on her mother's face when she had said this to her, her father had the same look of expectancy as if she was going to tell some good news about work. This cut Laura up even more knowing they were expecting so much of her.

As soon as they were all sat down together her father couldn't contain his eagerness. 'Come on then lass, out with it. What is this good news?'

'Mum didn't say good news, only news.' Taking a deep breath and thinking here goes Laura plunged on, 'I'm pregnant.'

Her father's face instantly changed from joy to despondency. 'Say that again?'

'I'm pregnant.'

Putting his head in his hands he mumbled, 'I don't know what to say, I really don't. This is the last thing I expected of you Laura.'

'But Dad, Mum and you had to get . . . ,' she got no further as her mother quickly jumped in, 'That's enough Laura.'

Realizing it was the best thing to do as she was told at this moment she just kept quiet.

'Dear, dear,' her dad mumbled. Finally looking at her mother he asked her, 'I take it

Laura has already told you this news Marjorie?'

'Yes, just before tea.'

'I see. Why didn't you tell me straight away?'

'I wanted you to enjoy your tea before you were upset by the news.'

'M'm. So what do you think we should do Marjorie?'

'There's no question, she must have it adopted.'

'Mum! No. I've already told you I want to keep the baby.'

'Be quiet young lady, you've done enough harm. Now you'll do as you're told.'

'But Dad it's my baby.'

'Enough! You're still a minor and we're still responsible for you as your parents. I don't want to talk about it anymore tonight. I want to sleep on it, then decide what's to be done.'

Laura realized it was best to say no more at this point as he had neither agreed nor disagreed to her keeping the baby. Just then her brother rushed into the room. 'Telephone for you Laura.'

As she walked out of the room her mother called after her. 'If that's Keith you can tell him you're staying in tonight and yes, you can tell him you've told us about the baby. But there's no more than that to say to him at the moment.'

'Oh Mum! What harm can I come to now seeing him tonight?'

'I said you are staying in tonight and that's that. Anyway at the moment you have a baby to think of so resting won't do you any harm.'

Rushing to the phone Laura could hear Mark say to her parents, 'Baby, what baby?' and her mother snap at him, 'None of your business, just you go and finish your homework.' Laura gave a hiccup and sob as she said, 'Hello Keith.'

With more concern than he usually showed he quickly asked her, 'Are you all right, Laura? Have your parents upset you? I'll come to see you now if you like.'

'No, don't do that. They're really cross and have told me I've to stay in tonight.'

'Well I could come to see you.'

'Not with the mood they're in. Leave it, then maybe tomorrow once they've got used to the idea of me having a baby they might want to discuss it properly.'

'Why, what've they being saying to you?'

Laura gave another hiccup with a sob as she said tearfully, 'They say I've to have the baby adopted.'

Keith exploded down the phone. 'How could they? I thought you said your Mother was pregnant with you when they got married.'

'She was and I pointed that out but it made her see red. Like I said to you before, they were already engaged and had saved up a good amount of money before they had to marry. After all, they'd to rearrange their wedding and bring it forward a few months. She still says it's a different situation.'

'I don't see how. I've said I'll marry you when I'm old enough.'

'I know, just leave it now until they cool down then they might see sense. I'd better go now, I don't want to make them crosser than they are already by staying too long on the phone. They said I hadn't to discuss it with you. I'll ring you tomorrow night once they've talked properly about it.'

Feeling he was missing out here Keith responded rather petulantly, 'If that's the way they want it I suppose it'll have to be that way, but I can't see the harm in us meeting.'

'I know but you know what parents are like. Love you and I promise I'll ring tomorrow.'

'If you say so, goodnight then.'

Laura came off the phone very despondent that Keith hadn't said he loved her. She felt so confused.

Her mother rushed into the hallway. 'Right

young lady, I hope you did as you were told. You were on the phone a long time.'

'I did. He was just trying to get more out of me, that's what took the time. I told him I would ring him tomorrow after we've talked it through further. I hope that's all right?'

'It'll have to be. After all, I've to admit he is involved in all this. By the way has he told his parents yet?'

'No, not yet. He thought you should be told first. He wanted to see what we'd sorted out before he told his.'

'M'm well, just as long as he does. Mind you, I can easily ring them myself and make sure they know.'

Oh no! Laura thought to herself, this is going to be real trouble. Trying to avert this she appealed to the better side of her mother's nature. 'That won't be necessary honestly, he'll tell them. I'm sure once we've sorted ourselves out, like I said, he'll tell them. Why shouldn't he? Anyway there are always enough gossips around and if he didn't tell them then one way or another they'd find out. That would be even worse than him telling them himself.'

'Enough said on the topic tonight. I said an early night for you and I meant it. Go and have a good sleep and don't start worrying it'll all sort out in the wash. Good-night love, by the way just one last thing. I was so shocked by it all I've never asked you how you are feeling. Are you sick with the pregnancy?'

Laura was rather taken aback by her mother's sudden change of tone but managed to answer, 'Not really sick. I just feel nauseous a lot of the time, but sucking glucose sweets takes that off.'

'Let's hope it gets no worse. I felt terrible most of the time I was having you. Not well at all, but look what a healthy baby I produced. Go to bed now, sleep tight don't let the bugs bite.'

Laura gave a smile at her mother as she had brought back childhood memories by what she said. But she didn't sleep tight, she tossed and turned wondering what conclusions her parents were coming to. She was sure they would be discussing her now they'd got her out of the way. At times she nearly climbed back out of bed and went to join them, after all it was her life they were meddling with. But common sense took over and she realized it was best to leave well alone. No doubt once they sat down and talked it through they would realize what she had suggested made a lot of sense. After all, she thought with annoyance, who were they to judge her? So their wedding had been a bit

130

nearer than hers and Keith's when it happened to them but even so they couldn't get away from the fact her mother was pregnant when she married. Finally, this thought seemed to settle her mind and she drifted off to sleep.

It didn't seem two minutes before she heard a voice, 'Laura, come on get up otherwise you'll be late for work.'

Slowly it dawned on her this was not a dream but her mother actually calling her to get up. Had she really been asleep so long? It seemed incredible, she hadn't expected to get a wink of sleep. Now her stomach turned at the thought of the day ahead she had to somehow get through. It was going to be very difficult to carry on at work as if there were nothing wrong. But she knew she had to. It would soon be evening and she was sure her parents would tell her to ring Keith and ask him to come around so they could all sort out the plan of action. This thought fair cheered her up and she jumped out of bed suddenly feeling as if a weight had been lifted from her.

Not wanting to get on the wrong side of her parents as they had told her she had to wait until that night before they would discuss the baby further, so she acted as if there wasn't anything any different during breakfast. Considering everything she was quite chirpy and when she was finally ready for work said a cheery, 'Good-bye' to her mother, leaving her staring open mouthed wondering what on earth had got into her. She had expected to see a miserable and glum face at the breakfast table, not somebody looking as if they hadn't a care in the world. Well, if Laura thought it was no problem her mum and dad felt differently. It had been the early hours of the morning before they had gone to sleep after spending a great deal of time discussing what to do. Both of them were going to be busy doing a lot of sorting out during the day, so they could put their final proposals to Laura that evening as promised. They also knew it was going to be a difficult evening because what they had to say would not be to Laura's liking.

Meanwhile, Laura had a good day at work. Somehow telling her parents had seemed to relieve her burden. She could give her job her full attention. Sally commented to her, when they had a quiet moment together. 'Was it a false alarm, you seem suddenly happy?'

'No, but I've told my parents and we're all going to get it sorted out tonight. I know everything will be all right now. I do feel so much happier.'

It seemed as if events were going her way, when everybody balanced first time and they were sent from work early. This pleased Laura as she felt she couldn't contain herself much longer waiting to hear what her parents had to say.

She gave a cheerful, 'Hello' as she breezed in home. If she could have seen the reaction on her mother's face to this she wouldn't have felt so confident all would be well. Laura was too wrapped up in her own thoughts to notice how unusually quiet her parents were during tea. After they had finished her mother quickly jumped up saying, 'I won't be two shakes washing up. Dad, do you want to dry for me then we had best go and sit down and get this business sorted out. Mark, you can go to your room to get your homework done.'

'Oh, Mum!' he quickly protested.

'You'll do as you're told. I want no nonsense from you.'

One look at his mother's face and he knew she meant it, so grabbing his schoolbag he made a quick retreat.

'Go and sit down, Laura. We'll be with you in a minute or two.'

'Okay, Mum.'

True to her word before Laura had time to really gather all her thoughts her parents joined her again. Her father didn't seem to know what to say, he just gave an embarrassed cough. In the end her mother broke the silence. 'Both of us have been very busy today getting things sorted out. We talked long into the night and once we'd decided what was to be done we thought it best to get on with it. That's right isn't it Dad?'

'Aye, to tell you the truth Laura I haven't been in work today. I was too upset by what you told us last night. I've always set great store by the fact you were going to make something of yourself. I felt fair sick, yes I did, by it all. Anyway, it has given me chance to sort one or two things out.'

Her mother again quickly jumped in. 'We do hope you have realized by now it'll be impossible for you to keep the baby.'

Laura just looked at them with puzzlement. 'I don't know what you are talking about! Of course I'm going to keep the baby.'

Her mother looked at her with a sad expression. 'Sorry love, you're not. It's going to be adopted once you've had it.'

Laura could only say, 'Adopted?'

'That's right, that's what I said. Your Father has been in touch with a home in Leeds and you'll stay there during the week. It's a home for unmarried mothers.'

Laura still couldn't fully comprehend what they were saying. 'It'll be a long way to travel to work from there.'

'You won't be working in the bank. They don't allow it. Have you got that paper Frank with the jobs in. Here look at this Laura, there are plenty of jobs in Leeds you could do. They needn't know you're pregnant until you're a bit further on.'

'Isn't that a bit deceitful?'

'Nay love! You'll need all the money you can get to help keep you in Leeds. You'll come home at week-ends to stay with us.'

'Oh! That's kind of you I must say.' Laura said sarcastically before she could stop herself.

'Now be careful what you say. It isn't our fault we're having to sort this mess out.'

Still feeling very annoyed, yet at the same time extremely worried by it all, Laura pointed out. 'There would be no mess if you just let me keep the baby and marry Keith when he is old enough.'

Both her parents said in unison, 'Impossible.'

Petulantly Laura looked at her parents and said in a flat voice. 'That's it then, that's what you plan to happen. Maybe Keith's parents will think differently.'

'No, they don't.'

With panic in her voice Laura scanned both their faces as she asked, 'What do you mean? You haven't been in touch with them have you?'

'Of course, they had to be told sometime and we didn't want to get things organized then them put their spanner in the works. But no, they agree entirely with us.'

'Thanks very much. You could at least have let Keith and myself tell them. I suppose Keith will be in trouble for that as well, not telling them before you. But you did ask me not to say anything last night. I didn't expect you to go behind my back. Anyway I'm going to talk to Keith now and see what he has to say about all this.' With these words Laura flounced out of the room and her mother's voice drifted after her. 'Remember, he is still under age for marriage, so whatever you say to each other you really can't do anything about it.'

These words were still ringing in her ears as Laura heard Keith's voice on the other end of the phone. She quickly jumped in with, 'I suppose your parents have already spoken to you?'

'Of course, what do you expect when yours have gone and blabbed everything.'

'Don't blame me. I didn't know they were going to do that. I'm as cross as you about it all. Anyway that's not what I want to talk to you about. What are we going to do now?'

'What do you mean what are we going to do now? We're going to do as they have told us. There's nothing else we can do.'

At these words Laura broke into tears. She felt she had been well and truly let down by him. 'What do you mean nothing else to do? I thought you said you would marry me when you were old enough.'

'Be sensible, Laura. Without our parents' backing and consent how can we? We have no money of our own, in fact nothing at all to set us up.'

Laura couldn't take any more of this, she just slammed the phone down and ran to the privacy of her room where she sobbed her heart out. Inside her she was hoping her mother would come to console her and relent at what she had said. But not this time. She was left on her own to mull over the true facts of what the future held in store for her.

11

A very subdued Laura came down to breakfast. Her mother still seemed unsympathetic to her predicament. 'I suggest you don't say anything at work, Laura, until you've found another job and it's time to hand in your notice. When you come in tonight, we'll start sorting through the job advertisements then you can get some letters of application sent off.'

Seeing no point in arguing further if she hadn't Keith's backing she just gave a submissive, 'Yes, Mum.'

How she got through the day she didn't know. Each small task she did made her realize how much she enjoyed the work. She didn't want to leave to go to another job. Laura felt she had only just learnt the duties here and got to know the people she worked with. The thought of going through all that again was too much to bear. Then, after all, she would be at her new job no time before she would have to leave that. She couldn't see the point of any of it. Why couldn't she stay here? Then she remembered her mum had said it was the bank's policy not to keep on any single, pregnant employees. So she had no choice about the new job. Still, she could have had some choice about the home and adoption. If she could stay with her parents at the week-end, she didn't see why she couldn't just carry on as now, just simply stay there all the time. There suddenly seemed a lot of unanswered questions. The more she thought about it as she went on with her work the more determined she was to have her say.

Tonight she was going to say more. Why shouldn't she? It was her life after all. With these decisions made she settled down to work, with what could have been taken for a cheerful expression on her face. Nobody would have deduced the concerns going on inside herself.

But once she arrived home and saw the set expression on her mother's face it somehow seemed a different matter. She just sat down quietly and wrote out the job applications as her mother directed. She was amazed that she was actually interested in these jobs. Some even sounded better than her present job in the bank. As she put pen to paper she got quite carried away and couldn't stop herself exclaiming. 'Hey this doesn't sound a bad job, Mum, and the pay is better than I'm getting now.'

Her mother soon shot her high spirits

down by reminding her the job wasn't going to be for very long. It all brought it back to Laura very acutely that this was all about a baby. Suddenly she looked at her mother and pleaded with her. 'Can I ring Keith and tell him about the jobs I'm applying for?'

'Most certainly not young lady. Don't you realize the less you have to do with him the better? He's messed your life up enough.'

'But we intend to get married.'

'Not without our permission you can't and you'll have a long wait for that.'

The stress of the situation made Laura revert to childish behaviour. With a tear dripping down her cheek, she slammed the pen down and jumped up from the table. 'Just you wait and see, we'll show you.'

Behind her she heard the words. 'I think you've already done that.'

Realizing showing her temper wasn't going to get her anywhere, Laura quietly sat back down and finished the letters.

She was amazed how quickly the replies came with interview dates. Her mother even took her out to buy her a new outfit for the interviews. But she did remind her, 'Mind, remember when you go to the interviews that you do not make any mention whatsoever about having a baby. First get the job then, unfortunately, they will find out soon enough once you begin to show.'

For some reason she wasn't that nervous about the interviews. At least not as much as when she had the interview for the job in the bank. Maybe it was this couldn't care less approach that made her appear more confident during the interviews. Whatever the reason, she was offered three different jobs. The decision which one she wanted was easy, the one with the insurance company. Somehow the whole pattern of events was slipping into place too easily for Laura's comfort. She still hadn't given up the hope of keeping the baby and eventually marrying Keith. Her parents couldn't watch her every minute, although they tried. Whenever possible she made an effort to contact Keith by phone which was better than nothing if she wasn't allowed to meet him. She was amazed at the lengths her parents would go to in trying to keep them apart.

One night after she had genuinely been to see a female friend, as she climbed off the bus she actually saw her father hidden around a corner watching for her. The more she kept her eyes open for them the more she saw them spying on her. It was terrible. She now decided she would be glad when her month's notice was up with the bank and she could move to Leeds. Maybe things would be better there after all.

She had gone through one or two funny question times at the bank. Her colleagues were curious why, when she seemed so happy there, she was leaving after such a short time. Then when they found out she was moving to Leeds, without her parents, they were even more curious. She simply told them she wanted to be more independent and left them to draw their own conclusions from that. Off course, as with any job, there is always the know-it-all and the Jane she least liked was quick to point out she could have always asked for a transfer with the bank. Laura simply got around that one by saying truthfully that she was moving to a better paid job. The management knew the real reason for her leaving and had offered to release her before her month's notice was up, but Laura didn't want that as it would definitely make her leaving look suspicious.

The month went quickly enough and before she knew where she was it was her last day. Unlike the happiness she had felt when she left school, now she felt quite tearful all day at the thought of leaving. This surprised Laura but there wasn't anything she could do about it. It was simple, she had to leave and that was that. She was amazed how, in such a short time, she'd seemed to have made so many friends and as she left they gave her a good luck card. Even the manager called her in to his office. 'When things are all sorted out, if you feel you'd like to come back to work for us, let me know and I'll see what I can do. You'd a very promising career here.'

Taken aback at this Laura didn't really know what to say. 'Thank you. I'll just have to wait and see what happens.'

The previous week, her parents had taken her to see where she would be living during the week days. All things considered, Laura decided it wasn't too bad. She would have a room of her own, which was something, but she had to share a bathroom with two other occupants whose rooms were on the same landing as hers. Meals would be provided for her and there was a communal dining room and a sitting room if they wanted more than the solitude of their own rooms. Her parents had promised to help her move some of her personal things into her room in Leeds to make it look more homely for her. Much to her surprise, one evening, her father showed her a large box. 'Just something for you, to go in your room.'

'What is it?' she asked in surprise.

'Look inside then you'll find out.'

Much to her delight it was a portable television. This kindness really touched her as she realized after all she'd done to her parents she didn't deserve gifts like this. With tears in her eyes she hugged her dad. 'Thanks, Dad.' Unlike most of the time of late he didn't pull away from her as if in distaste.

One way and another they had managed to keep her away from Keith for most of that last month at home. It was so unfair, after all it was his baby as well. Then again Laura wondered how much of an attempt he had made to contact her. Surely if he had really wanted to speak to her, he would have found a way. Little did Laura know he had received so many threats from his parents that he decided it was best not to attempt to contact her. They had told him he had to knuckle down at his school work and come up with some good results before they would decide where to go from there.

All was packed that she needed, it was time for them to set off to Leeds. As they hadn't a car her Uncle John, dad's brother, was taking them. Because both her mum and dad came from close knit families, her aunts and uncles had been told what was going on. Even Mark seemed sorry to see her go, she detected a glint of a tear on his cheek as he rushed up to her to kiss her good-bye.

'You'll see me again on Friday night, silly,' Laura told him sensing his sadness.

'I know, but it'll seem strange without you here all the time.'

'I'd have thought you were glad to see the back of me, seeing you're always shouting at me,' Laura laughed at him.

'Well, who'll stick up for me now?' Mark asked in petulant voice.

'Time for you to grow up and look after yourself, little brother.'

Before any more could be said between them, Laura's mother interrupted. 'Come on, you two break it up. I wouldn't have thought you had much to say to each other, you don't normally have. Why couldn't you have let life be more peaceful and talked to each other like this before, instead of just shouting and arguing.'

Mark looked at her, 'Oh come on, Mum, you know all brothers and sisters fight. Didn't you with yours?'

'Maybe. Anyway I haven't time to discuss the issue anymore as we must get on our way now.'

As they pulled away from the house, Laura found it hard to believe she would be back in just four days time for the week-end visit. It felt as if she was going away for a lifetime. As if sensing how she felt her mother took hold of her hand. 'It'll be all right lass, never fret. You know the old saying which I keep repeating to you, but it is very true at times, that it all comes out in the wash. It'll come right in the end you see. You'll realize all this is for the best.'

Laura couldn't really see any of this but she felt she couldn't take any more at the moment so she just added, 'If you say so.'

She was amazed how quickly she settled into her new routine. It wasn't like being at home but there again she soon made some friends. She was nowhere near as lonely as she thought she would have been. If she was honest with herself she actually enjoyed her job a bit more in insurance than the bank. Straight away she was given more responsibility and felt part of a team, not just a junior having to work her way up. There was more than a little amazement when she had to let the cat out of the bag and admitted she was pregnant. At first the bosses seemed hostile that she had tricked them into giving her a job, but that soon passed.

Each week-end she went home Laura put pressure on her parents to let her see Keith. Of course, whilst she was away in the week they couldn't monitor the phone calls. So at least the pair of them had managed a few chats on the phone. His parents hadn't managed to stop that. The only problem was, the more Laura spoke to Keith, the more she wanted to see him. If she was really honest, Keith didn't sound quite as convincing that he was missing her. Odd times he let things out that gave the impression he was enjoying himself going out with the lads. When she asked him, 'Do you still want me to keep the baby and us to get married when you are old enough?' He was quick enough to respond, 'Of course I do. Why do you think I'm working hard to get good exam results?' This made Laura feel happy and see a point in all she was going through.

So life surprisingly moved on for Laura. She couldn't say she was as unhappy as she thought she'd be. Lonely maybe for her family, although some of the other girls in the home were a good laugh so what with her television and them she always seemed to have some company. The only problem was she would make a friend then that girl would have her baby and leave the home. So it was back to making a new friend.

There were some nice young men where she worked and she did get asked out on dates until they knew she was pregnant. Then the offers stopped, but Laura could understand why even though the companionship would have been nice.

At times she felt resentful that Keith must be having more freedom than she was. She was sure he wasn't questioned about his comings and goings with his friends, although she knew he must be watched enough to stop him making any attempt at seeing her at the week-ends.

She was quite amazed that there seemed to be a thawing in her parents' attitude when she went home at week-ends. Each visit they became more like she had always known them before she had sprung this shock on them. Both would ask, with interest, about her work and life in Leeds. 'What have you been up to this week then?'

'Oh this and that. One person, Maggie, who I'd made particular friends with left this week. She had her baby the other week. I was sorry to see her go, it won't seem the same without her.'

'Somebody else will come surely in her place, then you might make friends with them.'

'I suppose so.'

In fact, at times her mum even broached the subject of babies. Laura decided if she bided her time and took it carefully she might once again be able to bring up the possibility of keeping the baby. Therefore there was nobody more surprised than herself when she heard a knock at the front door one Saturday evening. 'Go and answer that Laura,' shouted her mum.

She looked in open mouthed amazement as Keith and his parents stood there. Seeing the look of surprise and fear on her face, Keith was quick to reassure her. 'It's all right, Laura. We're here at your parents' invitation. They asked us to come tonight because they said they had something to discuss with us.'

Laura could only look at them and an astonished 'Oh!' escaped from her.

'Aren't you going to invite us in? It's a bit chilly stood here.'

Laura sensing somebody had come up behind her heard her mother's voice. 'What are you thinking of, Laura, keeping them standing on the doorstep in the cold. Come in quick, please do and get warm. Laura will take your coats for you.'

Laura was too stunned to do any other than her mother had bid her. Her mind puzzled over and over again what was going on. Not sure whether she was supposed to be in on this, although the discussion could only be about her and Keith, Laura paused hesitantly in the lounge doorway. She heard her mother call, 'Come in here Laura, we're waiting for you.' Moving quickly across the room she could see there was a bemused expression on both Keith and his parent's faces.

Even her mother seemed to be finding it difficult knowing how to start the conversation. 'Er, I suppose you are wondering why we invited you here. Well, it is like this. We've been doing a lot of thinking and maybe our first approach to Laura and Keith's problem was a bit rash. After all it's going to be our grandchild, now isn't it?'

Not sure where all this was leading Keith's mother simply replied with a hesitant, 'Yes.'

Her mother carried on. 'So we decided maybe there is another way around the problem after all. Now then, Keith, you said you were willing to marry Laura when you reach sixteen. Do you still stand by that?'

Looking a bit put on the spot he paused as he answered, 'Yes.'

Looking pleased about this and not noticing his hesitation, her mother carried on intent on what she had to say, 'Good. Well after much discussion we've decided to give our permission to the marriage.'

Both Laura and Keith said in unison with a shocked voice, 'You have?'

Then quickly Keith's mother jumped in. 'But what about our thoughts on the subject? After all, Keith's our son and in any case what are they supposed to live on?'

Laura's mother seemed to have all the answers. 'Again, we have thought about that.

Keith should have no difficulty finding a job when he leaves school. We've looked into it and even if he's not well paid they'll be able to afford to rent a small back to back house. But I thought maybe we could also help them with the rent so they're not on the breadline or at least until Keith gets better paid. Already we've had a lot of kind offers from relatives offering various items of furniture and things for the baby.' Looking really pleased with herself she looked around the sea of faces. 'Now what do you all think about that?'

Each of them showed a different reaction but all were of total shock and surprise.

Laura was the first to find her voice. 'You mean I don't have to have the baby adopted after all? We can keep it?'

'That's what I've said isn't it? Now then, Keith you don't seem to have anything to say for yourself.'

'Er, um, yes, well it's come as such a shock after your first reaction.'

Her mother looked at him keenly. 'You do still want to go through with this wedding as promised?'

'Yes, of course.'

Keith's mother at last found her tongue. 'Don't you think we should have had some say in it all as well? After all he is our son.'

'Of course, that's why we invited you here tonight, isn't that right Frank, so we could talk it through and try to get it all sorted.'

'But what if we don't agree?'

Quickly Keith jumped in seeing all this was leading no where. 'Oh, Mum, don't start now. Let's just get it sorted out. After all, I did promise Laura I would marry her if I could and it is my baby as well. Your grandchild.'

His mother gave an indignant sniff and turned to his dad who had kept silent so far. 'What do you have to say?'

'Well love, if that's what the lad wants, then let them. After all as it's been pointed out it's our grandchild as well. Aye, it'll seem peculiar being called Granddad, but still you've got to admit it, Mum, that it is rather exciting our first grandchild.'

Marjorie looked round them all again. 'So we're all in agreement?' Not waiting for an answer she carried on, 'Good, let's get the arrangements sorted out now whilst you're here. There's no time to be wasted.'

Laura sat very quietly, hardly able to take it all in. Once again they were organizing her life to suit themselves. Still, she did want to marry Keith and keep the baby, if this had to be the way so let it be.

12

As Laura could hardly change jobs again at this late stage, it was agreed she would carry on living and working in Leeds during the week. Once it was time to leave work she would go back home. Her mother said she would get on to the doctors for her, during the next week, to organize a hospital nearer home for her to go to have the baby. Laura had to agree it all made sense. When she and Keith had been asked how much they had saved up between them they had to admit rather shame faced, 'Five pounds.'

Both sets of parents had exploded. 'Is that it? What on earth do you both do with all your money?'

Laura was told by the parents that whilst she was earning she must try to save as much money as she was able.

Laura and Keith just looked at each other in despair. It had all been taken out of their hands. Wondering what Keith was really thinking, Laura gave him a timid smile. Seeming to sense some of her uncertainty he walked over to her and said in a kindly voice, 'It'll be all right, never fear.'

Laura could feel her eyes fill with tears. This was all too much for her, she had never seen such a gentle and understanding side to him before. Yet she felt happy inside as she now felt confident it was all going to turn out as she hoped.

After a few more details were settled Keith's parents suggested they leave as they felt they'd had a lot to take in all in one go. They needed time to digest it and talk to each other. They wanted to be certain their son was happy about doing what had been proposed, as it had been thrown at him so quickly. 'You will be all right with this marriage won't you?' his dad asked quietly to his son.

'I suppose so. After all I did promise Laura I would wed her if possible.' With a sigh he added, 'I'm too young for all this, but I know what's done is done. It's too late for regrets now there's a baby on the way.'

'We'll be there for you anytime you need us.'

'Thanks, Dad.'

When they had gone Marjorie turned to her daughter with a look of pride on her face. 'Well young lady, what do you think to all that? It's come right for you in the end hasn't it?'

'Er, yes, Mum.' Laura suddenly realized the

154

full impact of what had happened and she rushed over and gave her mother a big hug. 'Thanks, Mum.'

'Watch that first grandchild of mine. You fair knocked the poor baby rushing over to me like that.' Laura thought she was getting told off again but then she could see a twinkle in her mother's eye.

'Yes, it is your grandchild, Mum. Don't worry I'll take good care of the baby.'

Laura went to bed with a much eased mind now everything was sorted the way she wanted.

When she was back at work, after the week-end, she had a few comments from her work mates that she was like the cat who had got the cream. Somehow now being away from home in the week was different. She knew she could talk freely on the phone to Keith and see him when she went back home at the week-ends. Anyway she only had another month to work then she would be living back at home awaiting the birth.

When the time came to leave work she couldn't believe how upset she was. It was amazing how, in such a short time, she had become attached to the people she worked with. As Trina, the one she had become closest to bid her good-bye she said to her with tears in her eyes. 'You'll keep in touch won't you? Come and see me and you must see the baby when I've had it.'

'Of course I will silly. I wouldn't miss seeing it for all the world. Not after having sat opposite you all these months seeing the bulge grow.'

Saying this humorous comment Trina knew Laura would revert back to her usual cheerful self. With a final wave and 'Bye all,' she took her last step from that work place.

She knew life from tomorrow was going to be very different for her. But she hadn't realized how much so. When she had been at school she always longed to be at home, she thought it would be fun. It wasn't, it was lonely and boring. Her mum was at work much of the day and although Laura offered to do jobs for her, most of these offers were turned down for one reason or another. Then her friends were either at school or work and there again she didn't really want to see them, she felt ashamed of her grotesque shape. Her body no longer felt her own, she felt as if she had been invaded. Then somehow she didn't seem to have the energy to do much. Not that she exactly felt ill but neither did she feel well. A state of depression settled on her. Her grandma had taught her how to knit, so some of the time she spent making tiny garments for this little person who was to be her child.

Although it passed some of the time, it was still lonely having no-one to talk to whilst she was knitting. With too much time to brood she would start to think of the actual birth. She had attended anti-natal classes where she had been shown breathing exercises to help her relax during the birth. It was how the baby got out that puzzled her. Many a time she would say to her mum. 'I just can't believe it is possible for a baby to get out as it does. Are you sure that is how you have them.'

'Of course silly. I've had two haven't I? So I must know.'

Knowing how worried she was, her mother would try to reassure her as kindly as she could. 'Well, I won't say it doesn't hurt at all. Of course there must be some pain, but there again they have a lot more painkillers to help you nowadays than when I gave birth to you. Don't worry, they know what they're doing — all will be fine.'

This didn't entirely satisfy Laura but at least it put her mind to rest to some extent. Then she would be afraid Keith would lose interest in her when he saw her no longer attractive. She became very reluctant to be seen out because she felt so ashamed about what had happened to her. There were her friends working and enjoying life as she should have been. Already she felt bound and shackled. Yet she knew she should feel happy. After all, in the end she had got what she had wanted hadn't she? Her parents had given in and were going to let her marry Keith. What on earth was the matter with her? The nearer her time got the worse this feeling became.

She did make a friend or two at the anti-natal clinic. But then as slowly one and another didn't turn up because they had given birth to their baby, this made things seem even worse. Would she ever get rid of this encumbrance from her body?

Then she reached a point when she felt she could go on no longer. There were still ten more days to go before the baby was due, but as she was preparing to go to bed suddenly a flood of water came. Not knowing what was happening to her, Laura screamed, 'Mum, come here quickly. Something terrible has happened.'

Her mother rushed into her bedroom ashen faced at the same time calling, 'I'm here, hang on.'

When she saw Laura standing in a pool of water her face changed from fear to laughter. 'Your waters have broke that's all love. The baby is on its way.'

Laura just looked stunned and muttered, 'Oh, then coming to her senses she said in a rush, 'But I've no pains like they said I would.'

'You will, have no fear on that count.' Now fully in command of herself again her mother directed her to sit on the bed. 'I'll just go and ring the hospital. I'm sure they'll tell us to take you in now. If they do I'll get Uncle Fred to come and drive us there.'

Still not quite sure what was happening to her Laura needed reassurance. 'But will I be all right on my own? The baby won't pop out or anything?'

Her mother moved out of the room in hoots of laughter calling after her, 'Have no fear, you won't have it yet. It'll be hours before it's born.'

Laura sat down satisfied all was well and said in a soft voice, 'Well this is it then.' She kept mumbling over and over to herself. 'Come on mum, be quick.' In fact it was only a few minutes before her mother was back and telling her to get downstairs, she would get her case and coat for her.

Still in a daze by what had happened Laura paused to ask her mum, 'Have you remembered to let Keith know?'

'Of course I have, now stop fussing and just do as I tell you. You'll be all right don't worry.'

In some ways the labour was worse than

she imagined but parts weren't as bad as she had thought they would be. At least it was quick. She'd heard horrific tales of women being in labour twenty four hours or longer. It was only six hours and she had produced a perfectly healthy son.

The midwives were kind to her in what was called a G.P. Maternity Unit. Laura was lucky being able to go in there as it was one of the very few in the country. The midwives from the rounds ran it and came in on a rota basis. For such a young naive girl, not really sure of what was going on, they couldn't have been any kinder and sympathetic. Her own doctor came to see her after the birth. It was all as pleasant as it could be and took away any fright Laura might have had about the birth.

It didn't seem two minutes after both the baby and herself had been tidied up before she heard footsteps down the corridor and saw the door being very cautiously pushed open. Keith's face appeared around the door.

Laura feeling on a high after the birth shouted, 'Come in quick and see your son.'

Even Laura was surprised at his response as Keith exclaimed with great delight in his voice. 'But he looks like a miniature me!'

Laura burst out laughing. 'Don't be silly, you can't tell yet.' Suddenly her laughter turned to tears as she realized just what had happened. At seventeen years of age she had become a mother. She let out a sob as the thought came into her head, what was she doing here with a baby? She should have been out enjoying herself with her friends. She just couldn't believe the change to her life in such a short time.

Just then the midwife rushed back in. Seeing Laura's distress she quickly turned on Keith. 'What have you been doing to upset her?'

Turning a brilliant red at being put in this position Keith could only answer defensively, 'Nothing, nothing at all. One minute she was laughing the next she was crying.'

'Well, visiting time is over for you. Out you go young man.'

Looking sheepish now he turned to Laura. 'Bye for now. I'll come and see you again tomorrow. Mum and Dad will want to come as well.'

'Of course they will. They're grandparents now and don't you think we'd best choose him a name when you come tomorrow.'

Feeling a bit more relieved now that Laura seemed back to her old self he gave a cheerful, 'Of course, bye for now.'

Once he had gone Laura was really depressed. It had struck her again; here she was just seventeen with a baby and she would soon have a husband who would only be sixteen.

They had been right all along her parents, it would have been better to have had the baby adopted. Yet when she looked down at him, her son, something was there already. She could feel a pull at her heart strings.

The midwife rushed in again. Everything she did seemed to be in great haste. 'Now then dear, we'll soon have a go at feeding him at the breast.'

'I'm not feeding him that way. I'll need a bottle please,' replied Laura being very determined on this issue.

'Now what is all this? Not breast feeding!'

'That's what I said.'

'Come, come, surely at anti-natal class they explained all the reasons why it's better. Surely you want to give your baby a good start in life?'

'I said no; I'm not breast feeding. I'm sure he'll still have a good start to life.'

As the midwife could see Laura on the point of tears again she saw no use in pressing the matter. 'If that's the way it's to be then we'd better sort out drying up your milk. I won't be two ticks. I'll first have to go and get something.'

Laura breathed a sigh of relief as she realized at least she had got that point across. Somehow, although she knew she should be breast feeding, she felt better in her own mind that she wasn't. It still helped to keep some of her own independence. At seventeen she felt she couldn't cope with breast feeding as well as everything else.

As Laura was now expecting, the door swung quickly open as the midwife rushed in once more. 'Move on to your side dear so I can get to your bottom. Just a little injection then the milk will start drying up.'

Doing as she was bid Laura let out a loud, 'Ouch' as she felt the needle go in her. A little injection, she said to herself, I don't think she could have found a larger needle if she had tried. Laura felt as if the midwife was punishing her in her own way for not breast feeding. Luckily Laura knew, because it had been a normal birth, she would be leaving the hospital within forty-eight hours. Not too long to lie here impatient to be back home.

She was much surprised that before she left the hospital that she had a visit from a health visitor to tell her all about birth control. She found it quite hard to keep her face straight as she had it all explained to her in great detail. Whilst the dialogue went on she quickly thought to herself that there was no need to worry because she wasn't going to be caught out this way again, once bitten was enough.

13

It amazed her how, once she was home, Keith seemed to adapt to holding the baby quicker than she did. The little mite, who they had decided to call Richard frightened her, yet Keith could hold and bounce him up and down seeming quite confident that no harm would come to him. Her mum was a help in letting her get some sleep. She had no obligation to take turns in the night feed, yet she did.

Once she was up, dressed and pottering about the house her mother broached the subject of the wedding which wasn't in the too distant future. 'Time we started some planning for this wedding, don't you think Laura? Once you are out and about again I'll look after Richard so you and Keith can go and have a look at houses to rent.'

Suddenly Laura wasn't sure this was what she really wanted, but it was too late to retract from that decision. Her friend, Sally, had come to see her and the baby, this had made things worse for Laura. It made her wonder what she was doing with her life and realize what a mess she had made of it already.

Now her mother seemed to have got the bit between her teeth about the wedding there was no letting go. All the time she was behind Laura pushing her to get things organized. She even took the initiative into her own hands and booked for the viewing of possible rented houses for Keith and Laura. They were presented with the times they had to go and look at the places. Gifts, furniture and items for the baby were coming to them fast and furious. It was a good job they had an attic mused Laura, to put all the things in. It was amazing when friends and relatives looked at their own things how they realized that they had many spare and redundant possessions and these were willingly passed on to Laura and Keith for their new home. Laura's mum and dad did buy a beautiful new pram for Richard and from Keith's parents they got the cot.

Laura wasn't sure what the churning in her stomach was as they set off to view the first property. It could have been excitement at looking for the first time at a home of her own, or it could be fear at this new life ahead that she wasn't really sure now that she wanted.

Whatever the reason when she saw the

houses they had to look at it turned to a point that she had physically to control herself not being sick. Laura sensed Keith must be feeling the same as neither of them said anymore than the few obligatory words as they were shown around. All the houses they looked at were called what was known as back to backs. They were named this for the simple reason that it was exactly as it sounded, another house joined onto the back as well as adjoining houses on both sides. All but one they viewed were the back house so access to these was through a dingy, smoke covered, stoned walled passage which felt more like a cave. Very little light seemed to enter the houses, there was only one door in and that went straight into the kitchen or really scullery. She suspected the landlords had never heard of a fitted kitchen as each had only a pot sink, a metal draining board and cupboards fit into the alcove for the pots. There wasn't room to swing a cat around in the scullery. Then on further examination another door led to the lounge. This wasn't much better but at least a little more space. From the lounge lead a steep staircase upstairs. When Laura couldn't see any more doors she felt there was something missing so questioned one landlord, 'Where is the bathroom?'

The landlord gave a snort in the form of a sneer as he looked at her. 'There ain't no bathroom. What do you expect for the rent of these, Buckingham Palace!'

Being so young Laura didn't know where to put herself at such a comment so she stuttered, 'No,' then quickly added, 'But there must be a toilet?'

'Of course there is. That building at the bottom of the yard.'

'The bottom of the yard!'

'That's what I said. What's the matter with you? Can't you understand English or something?'

'Er, yes. It's just we have always had a toilet inside.'

'Well then aren't you the lucky one, but if you have this house the toilet is outside. You'll just have to get used to it. Anyway, if you don't want the house there are plenty of others that do.'

In fact Laura had really liked the only house that they had seen which had been at the front. But the disadvantage of that was the toilet was still around the back. There was no way she could face going through a passage way in the dark at night.

Laura glanced quickly at Keith and she could see the same look of distaste on his face, as she was feeling. Pulling herself together and trying to show she wasn't going to be pushed around particularly with the landlords attitude towards them, she showed courage in saying, 'Thank you for showing us the house, but we have others to view. We'll be back in touch if we want it.'

'Well mind you are not too long making your mind up, as I said before they're soon snapped up. Got a good reputation as a landlord I have.'

Laura muttered as she went out of earshot, 'I wouldn't like to see a bad one then.'

As they got outside and away from the horrible man Laura turned to Keith, 'Thank goodness that was the last to look at. I couldn't have taken any more looking at houses like that.' Then in a rather petulant voice she added, 'I'm not living somewhere like that, why should I? It's not what I'm used to. Anyroads they all felt too damp for a baby.'

Keith felt much the same and for once seemed in total agreement and joined in with her. 'I don't know what our parents think they were at sending us to look at houses like that. I really don't.'

Feeling more cheered now she knew that Keith felt like she did Laura linked his arm. 'Come on, let's go home and tell them none were suitable and that we'd better start looking again.'

Laura was quite shocked by her mum's reaction. She had thought when she told her all about the houses she would have felt the same as them. Instead she simply said, 'Beggars can't be choosers.'

Seeing Laura's look of puzzlement she then said in a more kindly voice, 'You have to see it from our point of view Laura. You nor Keith have any money and no wage coming in yet. You know full well Keith's parents as well as ourselves have agreed to pay the rent for you until Keith's earning. But you must appreciate none of us have that much spare money. We still have our own bills to pay. That's all we can spare to pay. What I will say is you know what the rent is for those houses. You look around yourself and if you can find anything you like better for that rent then you can have that. But that's your budget set. I don't think I can say fairer than that, do you?'

'No, Mum, thanks. I do appreciate what you're all doing, I really do. I'll go and have another look at the papers, see what else there is. After all whatever we get might not be for too long once Keith leaves school and gets a job.'

Her mum sniffed to herself as her daughter moved away, let her believe that if that's what she wants but she thought differently.

After much searching Laura did find a through terraced house, at least it had an inside bathroom and a little bit more space. To get to the back door a passageway had still to be gone through but at least it did have a front door. The only disadvantage was that it was not in a very good area, but Laura decided she could put up with this to have an inside toilet. The rent was no more expensive than the back to backs. So all of them were satisfied. Although her mother did have a few qualms about the area her daughter was going to live in.

As soon as they had got the house all the parents were very good and helped them smarten the place up with a lick of paint and emulsion. Then they started to move in all the furniture they had been given.

The day of the wedding was drawing nearer and Laura became more nervous and on edge the more she thought about it. She could often see her mother look at her with a puzzled look wondering why she was so moody. After all this should be the happiest moment of her life, she had got what she wanted hadn't she? All she could put it down to was wedding nerves, but she had to have a silent laugh to herself when she thought about it. It had all gone long past that stage surely, when she was a mother before she had even been to the altar.

Keith left school and as anticipated he quickly found a job as a shop assistant at a Co-op grocery store, with the promise to train him up for the possible post of assistant manager at a branch in the future. Considering everything none of them were that unhappy about his job, and at least it had prospects.

Laura began to hate it at home, she missed the companionship of her work colleagues, it seemed so lonely and everywhere she went, like the local clinic, all the talk seemed to be baby talk. She got fed up of hearing about babies and as Richard was thriving she decided there was no need to go and get him weighed there again. She could always nip into the local chemists for this. But in a sense this isolated her even more. Her mum was home part of the day but even she was so besotted with her grandson her main conversation seemed to be about him or the forthcoming wedding.

Laura decided things must improve when she had a home of her own. Surely there would be young women in the neighbourhood to make friends with and some young mothers must have more to chat about than baby talk.

The wedding arrangements had really been

taken out of Laura's and Keith's hands and because her parents had only one daughter's wedding to pay for they said she was to have the best they could afford. It now seemed to make no difference to them that the baby had come before the wedding.

So a church wedding it was to be and the reception afterwards at a nice local hotel. The only concession made to recent events was that Laura would wear an ivory coloured wedding dress instead of a white one. A friend and cousin were to be bridesmaids and she was even to have a pageboy, another cousin. She knew she should be thankful for what was being done for her, but in a way she felt it was all a sham. Keith didn't say much at all on the topic, he just went along with the tide of events showing a total lack of concern for what was happening. This made Laura even more anxious if she really were doing the right thing, but it was too late now to back out.

At least it was a summer wedding and the day dawned bright, as they had hoped. Laura didn't need waking, she was already up and starting to get dressed when her mum came in to rouse her. Richard was still quiet, so it gave them some time to get organized. All her milk had dried up, nearly straight after the birth, as the midwife said it would with the injection. Mind it had been a painful process. Laura was particularly glad that today of all days she wasn't feeding him herself. A neighbour was looking after him, for the day. She had said she would go and watch at the church, taking Richard with her, but she wasn't bothered about going to the reception. She was looking forward to looking after Richard, even for such a short time. In fact she seemed as excited about that as the wedding. As soon as he was up, fed and dressed she would take him off their hands so they were free to get ready in relative peace.

Seeing the time was moving on Laura asked her mum. 'Mum, do you think I should wake Richard now and get him fed so I can take him to Mavis's.'

'That sounds a good idea love, because we have to be at the hairdressers soon and we don't really want your Dad to get him ready. He'll never manage to get himself ready as well if he has to do that.'

As if he sensed what was going on Richard couldn't have been a better behaved baby for Laura that morning. He quickly took his milk and lay placidly as she got him ready. In no time he was safely dispatched next door.

As Laura and her mum walked to the hairdressers her mum linked her arm. 'Are you nervous love?'

'A bit. It all feels strange, everything feels topsy turvey.'

'It'll be all right once you're settled in your own place, don't fret.'

'I'm not, I know it will. I wonder how Keith's feeling this morning.'

'Like you no doubt. It would be unusual not to. I think all brides and grooms have pre-wedding jitters. After all, it's one of the biggest steps you take in your life.'

Laura let out a hoot of laughter. 'Now you tell me, a bit late in the day isn't it?'

'Well, at last I've brought that smile back onto your face. About time too.'

This dialogue seemed to have brought her more back to her old self. She could feel the first fluttering of excitement welling up inside her. This was her day, her special day that would never be repeated again.

The rest of the preparations seemed to pass in a haze to Laura. One minute she was slopping around in casual clothes the next when she looked in the mirror she was this girl she didn't recognize. Luckily she had soon regained her figure after having Richard, in fact she was slimmer than before. She didn't look like a new mum as well as a blossoming bride.

At last total peace descended on the house

as everybody else except her dad and herself had gone to church. 'All right love, not too nervous I hope. I never thought I would be giving you away so soon. We're going to miss you and that little fellow, you know. It'll seem strange here without you.'

Laura could hear a hint of sadness in her father's voice and tried to console him. 'I know, but that's life I suppose. You never know what's around the corner.'

'Aye that's true enough lass, by Jove it is.'

'But I'll not be that far away. Don't worry I'll visit Mum and you often.'

'I know you will. Just before we go I want to say you look lovely. Whatever has happened you are still doing me proud today. I also want to give you this to put away for a rainy day. I know you haven't much money.' Then he gave a slight chuckle, 'I mean any money. It's always useful to have something in reserve. Keep it to yourself though. I'm not being funny but you're both young and you never know what happens.' With this he handed her ten pounds.

This seemed a small fortune to Laura. 'Oh thanks, Dad. I do know what you're saying. But don't worry I'll work hard at making it work.'

'I'm sure you will, anyway enough said. Time to go now. The car is waiting for us.'

With this he proudly led his daughter out of the house.

Now Laura knew what it was like to be in a dream but awake. That's how the day went past for her. She could feel everything happening as if it was her, yet it also felt as if she was outside her body. That voice that said, 'I do'. Did that really belong to her? Even Keith couldn't keep a look of pride off his face as she walked down the aisle. That much she did notice.

However quickly the wedding had been organized Laura began to appreciate how much care had been put into its planning, as the whole day ran so smoothly. The meal was superb and all ready exactly on time. The only fly in the ointment was the odd comments Laura heard, 'Put the cart before the horse, haven't they?' But she wasn't going to let these words upset her, on this, her special day.

Although they had no money for a honeymoon both sets of parents had insisted they have one. They had clubbed together to pay for them a few days at Blackpool. Between them they would look after Richard whilst they were away. Laura could sense they were trying to make their start to married life as normal as possible.

Before she had time to take in all that was

happening at the wedding her mother's voice was at her side. 'Come on love, time to get ready now.' She felt a slight disappointment at this. Here she was enjoying herself for the first time in such a long time and now they had to leave all the festivities. She wasn't sure she really wanted this honeymoon, she could have enjoyed herself just as much here, if not more so. Anyway, she felt it was a bit hypocritical to have a honeymoon now.

Not having any money to spare she hadn't been able to afford to buy a new outfit for going away, but at least one thing she had been taught at school was to be a good needle woman. So she set to and made herself some new outfits, which she had to admit she was well pleased with. Once changed into one of these outfits she received many compliments how she looked. She decided it had been worth her time and effort to make them.

'Come on, the taxi is here. You don't want to miss the train do you?' she heard somebody call to them.

Both Keith and herself shouted together. 'No, we're coming now. Just saying our last good-byes.'

Laura hoped this being in unison was a good omen for all their marriage. That it was a prediction what their life would be like together.

Finally amid a shower of well wishes they took their leave of the wedding guests who looked set in to continue the party well into the night.

14

Once settled on the train Laura felt as if normality had returned. Taking her hand in his and whispering in her ear, Keith murmured, 'I can't wait to get you to that boarding house room.'

Quick to retort to him Laura said more sharply than she intended. 'Is that all you think of?' Then quickly putting her hand to her mouth she said in a panic stricken voice, 'Birth control! I forgot all about it!'

With those few words Keith understood what she was on about. 'Don't worry, I've taken care of it.'

'But you would think I'd know better after last time.'

'I think you'd enough on your mind with a new baby and the wedding arrangements, don't you? I've told you it'll be all right. Anyway we're married now so what are you fussing about?'

'I don't want another baby yet. I've only just got over having Richard and I'm far too young for more.'

'Sssh, stop it. This is our honeymoon. Don't start nagging as soon as we're married.'

Laura felt this last part was said with a rather snide tone and decided she had better shut up. She sat back and gave herself the opportunity to watch the passing scenery and suddenly it really clicked that she was a married woman, no longer a single girl. It all became rather exciting and she couldn't help but hold her left hand in such a way that anybody who would care to notice could see her wedding ring.

This suddenly felt like a real adventure. Laura realized she had never been away on holiday without her parents. In some ways everything new was happening to her too quickly for her mind to absorb it all. It made her stomach tremble both with fear and excitement. She heard a voice at her side, 'Nearly there now,' and suddenly woke up to the fact that this was her husband. She hadn't really noticed a great deal of the passing scenery, her mind had been too busy looking into her own life instead of the world going by.

She felt a quick tug at her arm and the voice again at her side, 'Come on time to get off. What did you think you were going to do, stay on and have a ride back?'

'No, I was miles away wasn't I? It just all seems so strange. Do you want me to carry a bag?'

'I can manage, you just look after yourself. Mum slipped me some money to use on a taxi to the boarding house. She thought we would be too tired after all the excitement of the day to want to walk there or to go by bus. Besides it's late now.'

'Thank goodness she did that. I don't think I could have made it. Look that's the taxi stand over there.'

It seemed only minutes and the taxi was drawing up in front of the boarding house and the driver turning around. 'Here we are then.' Laura wasn't sure if she liked the look he gave them, as much as to say I know what you two are up to. Keith had already paid him and they were getting out so Laura realized she might as well forget the incident. After all, she would probably never see him again so what did it matter what he thought. But he was wrong, Laura thought with sudden pride, we really are man and wife.

As they moved up the steps into the boarding house it came back to Laura again that this was the first time she had been on holiday without her parents. She knew she had stayed at the Hostel for Unmarried Mothers, but that was different. There they were all females together. She felt very strange and as she saw Keith sign the register for the landlady she could see his hand was shaking. Suddenly he did not seem a stranger, he had the same feelings as her. Laura could feel a silent giggle build up inside her as she looked at the stern face of the landlady. She hoped she didn't notice the hand shake otherwise Laura was sure she would also jump to the wrong conclusion. She looked a character that could easily be suspicious.

A gruff voice said, 'Room twelve, the stairs are around the corner. Breakfast at eight prompt.'

That was it, hard to believe this was supposed to be a place for holiday makers where it was assumed it would be fun. Keith picked up the cases and said, 'Come on Laura, this way I think.' Laura could tell he was thinking much the same as herself, 'What a misery.'

At last they found the room after much difficulty and as Keith shut the door behind them Laura glanced quickly around. It was no better furnished than her hostel room but at least it was clean. Realizing they were alone at last shyness took over. Not quite knowing what to do with herself she walked across the room and looked out of the window. Trying to distract Keith from herself she gabbled the first thing that came to her head. 'Isn't that Blackpool Tower over there?'

'Never mind the tower. Come here and

give me a kiss. I've been waiting for this all day.'

Laura suddenly came over all coy. She found it hard to believe she had done what she had with Keith and had a baby. Not quite sure what to do she just said the only thing she could think. 'I've never been up the tower, have you? Maybe we could go tomorrow.'

'What's the matter with you? Come on it's legal now. We can take our time and enjoy ourselves.'

Still feeling uneasy Laura tried to put off the moment. 'Did you see where the bathroom was as we came in. I'll have to go.'

'Next door but one. Now don't be long. I've waited long enough for this moment.'

Laura shot out of the door glad that she had a few minutes respite. She only hoped the bathroom was vacant. It was, she rushed in, locked the door and just sat on the edge of the bath in deep thought. What was she doing here, she should still be at home with her parents. What a fool she had been. It might have been better if she had stayed on at school like her dad had wanted, then maybe none of this would have happened. Giving herself a mental shake she realized this was her life now, her future. Deciding she could not stay here any longer she forced a smile on her face and set off back to the bedroom. As she shot out of the bathroom door she felt herself bump into someone. 'Oh! I'm sorry.'

'It's me Laura, are you all right? I was just coming to see you, you've been such a long time.'

'Fine Keith, just fine. Come on then this is our honeymoon.'

As soon as they were back in the bedroom Keith started to undress. Laura didn't know where to put herself. She realized the only thing she could do was turn her back to him and somehow undress without him seeing her. She heard a snort and laugh behind her as she fumbled under her nightie trying to get her bra off. 'Come on, you shouldn't be shy with me. Good gracious you've already had our child.'

'I know but that was somehow different.'

Keith being young and inexperienced himself hadn't thought to put her at ease. The only thing on his mind was to get into bed. 'Anyway what's that thing you've got on?' her questioned her.

'My nightie, of course,' replied Laura rather amazed at this question.

'You don't need that on, not on our honeymoon night, or any other night for that matter.'

'But I do. I feel better covered up.'

Getting rather impatient now to get her into bed, Keith decided it was easier to relent. 'Okay, if that's how you want it, but hurry up do.'

Quickly she jumped in bed and pulled the bedding up. Then she let out an exclamation. 'Oh! The light, I forgot to turn it off.'

'Leave it, I want to look at you.'

'Please Keith, let me turn it off.'

With a sigh of exasperation Keith snapped, 'Just turn it off then if that's what you want, but be quick.'

Not wanting to upset him anymore than she already had Laura quickly jumped out of the bed, ran to the light switch and started to run back to the bed, but quickly let out a cry. 'Oh! That hurt.'

'What have you done now?'

'I've stubbed my toe. I couldn't see where I was going.'

Keith replied with satisfaction. 'Well I told you to leave the light on. You would have it your way.'

'But you know why I wanted it off and I was only rushing to please you.'

'Come on then get in bed and I'll rub it better.'

'Thanks.'

But quickly his hand moved from her toes up her leg. Laura's natural reaction was to pull back. 'What is the matter now?' Keith asked nearly at the end of his tether.

'Nothing, er it just tickled.'

'Come on get close, join in then it won't tickle. You'll be enjoying yourself too much to think of that.'

Before she knew where she was Laura felt Keith's weight on her and his knees pushing her legs apart.

His voice snapped at her. 'Relax, stop being so tense. You're supposed to be enjoying this.'

Before she could reply Laura felt him enter her and all she could do was give a shocked, 'Ah.'

As before Keith seemed to move up and down a few times then gave a shuddering movement. 'That was great.'

Recovering herself Laura quickly asked, 'You did take care of everything?'

'What do you mean?'

'To make sure I didn't get pregnant again.'

As he rolled off her he said in an unusually quiet voice for him. 'I forgot. I just wanted you so much.'

'You what! But you promised me you would be careful.'

'Stop fussing it'll be all right.'

'That's what you said last time and it wasn't.'

'You know the old saying, lightning doesn't

strike twice. You'll be okay, don't fret.'

With a sigh Laura turned on her side and already felt the dye had been cast for her future. In no time she could hear the even breathing of Keith telling her that he, at least, had fallen easily asleep. Laura felt a tear fall to the pillow as the events of the last few months and this her special day came to a head.

Waking up to a bright sunny morning her new life didn't seem as frightening as it had in the dark of the night. Keith stretched his arm and gave a cheery good morning. He quickly turned on his side but Laura pulled away saying, 'It's nearly breakfast time, we had better hurry up.'

Keith gave a laugh. 'Who's hungry when they've got you.' Then seeing the look on Laura's face, 'I was only joking. Come on I will race you to see who can be ready first.'

He gave a quick pause as he put his clothes on. 'Don't think you'll always get away as easily.'

Again a cold shudder went through Laura as though someone had stepped on her grave. After a good traditional English breakfast Keith took hold of her hand and asked with good humour, 'Now what do you want to do to-day?'

There was no hesitation in Laura's reply.

'Go to the pleasure beach of course. I can't visit Blackpool and not go there.'

'That's a good idea,' he was quick to reply. 'I agree entirely.' Then pulling her along he shouted, 'Blackpool here we come.'

Laura soon forgot she was a young wife and mother and behaved like the teenager that she really was. As she relaxed and enjoyed herself so did Keith. Suddenly they were comfortable in each other's company. But all too soon the honeymoon came to an end and it was time to pack and go back home to reality. Laura could feel the dark cloud come back over her. This wasn't the life she wanted. In a way she was looking forward to seeing her baby again but in another way she resented him. He had tied her down, brought her to being a wife and mother before her time. She should be enjoying herself like she had in the last few days. Then with a guilty feeling she realized it was probably as bad for Keith as her. He was young, younger than her and must also have regrets about the life he should be having. Tentatively she moved her hand onto Keith's and gave it a gentle squeeze as much as to say, I know what you are feeling as with every turn of the wheel this train takes us nearer home.

15

It had been decided that Keith and Laura would go straight from the station to their new home. They were to spend that first night alone before picking Richard up the next day. Both sets of parents had agreed this was a good idea, giving them a chance to settle into their new home, at least, for a few hours on their own.

Laura let out a loud exclamation as she went in the kitchen door. Instead of the usual cold and damp feeling she had experienced inside the house, fragrant smells of cooking food touched her nostrils. Thinking something was amiss, she quickly rushed forward to see a note propped up on the table. Picking it up she instantly saw it was her mother's writing and she let out a sigh of relief that the landlord hadn't put somebody else into the house whilst they were away.

She heard Keith's voice behind her. 'What's going on here?'

'Shh, I'm reading this note from Mum.'

Sensing Keith's impatience once again, as soon as she had read the note she turned to him. 'Mum says she has left us some dinner slowly cooking in the oven and wishes us a nice welcome home. Isn't that kind of her?'

'Suppose so, but it wasn't dinner I had on my mind. Anyway, seeing it's there we might as well eat it. I think I'll go to the pub afterwards to see my friends.'

'Keith! This is supposed to be our first night in our new home. Anyway you're not old enough to drink.'

'There'll be plenty more nights to stay in here. I want to see what's been happening whilst I've been away. If I'm old enough to get married then I'm old enough to have a drink. Anyway, you'll have peace and quiet so you can get the unpacking done.'

With this comment Laura knew the honeymoon was well and truly over. This seemed to settle how her future life was to be. After Keith had gone to the pub she set about unpacking. But that didn't take her long and she moved around aimlessly, tweaking an ornament here and there, trying to make the house look more like home. She was upset. She had to admit it to herself at being left alone like this on her first evening in her new home. In fact, when she thought about it she had never really before been in a strange house on her own. It was rather frightening. She wished Richard was here, because as small as he was, at least he was company.

Laura had worked herself up into such a frenzy that by the time Keith came in she couldn't stop herself snapping, 'About time too. Had you forgotten I was here waiting for you?'

Keith just looked at her and snarled back. 'How could I?'

But Laura couldn't leave it. She was so cross yet at the same time upset. 'What did your friends think of you leaving your wife on your first night at home together?'

'They thought I'd a lot of sense. You don't expect me to forget my friends, do you now?'

Realizing she might have gone a little bit too far she said in a calmer voice, 'No, but it is our first night here and I was lonely.'

Taking the opportunity now she was calm Keith quickly responded, 'Come over here, you won't be lonely any more.'

'I don't know. Is that all you think about?'

'Course not. Come on, let's make the most of being on our own.'

Wanting the reassurance of his affection Laura was quick to go into his arms.

All too soon life settled into a pattern. Once Richard was back home each day she cleaned their little family home with pride whilst Keith was at work. Then every afternoon she would try to take Richard out for a walk in his pram. Her eyes would look around hoping that some other young mother would be on her own and want to seek some companionship. She soon realized how lonely she really was. Many an evening Keith would have his tea then instantly jump up from the table stating, 'I'll just go for a quick pint with the lads.'

Laura had soon learnt not to make any comment on this. If she did it only led to an argument. But it wasn't just the loneliness, it was the money. Paying for the beer left the housekeeping money short. More and more Laura could see the possibility of them getting into debt so soon into their marriage. She thanked the day her father had had the foresight to give her the ten pounds, at least that kept them solvent. Not that Keith seemed to care how she managed, as long as his meals were on the table each night and he had his beer money.

Her worst fears came to fruition when all too soon Laura realized she was pregnant again. Keith had been wrong, lightening does strike twice. It had only taken that first night on her honeymoon to cause this. She was frightened to tell her parents. More so than the first time, which she knew was silly seeing she was a married woman now. But she knew she would have to do so before long. Her mother would soon enough guess.

When she told Keith he was none too pleased. 'You fool! Why do you want to lumber us with another kid?'

Laura could only stammer back, 'Well you did tell me it was safe — that it wouldn't happen twice. After all, it does take two to make a baby.'

'But you could have made sure it didn't happen,' he snarled back at her.

'Well it has and that is all there is to it. Anyway you don't have to suffer nine months of discomfort and be shut up in this house day after day. Not only the days but the evenings as well.'

Before she realized what was happening she felt a sharp slap across her cheek which sent her reeling backwards. 'If you feel you're shut up here, how do you think I feel? Well I'll tell you.' Not waiting for a response he continued, 'Trapped, snared by you. I should be out enjoying myself not tied to you and your brat.'

Despite the sense of shock, Laura could feel anger well up inside her at being accused of this and started to defend herself yet afraid to mention the hitting in case he attacked her again. 'I didn't want it either you know. I could have made a career for myself.'

Keith just laughed at her. 'A career for yourself? What waiting for somebody to get into your knickers? That was all you wanted.'

Indignantly Laura replied, 'It wasn't, you know it wasn't. You begged and pleaded with me to do it.'

'Oh! Just shut up you bitch. I'm listening to no more of this. I'm off to the pub where I can have a sensible conversation and a laugh with my mates.' With this Keith marched through the door and slammed it shut behind him.

Laura let out a sigh of relief. She suddenly realized it was better with him out of the house than in a mood like this. She was only thankful Richard had been safe in his cot and had not witnessed any of what had gone on. Now it dawned on her that her face was stinging and smarting badly. Running up the stairs she went to look at it in the bedroom mirror. She stared in horror as she saw the red weals where his hand had hit her. She just burst into tears in utter despair at where her life was going.

Laura daren't go near her mum's for a few days in case she saw the marks. She knew she was astute enough to quickly realize what had been going on.

Yet as soon as she dared she did go to see her mum. She suddenly had an urgent need to tell somebody else about the pregnancy.

'Er, Mum, I've something to tell you.'

Giving her a suspicious look her mum said, 'Oh yes?'

Sensing what her mother was thinking Laura was quick to reassure her. 'No, all's fine with Keith and me, it's not that. You're to be a grandparent again. I'm pregnant.'

'Oh Laura! How could you so soon after Richard? Surely you'd more sense after getting caught so easily once. Didn't they tell you at the hospital or clinic about family planning?'

'Of course they did, but with all the hectic arrangements for the wedding I forgot, that's all.'

'In this day and age the boy can take care of it as well as you. Didn't Keith think about that?'

Laura could feel herself going red at talking about such personal things with her mother.

'You know how it is at the heat of the moment. Things like that are forgotten.'

'Well, young lady, they'd better not be forgotten too often otherwise you'll soon produce a football team of your own.'

'Don't worry, I've really learnt my lesson this time.'

'We'll see, we'll see,' said her mother in rather a sad and resigned voice. 'Anyway back to practicalities. Have you seen the doctor yet and had it properly confirmed?'

'No, I'll go tomorrow but I know I am like I did last time. I just know. You agreed with me before about that. Anyway I've got a craving for chips and you know I'm not usually keen on them.'

Her mother let out a laugh. 'Well, I suppose there could be worse cravings.'

Laura carried on that craving for the whole of her pregnancy. The more lonely she got; the more chips she ate. She was constantly told off for her weight gain by the Midwife, Sister Rose, as she went for her regular check ups. But she couldn't stop herself, unhappiness just made her crave all the more and eat and eat.

There were very few evenings that Keith was in with her. In fact, he hardly noticed her, which was some relief. Since the first smack on her face there hadn't been a repeat of that, at least not until well into her pregnancy.

She felt so lonely and depressed that one evening, after one of his usual drinking bouts, as soon as he entered the door she ended up saying in despair to him, 'I hope once this baby is born you're going to stay in a bit more with all of us.'

'Are you joking? What sitting looking at a fat cow like you.'

'That's not fair. Once the baby is born

I'll be thinner again.'

'H'm, fine chance the amount of chips you eat and if you think it isn't fair, what about me? It isn't fair me being snared by you, young lad that I am.'

'What do you mean?'

'What do you think I mean? You got yourself pregnant so as to trap me into marriage.'

Indignant now at his accusations and feeling she had to defend herself Laura snapped back. 'I didn't do that at all and you know it. We've been through it all before. I no more wanted to be pregnant with Richard than you wanting it. But that's in the past and it can't be changed.'

'But it wasn't only that,' said Keith his speech slurring. 'As if once wasn't enough. Oh no! You have to go and do it again.'

Laura began to feel really indignant now at him laying all the blame at her door and cried out, 'You told me it would be safe, you know full well you did.'

Grabbing hold of her Keith pulled her quickly to him and started to shake her. 'You know you were told at the hospital to get sorted out so we were using birth control. But could you be bothered, oh no, you lazy cow. Can you be bothered about anything apart from yourself?' With this his hand met her face again and he gave her a sharp push.

Laura held on to her stomach with one hand fearing for the baby and with the other she tried to grab the back of the settee to stop herself falling on the floor. She let out a sharp exclamation. 'The baby, don't hurt the baby.'

With a grunt Keith turned away and tottered upstairs. She could hear him mouthing obscenities as he went but wasn't as frightened by these as the physical harm he seemed to want to do her.

With her whole body shaking she moved around and sat down on the settee. Gently she felt her stomach and as if to reassure and comfort her she felt the baby give a kick against her hand. She let out a sigh of relief as she realized, at least, the baby was unharmed. But the tears started to fall as she now thought about the life she was bringing it into. At least she hadn't many more weeks to wait until the baby was born and now Keith seemed indifferent to her for the present time which meant she was left in peace.

Her mother did give her a few strange looks when she asked for her instead of Keith to be with her and hold her hand during the birth. Laura tried to think up excuses why he was not there so at least not to discredit him in her parent's eyes. She was too ashamed to let them know what her life was really like. Much to her joy, she gave birth to a lovely bouncing daughter, no worse for wear with what had happened whilst she had been in her mother's womb. They named her Katie. Luckily she couldn't have been a better behaved baby. It was as if she felt her mother's pain and wanted to do everything she could to ease it. Just to hold and love her took some of the hurt away. After her birth Keith once again seemed to notice Laura more and each time he did he became more and more aggressive. The bruises came fast and furious as he kept on hitting her. Each time she felt his hand make contact anger built up inside her until she wanted to hit him back, but she was afraid. He was so uncaring that she thought if she tried to hit him back he might actually kill her. Then what would happen to her lovely children? Her mother started to get suspicious and questioned her one day. 'You are becoming very clumsy Laura, look at all those bruises.'

Trying to cover up the real reason Laura was quick to respond, 'I know, I just seem to rush around so much after the children and forget things are in the way. Then bump and another bruise comes.'

'Um, well you want to be more careful in future. You must take care of yourself as well as the children. After all, they need you there with them.'

Laura knew better than to argue the issue so just said meekly, 'Yes, Mum.'

This time after the birth she made sure she saw to the family planning. Straight away she went on the pill and she was glad she had. Whilst she was pregnant Keith had left her alone that way, it was as if he couldn't bear to feel what they had produced. But once she had given birth he was soon forcing his way into her. Laura knew it amounted to rape even though it was between husband and wife, but she was getting more and more frightened of his violence to do anything about it. Not only was he physically he was also verbally abusive. He rarely spoke a civil word to her and every sentence seemed to finish with, 'You fat, sloppy cow.' Laura knew she was fat but the more unhappy she became the more she seemed to eat. That was until she was violently sick after a binge and realized what a glutton she had become. But it wasn't the food, she had a virus. Not that Keith cared. Somehow she had to haul herself out of bed and between being sick care for two babies. But no matter what, she didn't forget to take that little pill, and she felt at least safe with this knowledge. She couldn't believe it when she was moaning and groaning with pains in her stomach and Keith forced himself on her. It was too much. She knew if there had been a knife at hand she would have plunged it into him. But at least she felt safe in the knowledge that he couldn't make her pregnant again.

Then why, she questioned herself, a few weeks later had she missed and felt sick again. No! No, she couldn't be pregnant again, not with Katie only four months old. Anyway she'd taken the pill regularly. It must have just caused a change in her. But even with telling herself this, the panic would not subside. What should she do? She daren't talk to her mother, she was sure she would be furious with her. Not in the true sense of being cross but with worry for her, and of course, she would blame her for being careless. But she hadn't been.

There was only one thing for it and that was to take the bull by the horns and visit the doctor. This was nearly as bad as telling her mum but at least he would confirm her suspicions one way or another. Carting the two young children with her she set off, once her mind was made up on this course of action. Being rather late arriving at the surgery there were already many patients before her and it was still first come first served basis to see the doctor. She settled herself for a long wait with two restless children. A few times, when it became really hard work entertaining them, she had to stop herself from walking back out and home. All the time of the wait her mind swung back and forth what it could really be and whether it was worth persisting in this visit to find out.

At last it was her turn. As she faced the doctor she said in a very soft voice, 'I think I'm pregnant again.'

'Speak up Laura, what's that you say?'

'I think I'm pregnant.'

Tut tutting the doctor looked at her carefully now. 'Haven't you been taking the pill as instructed?'

'Yes, doctor. I've never missed one even when I was sick with a virus, I still made sure I took it.'

'What that's you say? You were sick?'

'Yes, I'd a tummy bug. I didn't want to bother you but I was ill. Still it passed.' Then looking hopeful now she quickly added, 'Maybe it hasn't passed after all?'

'But Laura when you were sick you would have brought the pill back up. Didn't you think of that?'

Shame faced she had to admit she hadn't.

Giving her another look the doctor continued, 'Anyway I thought you said you were really ill; I wouldn't have thought you felt like sexual relations.'

Not knowing how to answer this without giving away the truth, that Keith had raped her, she quickly gave a small embarrassed giggle and said, 'Well you know how it is.'

'Well, what's done is done, I suppose. You'd better get on the bed whilst I examine you.'

'Will the children be all right in the pushchair?'

'Oh yes fine. No worry. Come on let's see if you're right.'

Laura tried to blank all thoughts out of her mind, even the hope that he would cause a miscarriage, as he examined her. She didn't want this to be true again.

All too soon the doctor's voice penetrated her thoughts. 'Well I'm afraid you were right with your diagnosis. You're pregnant again.'

Reaction to the shock just made her burst into tears. Taking a fatherly role the doctor put his arm around her. 'Now then, lass, don't take on so. I see people with far worse things than bringing a new life into this world.'

Between sobs Laura managed to say, 'But three young ones. How will I cope?'

'You will, you will and after all you're young and fit yourself. But you'll have to definitely make sure there are no more after this.'

Seeing the sobs had stopped the doctor asked, 'Are you feeling better now?'

Laura managed a weak smile. 'Yes thanks.'

'Right then, let's get all the details sorted out.'

It was all done soon enough but Laura had only half a mind on it as she kept thinking how Keith would react with this news. He would blame her, she knew. To him he would not be at fault, only her.

Finally she heard the doctor say, 'Now I hope you've listened to all I've told you. You don't seem at all with it today.'

'I am, I've listened. I'll see you again then at my next check up.'

'Take care then and remember there's a new young life inside you.'

Laura just gave him a look as if to say, 'I don't need reminding,' as she bid him good-bye.

With weary footsteps she made her way home wondering all the while how she was going to break the news to Keith and her parents.

16

Laura decided the best way to tell Keith was to try to get him in good humour. She had made a special effort with tea and made his favourite meal, home made steak and kidney pie with chips and a nice apple pie to finish. She had even managed to get the children bathed and in bed, so they could have a peaceful evening together.

As she heard his footsteps coming down the path her heart became heavier with each resounding tread. Trying her best she put a smile on her face as he came through the door and asked, 'Had a good day at work?'

Her only acknowledgment was a grunt. Her heart sank further in her boots. This was going to be difficult. Still trying to be pleasant she told him, 'Go and wash your hands whilst I serve tea, it's all ready. I've made a nice surprise for you.'

At last she had his attention but he still said only a few words. 'Oh yes! What's this all about?'

Stammering slightly Laura looked at him. 'Nothing, but I know how hard you work. Anyway, I'll only be a few minutes serving it so don't be long washing.'

Laura knew if she didn't want him to suspect anything she would have to eat her tea. But she didn't know how, her stomach was heaving at the mere thought. Still trying to be pleasant as Keith tucked into his pie she asked, 'Is it alright for you?'

'Yeah. Okay.'

'Good, I thought you'd enjoy it.'

Again he only gave a grunt in return.

Laura had decided to let him have his tea then tell him, but finally it all became too much for her. 'Er, Keith, I've got something to tell you.'

With that here we go again look on his face he snarled, 'Not pregnant again are we? You'd better not be.'

Put off even more by these words she just answered very quietly. 'Well actually yes.'

Before Laura knew what was happening the plate, with the rest of his dinner on it, was heading her way. As she ducked to avoid it she heard him say, 'You stupid bitch, I thought I told you to take care of it.'

Crouched down she managed to mumble, 'I did.'

'Silly cow, what do you take me for? You can't have if you're pregnant again like you say.'

'It was when I was ill. The doctor said the

pill would have come back up when I was sick.'

'Well, you know what you should have done?'

'What?'

'You should have kept your legs shut then shouldn't you?'

Laura felt sick to her stomach as she forced herself to sit back up in the chair. She was trembling with fear as she said, 'It wasn't my fault. If you remember you forced your way on me.'

She felt her head snap back with the force of his fist as he hit her. 'What are you trying to accuse me of? Come on spit it out, you silly cow.'

As Laura felt around her mouth she realized not only were there words to spit out but a tooth that was loose in her mouth. He had actually knocked a tooth out. Not wanting to aggravate him more she tried to say gently, 'Nothing Keith, nothing at all. Of course it was my fault. I'm sorry.'

'Get rid of it then.'

'I can't. The doctor won't do anything.' Then she added more hopefully, 'but he did say he would help us to take more permanent steps so there are no more.'

'I'm listening to no more of this nonsense. Get out of my way.' With this he gave her a violent push that knocked her head back against the wall. Laura slid to the floor as stars shot before her eyes. For good measure he gave her a kick with his foot as he went past her. As the room stopped spinning she began to recover her senses and she heard the back door slam. Laura let out a sigh of relief as she realized she would see no more of him until pub turning out time.

She had never known an evening seem so long. She alternated between anger and tears. She couldn't stand any more of this treatment but didn't know where to turn for help. Deciding it would be best if she was out of his way when he came back she finally went to bed but lay in agony both in body and mind. She wanted to see her mother to tell her about the baby, yet how could she looking like this. There again, in some ways she wished she could show herself to her mum, as she was now, so her mum and dad would know what was really happening in her life. But they would be heartbroken if they knew, and more likely than not blame themselves as they would feel it was with their help that Laura was married and in this position. Oh! What was she to do? She knew now what a fool she had been. Of course she loved Richard with her whole heart and wouldn't be without him or Katie for that matter, but perhaps her parents had been right, it would have been better to have had him adopted. Each time she bumped into an old school friend who was making a career for herself it felt like a knife was being plunged into her with the pain of what she was missing. With all these thoughts she sobbed into the pillow and eventually fell asleep.

When her mother did see her, when she actually looked a bit better, she still let let out a gasp of amazement. 'Laura, what on earth have you been doing?'

'Do you mean the tooth or rather should I say the lack of it?'

'Of course and you seem to have a lot of bruises.'

In the end Laura decided it was still best to evade the truth. 'I'd bad tooth ache and had to rush to the dentist. The tooth was badly decayed so he took it out. As for the bruises, you know how it is running after little ones, they're so quick. One minute they're with you and the next where they shouldn't be.' Giving a laugh she added, 'I seem to manage to turn too quickly to run after Richard then I bump into something. It's so easily done. Anyway I told you all that before.'

Her mother looked at her as much as to say she didn't believe what she had said, but at least she left the matter at that.

Laura felt she had to say what she'd come to say before she lost courage so she plunged straight in. 'I know this will come as a shock, but I'm pregnant again.'

'Oh Laura! You silly girl. I thought they'd put you on the pill to make sure there are no more babies or at least for the time being.'

'They did.'

'So what have you done, forgotten to take it?'

'No, Mum, I'm not that much of a fool. You remember when I'd that virus, apparently I must have brought it back when I was sick.'

Looking at her with a rather prim and proper expression her mother said, 'I see,' then after a pause added, 'I'd have thought you were too ill to get up to that kind of thing.'

Laura looked rather embarrassed not quite sure how to reply. 'That's what the doctor said as well but you know how it is?'

In a stern voice her mother questioned her. 'Do I? Well at least I've only two children.'

Laura just burst into tears and ran into her mother's arms. 'Oh, Mum! What am I to do?'

'I don't know love, but you know we're always here for you.'

Between sobs Laura managed to say, 'The doctor did say he'd help me make sure there were no more babies after this.'

'Come on love, don't take on so. After all you must think of the baby. You'll be upsetting it. We don't want a sad baby, now do we?'

'No, but I don't know how I'll manage.'

'You will love, you will and after all you're young and strong. Dad and me will always help. Now come on, let's see a smile.'

Laura just managed to give a watery smile. 'Thanks, Mum, for being so understanding. I do love you.'

All through the pregnancy her mother gave her the support she needed because she certainly got none from Keith. He alternated between a sulky silence to verbal abuse resorting to hitting her when he had been drinking. He did seem to respect the fact she was pregnant and he could hurt the baby, so any physical attack was only superficial. Laura knew her mother looked at her strangely more and more, as if to say she knew what was going on. But Laura was too proud to admit her marriage was a failure. She did acknowledge to her mother that she was unhappy at having three children at such a young age. Each time she saw a reflection of herself she felt more depressed at her grotesque figure. It was bad enough before this pregnancy. Somehow she had never lost the weight after Katie's birth. Try as she might, she couldn't help her weight ballooning. The midwives repeatedly told her off, but it was as if the sadness weighed her down not only mentally but physically. The birth didn't come a day too soon, she was in despair. Try as she might to be cheerful during the pregnancy in the hope of producing a happy baby, she couldn't cheer up.

As with the others, Keith was nowhere to be found when she was rushed into hospital to give birth. But she was past caring. She knew the other two children were being well looked after by her mother. Except for having to endure the pain once again, it was a relief to be away from Keith. She wanted to stay in hospital as long as she could and have a rest. As it was her third birth in such a short time, it wasn't a particularly hard labour and in no time she produced a healthy bouncing girl. One look at her and for some reason she instantly became Rachel to her. She knew it made no difference to Keith what she called her, to him they were all brats.

Once she was back home and busy looking after the young ones, she'd barely time to think about her life. The only time she would do this was when she was alone in bed, whilst Keith was still out drinking with his mates. She had to admit she was frightened. He had become more violent again. Not that he touched the children, but she was afraid that one day he would. She could see it in his eyes, the anger he was holding back when they became boisterous and behaved as normal children.

For days on end she would have to go without seeing her parents for fear they would see the physical evidence of what was happening to her. Finally she reached a point where she didn't care any more and when her mother saw her poor bruised face and let out the exclamation, 'Good gracious girl! What's been happening to you?'

Laura just sadly replied with one word which said it all. 'Keith.'

Her mother looked keenly at her. 'It's been going on for a long time hasn't it?' she asked gently.

Laura let out a sob of despair. 'Yes.'

'Come here, love.' With this she gathered her daughter into her arms and gave her a love. 'Don't worry we'll sort something out.'

Her mother was as good as her word and they quickly moved Laura and the children out of the home with Keith and back with them. It was rather a squash but at least her brother had left home to go to University, so there were two empty bedrooms, her old room and his.

Luckily being an old house it also had an attic which her parents only really used to store junk. They quickly converted it to a bedroom and Richard thought it was great fun and made him very grown up to get his own room on a different floor from the rest of them. Laura wasn't sure this was really a good idea and said as much to her parents, only to be told that she was being too protective.

She had good reason to feel protective, because they had no end of threats from Keith. Her parents had tried to protect her by dealing with him themselves, but it was impossible at times for her not to know what was going on. He was worse when he was drunk. He would come to the house and stand outside shouting obscenities for all the neighbourhood to hear. He would bang on the door shouting Laura's name and saying he wanted to see her. At one point it became too much for Laura and she persuaded them he would quieten down if she spoke to him. They regretted listening to her. No sooner had they left the room than he started hitting Laura and by the time they had run back in, when they heard her scream but he had already hurt Laura. He had gone too far this time, she had two cracked ribs. Finally, they realized enough was enough and despite

Laura begging them not to, they called the police. When Keith appeared in court a restraining order was issued and he was given a suspended sentence on the condition he went nowhere near Laura and the children.

As they came out of court and her mother saw the distress on her face she told her, 'It's for the best love, you couldn't have carried on like this. Now you're still young enough to move forward with your life and make something of it.'

Once Keith had been restrained from seeing her or the children he decided he no longer needed to provide money to help keep them. Laura was totally dependent on her parents for their keep. She felt terrible that she had brought all this on them. If only she had listened to them in the beginning, they'd known best after all.

She decided her mum was right, now was the time to get her life back in order. Even though it was already term time, the first thing she did was enrol at the local college to study for another 'O' level. Then she applied to the local teacher training college for a place the following academic year.

Much to her delight she was accepted and was also awarded a local authority grant. It wasn't going to be a great deal of money but at least when she started her training she wouldn't be totally dependent on her parents. The next big problem to be faced was who would look after the children whilst she was at college. It took a bit of courage for her to tell her parents what she planned to do. Partly because she was afraid her father would tell her, 'I told you so. That was what you should have done in the first place.' Then secondly because she knew she was going to be dependent on their help in looking after the children. But it was her mother who came up with some of the solutions and there were no recriminations from her father. Instead he simply said, 'Aye, I'm proud of you, lass.' This instantly brought tears to her eyes as she asked, 'How can you be when I've brought all this on you?'

But he took her hand and said, 'All what? Three lovely grandchildren and you. After all, you've done it all on your own getting sorted out like this.'

'M'm, but I'll need your help with the children you know.'

Her mother chipped in, 'I hear there is a good nursery not far from the college. It's linked to the university so their students can observe the children at play. This means they don't charge a lot. What I hear tell is that it's an ex-headmistress who runs it, so it should be well organized. At least Richard and Katie should be old enough to go if they have vacancies and I'll have to sort out my work times to fit in with your timetable so I can look after Rachel.'

'Oh, Mum, what can I say? That's great! Can you find out who I contact at the nursery and where? Then I'll get straight on to them to try to sort a place out for them. Thanks again, Mum. I do love you.'

Now she decided it was also time to take stock of herself. She was grossly overweight and looked much older than her years. This was the time to do something about it before college started. There was no point in thinking about new clothes until she had done something about her weight. She hadn't expected the co-operation her mother gave in her help in dieting. 'Good idea, love. I could do with losing a few pounds myself. We might as well do it together.'

This helped spur her on, having somebody else to share it with her and as soon as she made a real effort to lose weight, it just rolled off her. As more came off, this gave her the boost she needed to carry on and show it was not just a nine days wonder.

Not a word was heard from Keith in all this time. She was amazed how quickly the children seemed to forget him. It was only Richard who asked once or twice, 'Is Daddy coming to see us?' and she had to answer honestly, 'I don't know. We'll just have to wait and see.' But of course she knew the court had put the injunction on him to stop him coming around. Still, if he had really wanted to see them, she was sure he could have done something about it through his solicitor.

Much to Laura's amazement she passed her 'O' level with the highest grade possible. This was even more remarkable since she had started one term after the course had begun, Not only did she give herself a pat on the back, but her parents did as well.

She decided that now she had lost so much weight and was moving ahead with her future, it was time to kit herself out with some up to date clothes. Although she was going to college and she knew most of the students would wear denim jeans, this had no appeal to her. Maybe it reminded her too much of a uniform and she'd had enough of that both at school and in the bank.

One good skill she had acquired at school was needlework so she was quite capable of making herself some outfits. This was what she would have to do as she had little spare money. Her mum had lent her some money in order to get herself sorted out on the understanding she would pay it back when she was paid her first instalment of her grant. But at least she felt happy again. She had something important now to live and move forward for.

17

This was it then, the start of the next chapter in her life. Laura was frightened, she had to admit it. She knew there weren't many years difference between her and most of the other students, yet she felt years apart in experience. Would she fit in? Would they accept her? These were all questions that kept going around and around in her mind. She desperately felt she needed them to because she wanted this to be the start of her new life and the start of new friendships. As luck would have it, when she sat herself down in the big hall, where they had to assemble, somehow she had managed to be amongst a group of mature students, like herself. This helped to still some of the butterflies in her stomach. It seemed a natural process how the groups formed and Laura, in some ways, was rather disappointed not to be grouped with the young ones. But maybe this was wishful thinking on her part, trying to recapture some of her lost years of youth. She had to admit her group were a friendly enough lot.

'Hello my name's Jackie, what's yours?' asked a voice at her side.

'Laura.'

'Pleased to meet you Laura. I'm glad to find there's others here in my age group. I thought I was going to be the odd one out.'

'Er, no, it seems as if we're in good company.'

This was the start of this particular friendship and in fact she was to stay friends with Jackie for many years to come.

At the end of her first year, which had seemed to fly by, she had a great deal to be grateful for that this had been her crowd. It was a shock to many of the young ones, who'd wrongly thought college life was about socializing and enjoying themselves, not studying, when they failed their exams and lost their place at College.

But to Laura it was imperative for her to succeed. It had been a hard first year, trying to study and look after three young children but she'd done it and passed the first three exams with flying colours. This gave her the much needed incentive to carry on.

It was probably a good job the teaching practice wasn't in the first year of study. If Laura had known how exhausting this could be she would, in all probability, have given up the course. But by the time she did her first teaching practice she was half way through the course and knew she couldn't let go now.

There was no chance to express their personal choice about where they would like to do their teaching practice. When Laura saw the name of her allocated school she just gave a groan and turned to Jackie her friend. 'Oh no! Why does it always happen to me. That must be one of the worst schools to go to.'

Jackie quickly tried to reassure her. 'Look at it this way, it can only get better, and if you survive this you can survive anything.'

'It's all right saying that, but I've to survive three weeks at that school.'

'Come on, it can't be as bad as all that and, after all, you've experience in looking after your own children.'

'True, but it's somehow different looking after your own to teaching other people's.'

'You'll be all right I'm sure.'

But none of this did anything to quell her nervousness at what she was letting herself in for. Some premonition must have told her it was going to be bad and it was. It was not only the children but the teachers' own attitudes. Particularly the one who was her mentor whilst there.

Laura couldn't believe it when she saw the class teacher wedge open the classroom door and pull a desk outside. She had thought she'd be left on her own at this first attempt at teaching but this illusion was quickly dispelled. 'I'll be sitting out here. I much prefer to do this as I've to be honest, this is one of the hardest classes in the school,' stated Mrs. Bennett.

With these words Laura's heart sank further, but the class teacher hadn't finished. 'Unfortunately there's one young girl in the class who's an arsonist.'

Laura could hardly believe her ears, the eldest child was only twelve years old, yet there was an arsonist amongst them.

'An arsonist?'

'Yes, that's what I said.'

'Oh!'

But again the teacher continued, 'You must appreciate that many of these unfortunate children come from very poor backgrounds. Yes, that helps make them what they are, I'm afraid.'

'Right. Thanks for the warning.' By now Laura was beginning to decide maybe it wasn't a bad idea after all that help, if needed, was close at hand.

'Well, my dear, all over to you now. Good luck, relax and enjoy the experience.'

It was only a basic exercise in English that Laura was taking for her first attempt and looking back afterwards she could never really remember what she did talk about and teach to them. It all became a blur as she tried to put everything she had been taught into that first practice, yet at the same time keep at least some class control.

What never went out of her mind was the end of the lesson when the class teacher approached her after the children had been dismissed. 'Not bad, my dear, for a first attempt but I'd like to point out a few things to you. First of all we never use loops in our writing when we put things up on the board. We teach the children no loops in their joined up writing so we must set a good impression by doing the same.'

Here Laura had to bite her tongue to stop herself making a sharp comment back. This annoyed her, particularly as all her school life it had been drummed into her that writing must always have the loops. So this and other comments went on in such a fashion that Laura's head began to reel and she wondered what she was doing there. She must be wasting her time. There was no way after all these critical remarks that she was cut out to be a teacher. She therefore couldn't believe her ears when the final words came. 'Not bad at all considering it's your first attempt at teaching. No, not bad at all, keep up the good work and you'll get there.'

Not really sure how to respond to all this, in the end Laura simply said, 'Thank you.'

By the time she arrived home she felt totally drained as if she'd done her three weeks teaching practice in one day. As she opened the door her children ran to her with her mum quickly following behind. She could hear their voices eager to know how she'd got on. 'Well, Mum, are you a teacher now?' asked Richard innocently.

Giving his head a pat Laura had to disappoint him. 'Not quite yet, it takes a bit longer than a day, unfortunately.'

Catching her mother's eye she said, 'It's tiring, Mum. Far harder than I ever imagined it would be.'

'Don't worry, love, it's always strange on a first day whatever you do. I'm sure I once told you before that it can only get better,' she said to reassure her as if she could sense some of Laura's thoughts.

Maybe it did get better but Laura wasn't always sure about that at times. She began to have doubts whether, after all, she had chosen the right career for herself. But then she did feel so tired so maybe that accounted for her reaction. Her mother tried to point out to her. 'Don't you realize you're doing far more than many of your fellow students doing their teaching practice. Not only are you doing a day's work, preparing work in the evening for the next day but you are also seeing to three

225

small childrens' needs. No wonder you're tired. Just give yourself time.'

In her heart Laura knew what her mother had said made sense. She did stick the practice out but was relieved when she was back at College. Talking to her friends, she found out they felt just the same and had thought it as difficult as she had. What else she realized by talking to them was that she had, as she had originally thought, been in a particularly difficult school to teach in. Maybe next time it would be better.

In all that time she hadn't heard a word from Keith. Not that she was really bothered because in her own way she was happy with the way she had chosen to go. Despite any doubts she might have at times she knew she had made the right decision for herself and the children. Not that times weren't hard for her. She certainly could have done with money from him but he had hurt her too much for her to go begging to him. No, somehow she would manage. Despite her shortage of money at least she felt at last she was doing something with her life. She realized just how much more she was becoming than a mother when Richard announced with great pride, 'I told Mrs. Fairburn, my class teacher, that my Mummy's going to be a teacher too.' Her heart swelled with pride at these words.

As her friends had predicted her next teaching practice was a lot better. It was a nicer school and altogether it was a much more pleasant experience. She was there just before Christmas and this seemed to make it all the more special seeing the children doing their various little plays. She was even invited to their Christmas party and she always remembered the record Under the Moon of Love by Showaddywaddy, as the children demonstrated the dance to her that went with this tune. It made her realize how much of her youth she'd thrown away. Never again would she waste her life. All too soon the course was nearing its end and all that was left was to pass the final exams. At least here she had done better than school. Each year she had steadily passed all the modules taken.

When the day of the results dawned Laura was no different to any other student in her nervousness. She was at the notice board long before the results were pinned up. Her heart was in her mouth and she felt sick with tension. As the results were put up her legs suddenly became immobile. She couldn't move to look until suddenly a voice said in her ear, 'Look, Laura, you've done it. You're a qualified teacher.'

Swiftly now she moved forward to make

sure there was no mistake and sure enough it was all up there in writing. To nobody in particular she said, 'Thank goodness I've done it. Now I can go ahead and go and get that promised job.'

This had been a concern to her, as teaching jobs weren't so easy to come by at that moment. But luck seemed to have been on her side as at her last teaching practice she had heard of a job coming vacant at that school so had enquired about it. She still had to go through the normal formalities of applying and being interviewed but she was convinced that actually having been there and their seeing her in practice had all been to her advantage. At last she had also felt that a little bit of maturity and having her own children had brought her into her own.

When she arrived back home her mum opened the door straight away. 'Well, how did you get on? Are we looking at Mrs. Bowes the teacher?'

With great pride in her voice Laura answered, 'Yes.'

Before she knew where she was her mother had her arms around her giving her a big hug. 'Well done, love, I'm so proud of you. I know it's been hard work, what with the children and the lack of money, but you've done it. Well done!'

With this she moved away looking embarrassed and quickly marched into the kitchen to get on with her jobs. Hearing all the commotion Richard ran out. 'Are you really a teacher now, Mummy?'

'I guess so, love. Yes I'm a teacher,' she said with a new found pride. Now she couldn't wait for her dad to come in to tell him the good news. At least she'd eventually given him something to be proud about. 'Dad's late isn't he?' she called to her mother.

'No, he isn't. Stop fussing he'll be here any minute.'

No sooner were the words out than she heard the front door open and quickly ran down the hall. He just looked at her, 'Well?'

With this she ran into his arms. 'I've really done it. I'm a teacher now.'

'Great, I always knew you could.'

With this he turned and shouted, 'Marjorie, did you organize the baby sitter as I asked you?'

'Of course.'

'Come on then the pair of you, get your glad rags on. We're off to celebrate.'

'To celebrate?'

'That's what I said. I think you deserve it. Now come on get ready. The table's booked for 7.30.'

'How did you know I'd pass?'

'Just confidence. I knew you'd do it. I always told you that you could.'

As she ran up the stairs Laura couldn't stop herself letting out, 'Whoopee.'

When the award ceremony day came around she knew her true moment of glory had come when she heard her name called and she walked up onto the stage in a cap and gown to be awarded her degree.

Her mum and dad were there watching and she hoped this made up for some of the heartache she had caused them. They certainly had a look of pride on their faces and that alone made all the hard work she had done worthwhile.

As a present from them for her efforts they had her picture taken to be made into a portrait. Her mum said, 'You'll have something there to always remind you of this day and as the children grow up and see it they'll understand your efforts.'

'Thanks, Mum, I'll always treasure it.'

With all this she felt a glow of happiness inside her, something she hadn't felt for a long time.

18

It was amazing how quickly the summer holiday went for Laura. She tried to do all the things she could, within her limited finances, to occupy and amuse the children. They went on day trips to the park and really she just fell in with their plans. She wanted this to be their special time and for once to have the opportunity to spend long spells of time with her.

But all too soon it was another first day, this time as a teacher. The first day nerves were no less than when she had started college. The night before she questioned her mum. 'But what if I can't do it? It's different going into a school for three weeks teaching practice.'

'Come on, love. Don't be silly, you'll be all right. If they hadn't thought you were cut out to be a teacher you wouldn't have passed your teaching practice.'

'I suppose so, but it's a funny feeling.'

'Of course it is. Whatever job you start, it feels strange. It wouldn't be human not to have doubts and fears. We all do when we're going into the unknown. But I've confidence in you, look how you manage your three. Come on, give me a smile. After all, they don't want to see a miserable teacher.'

'Thanks, Mum.'

'What for?'

'Just for being you and always understanding everything.'

Her mother's intuition had been right. As soon as she was with the school children she forgot her nerves and was soon in full swing putting all her efforts into teaching them. She was amazed how quickly she got to know all their names and in no time felt as if she'd been teaching all her life, not just for a matter of weeks.

When the first pay day came it really sunk in, at last she was earning money, proper money of her own. Not that she would be well off but at least now she could pay her own way in comfort. It started her thinking that perhaps now was the time she should set up a home of her own for herself and her children. She knew her mum and dad would be upset, but she needed to get some independence.

Finally she plucked up the courage to broach the subject. 'Mum, I think it's time I looked for a place of my own for me and the children.'

Rather indignantly her mother quickly

responded, 'What's wrong with it here young lady? Haven't we looked after you all well enough?'

Before she really upset her mum Laura knew she had to be quick to reassure her. 'Of course you have. It isn't that at all. I don't really want to leave but you must realize I'm a grown woman with three children of my own to look after. It's time I became independent again. It would be so easy to stay here but I think I should try to make my own home for the children.'

Realizing there was some sense in what Laura said, her mother began to calm down a bit. 'I suppose I can see what you're saying makes sense but we'll miss you all so much. It seemed chaotic when you all came but now we've got used to the noise and disruption. I wish you wouldn't go or at least think very carefully about it. I don't know what your dad will say, I really don't.'

'I've thought about it long and hard and that's what I want to do. But don't fret I'm not leaving tomorrow. It might take me a while to get sorted out and I need to save up some more money before I can do it. I'm only giving you plenty of advance warning. But you know you can't get rid of me or the children that easily. We'll always be around here to see you and you'll always be welcome to come and see us wherever our new home will be. By the time we're ready to go, you'll have got used to the idea and might even like the thought of the peace again.'

'I suppose so, but break the idea gently to your Dad, love. He'll be upset.'

'I will, don't worry. Thanks again, Mum, for all you've both done.'

'What else could we have done? You're our daughter after all.'

After this conversation Laura wasn't quite sure whether she was really going to be doing the right thing. The children doted on their grandparents and it made life much easier being with them. At least they were getting a man's influence even if it wasn't their father's. Maybe after all she wouldn't rush into anything but one thing she would and could do was have the driving lessons she'd promised herself so long ago. Her mum and dad had a car now and she knew how much easier it was for her dad to drive her or the children to places. But this was one area she could gain her independence from them without causing upset, by getting her own car. Her mum being fully supportive of this idea gave her the name of a driving instructor recommended by a friend.

Laura had nothing against people being older but as soon as she saw him she couldn't believe he was a driving instructor. He seemed past it, his hands shook as he spoke and even his own driving seemed erratic. How could he teach somebody else? But there again Laura quickly decided, seeing she couldn't drive herself how could she really judge somebody else's abilities. He was a good talker, she would give him that. He never shut up barely giving her chance to answer his questions.

Laura was disappointed that on her first lesson she only had a very few minutes behind the wheel and he never let her move fast enough to get out of first gear. This seemed to set the pace of future driving lessons. It didn't take her long to realize that at this pace she would be an old woman herself before she was entered for her first test. Tactfully she tried to explain to her mum that she was changing instructors. Much to her relief her dad supported her in this and even more to her surprise offered to take her out himself for drives in his car to get extra practice.

Her mum just sniffed. 'You'll not last two minutes together with Laura behind the wheel. Just you both wait and see.'

But she had to eat her words — not one cross word was ever said between the pair of them the whole time of the driving practice.

Now with this help and her new instructor she made great steps forward and in no time it was the date of her test.

As the examiner walked out to them she saw the instructor's face suddenly look despondent and instantly decided it looked as if she wasn't going to pass her test that day. Much to her surprise once she was sat behind the wheel he started to chat. It must have been the weather, because it was one of those infrequent glorious sunny days in February. The examiner kept saying, 'I feel as if Spring is here. I do like the sunshine.'

Whatever the reason as she drove he chatted away which totally relaxed her and she knew she had put on one of her best performances in driving. As they were talking she mentioned children and he exclaimed, 'Come off it, you're not old enough to be a mother.'

Laughing she answered, 'I am. In fact I've got three children and they're all old enough to be at school now.'

'Never! I just can't believe it.'

'It's true enough, but I admit I was very young when I had the eldest.'

'You must have only been a child yourself.'

Rather ruefully she answered, 'Aye, you're right there.'

Maybe this helped her or it was that her

driving was just good. Whatever the reason, much to her delight she passed her test.

Now she had real freedom. She managed to buy a little Mini all of her own. Not that it was much to look at but it got her and the children round, that was all that mattered. Suddenly she felt she was making up to the children for what they had missed before. Nearly every Sunday, weather permitting, they would pack up and go on some jaunt or other. It gave Laura real pleasure to see their little faces bright and laughing. She felt normal herself as if many of the horrors of the past had belonged to somebody else. What she did appreciate was that money gave her freedom and independence. Now she had tried a taste of this freedom she wanted more. She became very ambitious to further her own career because to her anything would then be possible. She wanted to give the children all they asked for and more. After all, who deserved it more than they did.

But as with all good things there is always something or someone who comes along to spoil it. Laura had been to the seaside with the children and it had been one of their best days out together. As soon as she opened the house door she could sense there was something wrong. Her mother walked quickly out of the front room. 'Laura you have a visitor,' she said quietly so the children couldn't hear.

Still being in high spirits from the enjoyment of the day Laura answered in jovial voice. 'Oh yes, and who might that be?'

Marjorie turned to her grandchildren. 'Go on upstairs and take your coats off and I'll come to see to you in a minute or two. Mummy must be tired.'

Turning to Laura her mother just looked at her and said in a soft voice, 'Keith.'

Laura could feel all the colour drain out of her face and like a parrot she repeated, 'Keith?'

'That's what I said. He insisted he waited until you came home. You'd better go in and see him. You should be all right as he seems calm enough.'

'But I don't want anything to do with him.'

'Ssh, keep your voice down. Just go and see what he wants then he might go away again with no trouble.'

'I suppose so.' Laura gave a quick glance in the hall mirror and marched into the front room.

Though it was unusual for her, before she knew where she was she said in a sarcastic voice, 'Long time no see Keith.'

Looking sheepishly at her he replied, 'You look well, Laura. I like the outfit.'

'Yes, well I'm sure you haven't come to tell me that. What do you want?'

'Why must I want anything? Can't I come and see my wife and children?'

Laura gave a bitter laugh. 'Well actually, according to the court you can't. A pity you didn't think of that before I needed to report you to the police and take such action.'

'I've had a lot of growing up to do. I admit that now and at least I can see my mistakes.'

'Can you now?' said Laura with a sound of disbelief in her voice. 'It would have helped us all if you had grown up a few years before.'

'I know, I realize that now. But I'm willing to try now. I thought we might be able to get to know each other again and get things sorted.'

'How do you mean sorted?'

'Let's take things a step at a time, that's all I ask. Will you let me see the children again now?'

'Not tonight, they've had a lovely day out with me but they're tired now. Mum will have been getting them ready for bed whilst we've been talking. In fact they'll most probably be in bed now. Mum will have seen to that.'

'I realize that, but can I see them sometime soon?'

Rather reluctantly Laura agreed. 'I suppose so, you're their Father after all.' Laura with her usual honesty added the snide remark, 'Though you wouldn't believe it if we're really honest.'

'I know and I've already said I'm sorry and regret all that.'

'Come next Sunday afternoon then. Let's take it from there. They might not want to see you. Rachel won't even know you, so we'll have to see how it works out. I don't think I can be any fairer than that, do you?'

Looking rather humble he said, 'No I don't. Thanks, Laura, I really do appreciate that.'

'Now I think you'd better go. We've said all we need to each other at the present time.'

Still being quite humble, not the aggressive person she was used to his response came as a surprise. 'Of course I'll go now. See you on Sunday about two if that's okay for you?'

'Yes, they'll be ready to see you then. You know your way out.'

No sooner had he gone than her mother was back in the room. 'Well! What did he want?'

'To see me and the children again.'

'I hope you said no.'

'Please understand, Mum, it's difficult and he is their father after all.'

'So you're telling me that you agreed to it.'

'Only for a short time on Sunday

afternoon. Then I said I'd have to see how it goes with the children. After all, it's a long time since they saw him and they might not be bothered about knowing him now.'

'H'mm I don't know what your Dad will say, I really don't. Remember what he was like with you before. All this time he's never been near, never sent you a penny piece. Then turns up like a bad penny himself. It fair gave me a funny turn waiting on my own with him. A pity your Dad had to go to uncle Fred's today of all days. I could have done with him here. Mind, I bet he'd have given him his marching orders.'

'I know, Mum, but you've got to see it's difficult for me. It really is. What do I do for the best particularly for the children? Rachel keeps asking why she hasn't got a daddy like her friends at school. I thought it might be good for her to see him. Anyway, as I said we'll see how it goes. I'm just taking it a step at a time. Then it's only him seeing the children. It's not as if I've any intention of us getting back together or any such thing.'

In actual fact Laura didn't feel as calm inside as the impression she pretended when she had spoken to her mum. She was worried as well, if she had really done the right thing for them all. That niggling doubt never left her all week despite the children's excitement at the thought of seeing their dad again. She could hardly control them by the time it reached Sunday lunch and she had to get quite cross saying she would call the meeting off if they didn't settle down a bit.

At last the knock came at the front door and suddenly they turned from being boisterous children into shy ones. Rachel hid behind her mother's skirt and Laura tried to move her back in front of her. 'Come on, don't be silly now. You know you've all been waiting for to-day.'

Finally she managed to get to the door. 'Come in Keith, they're all waiting to see you.'

'Hello, kids, remember me?'

Not a word was spoken from any of them.

Feeling uncomfortable by it all Laura turned to Richard. 'Now you remember your Dad.'

He looked very subdued now. 'Yes, Mum.'

'Well come on then, say hello.'

Very quietly Richard looked at his father and stammered, 'Hello.'

'Hello there yourself, young man. By, you've grown since I last saw you. In fact you all have. Now what do you say we all go to the park for an ice-cream. That's if your Mum wants to go there.'

Not wanting to cause any disagreement

Laura was quick to say, 'That's all right by me. They're ready to go now. I'll just tell Mum we're off. I won't be a minute.'

After the afternoon in the park Laura began to wonder if she had misjudged him and he had really changed and now did care about the children. But for some reason the more they saw of him she still had a niggling doubt that there was something wrong somewhere. Rachel and Katie were thrilled at getting to know their dad and to tell all their friends about him but Richard was still more reserved when his father was around.

Finally, as summer drew to a close he suggested that he and Laura went out for a drink because he wanted to talk to her. So far they had always had the children with them as company. Hoping, at last, he had seen sense and was prepared to contribute towards their upbringing she agreed. Her mother made a lot of protests about her going and even Laura had to admit she wasn't that keen. But she knew she needed to try to reassure her mum. 'Don't worry so, Mum. It's only for the children's sake I'm going. He means nothing to me, nothing at all. I'd much rather be spending an evening in with you, but I think it's time I sorted a divorce out so it might be as well to go out with him to see what he's to say for himself. Hopefully we can then sort everything out on a friendly basis.'

Even to her own ears this didn't ring quite true, but her mother, much to her surprise, said no more on the topic.

Still when the evening came around and it was time to meet him she couldn't stop the butterflies in her stomach. She wasn't sure whether these were in anticipation of trouble or just the thought she was going out. It was so rare to have an outing like this, without at least one member of her family with her.

He was cheerful enough when they met and Laura began to relax. Once seated, with a drink, before Laura could say what was on her mind Keith plunged straight in questioning her how well she was doing financially. This wasn't what she'd expected at all and she couldn't help but be rather vague in her answer by saying, 'I earn enough to get by, at least the children don't go short.'

'I see you've got yourself a car, as well.'

Laura laughed. 'It's only an old banger but it does make it easier to get the children around.'

'To me you seem to be doing nicely for yourself. I've been thinking that we've been getting on well enough these times we've taken the children out. How about having another go?'

Before Laura could stop herself she replied

more sharply than she intended. 'You must be joking!'

Now the sulky expression she knew so well from the past came back on his face. 'You're doing all right now and earn good money. I kept you and those brats, in the past, with my money so why shouldn't you share some of yours with me now.'

'I see now what this has all been about. You're only interested because you think I've got something now. You weren't interested in me when I was a wife and Mum, that wasn't good enough for you then. Sorry Keith, no way. In fact I wanted to talk to you about a divorce.'

She could see him changing to the person who had frightened her in the past and felt the need to move back to be further away from him. She was glad she had as she saw his hand come up as if to hit her, then as if remembering he was in a public place it fell back to his side. He snarled, 'You bitch, always were. You never gave anything away.'

Laura quickly jumped up. 'I'm going now. Don't try to follow me because I wouldn't hesitate to go to the police. You've already been in trouble for this.'

As she left she could hear his voice calling abuses after her, but she simply moved as quickly as she could without looking at any of the people she passed.

By the time she arrived home tears were streaming down her cheeks. As she opened the door she heard her mother call, 'Is that you Laura? You're home early.'

As she went into the room her mother quickly jumped up and came to her. 'What's wrong? Quick tell me what's happened.'

'Only Keith showing his true colours again. He wanted me back for the money I'm earning. He turned abusive as soon as I refused.'

'I always knew he was a bad lot. Are you going to call the police?'

'No, I'm sure there's no need. I don't think he'll be around to bother us again now I made it quite clear what's what.'

Her mother just gave a sigh and sat down. 'I suppose you know what's best.'

Her father was furious and all for going to the police but Laura pointed out she didn't want to upset the children any more than she need. In the end he relented leaving it up to her.

It was more difficult talking to the children than her mother. How to tell them they wouldn't be seeing their daddy so often, if in fact, ever again. Laura herself felt disappointed that she had lost the companionship of another adult when she took the children on their Sunday outings. She was lonely and had to admit it, despite the fact other parts of her life were coming together.

Katie and Rachel took the news badly and blamed her and became hostile for a while but with the resilience of the young soon bounced back to be her loving daughters. As Richard had never said much about seeing his father again so he kept his own counsel about not seeing him in the future. But secretly he was glad as his young mind could still remember having a fear of him.

19

What was she to do with her life to liven it up? Yes, she had to admit she could now buy the things she really wanted to. She had plenty of clothes, her little car and the children went short of nothing they wanted. In fact, she even had money to spare. But that didn't buy the companionship she so desperately needed. Her life seemed to comprise of work, home, bed and back to work. That was until Pat joined the teaching staff at her school. They were of similar age and both new to teaching and hit it off instantly. At last she had some female companionship and somebody she could talk to, but there was still a man in her life missing. Pat was quick to sense this and suggested an evening out. She said her husband had a nice, presentable, single friend who she would get him to bring along to make up a foursome. Laura laughed at this suggestion and asked, 'If he's as nice as you say, why hasn't he been snapped up before now?'

Looking serious Pat thought about this. 'I don't know why. I really don't because I honestly mean it when I say he's ever so nice. In fact if my Peter wasn't a bit of all right I could fancy him myself. There's one thing that I must warn you.'

Here Laura jumped in quickly. 'I knew there was some catch.'

Pat went on to reassure her, 'No nothing like that, only he is a few years older than us. That's all.'

'That makes it more and more curious why he's still single, or has he been married and he's now divorced?'

'No, he's never been married.'

'Um,' pondered Laura, then quickly asked, 'By the way you haven't even told me his name.'

'Silly me. It's Steven.'

'Well, all right you've convinced me, I'll come. It'll make a nice change — better than staying in but I'm sure nothing will come of it. But thanks for thinking of me and asking me along. You'd better warn him that I've three young children.'

'Don't be silly, that makes no difference. Anyway, as you said let's see how it goes. I'll get Pete to find out when he's free then we'll sort out a date that suits us all.'

'There's the bell, back to class once again, but at least I've something to look forward to now.'

As the time came nearer to going out Laura started to panic. It was a long time since she'd been out like this. What should she wear and even worse what should she say? She knew she would be tongue tied, never in her whole life had she been on a date like this.

As usual her mum was her supportive, reassuring self. 'You look lovely, lass. Any man would be proud to be seen with you. Now you go and have a good evening, whatever the outcome. It's about time you enjoyed yourself. Don't worry about the children, you know they're all right with us.'

Her dad quickly added, 'Your Mum's right. Go out there and enjoy yourself. Are you all right for cash?' he asked out of habit, forgetting she was quite self sufficient now.

'Of course, Dad,' laughed Laura. 'I'm a woman of means now you know.'

Her dad joined in the laughter. 'I must be getting forgetful in my old age, of course you are. Off you go then and enjoy yourself spending some of that hard earned money.'

Just then the tooting of a car horn could be heard. 'They're here! I'll be off then. See you both later, but I don't know what time I'll be in.'

Both her parents replied in unison. 'Be off

with you, it doesn't matter what time. Just enjoy yourself.'

Much to her disappointment there was only Pat and her husband in the car, and she was informed Steven was meeting them there. After Pat had introduced Laura to her husband Laura felt the need to ask, 'He will turn up won't he? Otherwise I'll feel like a gooseberry.'

'Don't worry,' Pat's husband was quick to reassure. 'If he says he'll be there he will. He's one of the most reliable people I've ever met.'

Laura began to think he sounded too good to be true yet she already felt a deep interest just by what she knew about him. She settled back in her seat and let her mind imagine what the evening would be like but more importantly so, what he'd really be like.

For the rest of the journey she let her mind wander and was awoken sharply out of her dreams by a voice saying, 'Right, here we are then, ladies. I'll let you get out here then I'll go and park the car. I can't see Steven's car around so he mustn't be here yet. Anyway watch out for him when you get in Pat, in case I've missed it.'

'Okay, then,' Pat answered cheerfully.

Laura couldn't quell her impatience and as soon as they'd entered the building she quickly asked, 'Well, is he here then?'

'I can't see him. Look there are some seats over there, let's go and sit and wait.'

All the while Laura was looking at the door and each time somebody entered she wondered if it was him. Finally Pete came in and Pat exclaimed, 'Look, Steven is here with Pete. They must have met in the car park.'

Laura could feel her eyes drawn to him and as if he could sense her looking at him, he gazed across the room at her. Instantly she felt a magnetic pull as if she had known him all her life. He quickly moved to her side and held out his hand. 'Hi, I'm Steven and you must be Laura?'

She could barely manage to reply 'Yes', she was so mesmerized. It came to her in an instant flash that this was the man she'd waited for these last few years. She couldn't remember what she ordered to eat or hardly in fact if she did eat anything. She must have done everything by an automatic reaction. The only thing she knew was the evening passed all too quickly. Before she knew where she was the meal was at an end and the waiter was hovering to clear the table.

Pat suggested, 'Let's go and sit over there and have another drink.'

Steven looked rueful, 'Afraid not. I promised my Grandma I wouldn't be late in and besides I want to take Laura home myself.'

Cheek she thought, he hasn't even asked me, but inside herself she was thrilled he had suggested this. Then suddenly she had to stop herself laughing out aloud when she realized a grown man had said he wouldn't be in late to his grandma.

'Come on Laura, are you ready to go now? I think we're stopping this young man from doing his job of clearing up.'

Waking out of her dream Laura looked at Steven. 'Yes, of course. Are you sure it's no trouble taking me home? Pat and Pete have said they would.'

'It's no trouble. I want to take you so let's hear no more about it. Come on, is this your coat?'

'Yes, thanks.' Being the perfect gentleman he helped her on with it.

'See you on Monday then Pat, at work.'

With a gleam in her eye Pat answered, 'I hope so, that's if you get home safely.'

'Come on, take no notice of her. I'm used to her teasing comments. She loves to wind me up,' Steven laughed.

Somehow she imagined him with a flash car and was rather surprised when he led her over to a Morris Minor. 'Is this yours?' she asked in amazement.

'It is, but don't look so worried. It's not my choice of car but my Grandma knew the person selling it and nagged me to get it. Anything for a peaceful life and to pacify her so she keeps in good humour.'

It suddenly struck Laura that his grandma seemed to play a large part in his life and she felt she needed to know more if she did keep on seeing him.

She was amazed how easily they chatted all the way home, there was never a silent moment. Again this reinforced the feeling of having known each other a long time. All too soon the journey ended. Quickly he said, 'Look if you don't mind I need to get off now. As I said before, I promised not to be too late but I would like to see you again. Will you meet me on Wednesday night at 7.30 outside the Odeon cinema in town?'

'Yes, fine thanks,' she replied as she opened the car door taking the hint that he wanted to be off home now. Looking back she waved him off.

As she shut the house front door a voice shouted, 'Is that you Laura?'

'Yes, Mum.'

'You're home earlier than I thought you'd be. Is everything all right?'

As Laura entered the room her mother looked at her sharply. 'What's amusing you, young lady?' she asked as she saw tears of laughter running down Laura's cheeks.

'He had to be home early, Mum, because he promised his Grandma. It seems funny that's all when he's a mature grown man.'

'Well, I think that shows what a really thoughtful person he must be.'

Sobering up at this statement Laura quickly said, 'Actually he is. Oh, Mum! Already I've fallen for him. He's really great to be with.'

'Now not so hasty. Just take it steady. Just remember this is your first date for a long time. I take it you are seeing him again?'

'Yes, on Wednesday night.' Then she quickly added, 'If that's all right with you to look after the children again?'

'Of course. When have we been known to refuse?'

All that Laura worried about before the date, even though it had been instant attraction, was whether she would recognize him again easily amongst the crowd waiting to go into the pictures. She did hope he wore that distinctive coat again. It looked like a sheepskin coat, but she could tell it wasn't actual sheepskin. Somehow with the collar turned up it gave him a look of his own that she was sure she would easily know again. But what about herself, would he recognize

255

her? Should she wear her hair the same to make sure, what coat should she wear — would he be looking for hers as recognition? All these thoughts kept passing through her head until she had to give herself a mental shake to tell herself to stop being so silly, she was actually behaving like a teenager not a mature woman with children of her own. It would be all right. They would just walk up to each other at the time and place as agreed and carry on from where they had left off.

Why had she worried? She had no sooner turned the corner than she saw him standing there. That old familiar feeling of knowing him for a long time, despite it actually only being such a short time, was back. As he saw her he rushed over to greet her. 'I didn't ask what you wanted to do tonight when I left you so hastily the other night. Sorry about rushing off, but my Grandma is old and worries about me. Silly I know when I'm a grown man, but there you are. Now do you want to go to the cinema or for a drink and chat?'

'I think a drink and chat would be nice. It makes a change to have some adult conversation after being with children all day.'

'A drink it is then. Any preferences where you go?'

'No, I don't really know the places around here. To be truthful, I don't often get out on an evening.'

'No, I don't suppose you do with having your children to look after.'

Laura was rather taken aback by this comment because she hadn't yet told him she had a family. Still she had been wondering how to break this fact to him, so at least he now knew and this problem had been solved. Then she remembered asking Pat to make sure he knew, so in all probability Pat or her husband would have told him.

It was amazing how they chatted all evening with no inhibitions. It brought a warmth inside Laura, making her so happy. She had never communicated in this way with Keith even though she had longed to. She felt as if she had known Steven longer than Keith already, whereas in reality she had only known him for a few hours.

She did find out that he was a joiner and had been in the same job since leaving school. What she also deduced from his tone that it was that it was more to please his grandparents than himself that he had trained for this job. Here was a kindred spirit, somebody else she could sense wanted to achieve the nice things of life. It appeared he had been brought up with his grandparents, but for what reason she didn't like to ask. But it seemed strange he had two sisters who were both brought up by their parents. Still she was already sure there was time enough to find out all the details. Before it was very late he was looking at his watch and once again apologizing that he mustn't be late home. Laura was quick to reassure him. 'I told you before it doesn't matter. I don't want to be home too late myself. I can't cope with late nights in the week, not when I've got work the next day.'

On this note they parted with Laura promising to meet him again on Saturday evening. It quite surprised Laura that he wasn't calling at her home to pick her up. But then she decided this was probably out of consideration for her and the children.

This time it was her dad who asked the question as soon as she got in home. 'Well, how did your evening go?'

'Excellent, he's really good company and despite only just getting to know each other we seem to have so much in common.'

'I'm glad, it's time you met somebody nice.'

'Now don't go rushing ahead, Dad. After all we've only just met. At least that's what Mum reminded me when I was excited about it all on Saturday night.'

'You're seeing him again though aren't you?'

'Yes of course.' Laura gave a laugh, 'That's if you don't mind baby sitting on Saturday evening? You see all this encouraging me to go out gives you more baby sitting.'

'We don't mind. All we want for you is that you have a life again. We know it isn't easy with three children. By the way, I take it he does know about the children?'

'Oh yes. Pat or Pete must have made sure of that, which saved me the trouble. But it doesn't seem to bother him in the least.' Here she gave another laugh, 'Mind you he hasn't met them yet.'

'He'll like them, they're good children and that's not just me being biased as their Granddad. Anyway it won't be long until Saturday when you see him again.'

Laura was delighted when on Saturday Steven suggested that he would like to take Laura and the children out for the day on Sunday. She was a little bit concerned what the children's reaction would be, as this was the first man she had dated. There again it did seem a good idea for him to get to know them as soon as possible.

When she told them on the Sunday morning, the two girls jumped up and down with joy, 'Goody, goody,' was all they could say. But Richard was a bit more reserved. 'Do I have to go, Mum?'

'Yes, Steven said he wanted to meet all of you and that's what he meant.'

'Well, if I must I suppose I'll have to come with you, but I don't know if I'll enjoy myself. What's he like?'

'You'll like him.' Seeing the look of disbelief on her son's face she added, 'You will like him, honestly.' She kept her fingers crossed behind her back hoping this would indeed be the case. She knew it was difficult for Richard, being the eldest he could remember his dad the most. Any other man in his life was going to be difficult after the experience of his father.

In fact, the day went a lot better than she had imagined and it was no time before Richard had lost his reserve and was joining in the fun. Steven, in his wisdom, had bought a kite for him. This helped no end to cement the friendship. In no time he was behaving as the young boy that he really was, running around and yelling as much as the girls.

The outing set the scene for many more Sundays. It became a set pattern that they all went out for the day. Each time they enjoyed themselves as much as that first Sunday. In fact Laura and Steven were finding it difficult to be apart, but with all the marking she had to do each evening, it was impossible for them to meet every night. Steven would try to make up for this by seeing her in their lunch hour. One way and another they seemed to be seeing each other every day.

The only thing that disturbed Laura was the fact she still hadn't met his grandma. That was until one Saturday evening when he said, 'Laura I hope the children won't be too disappointed tomorrow but I can't take them out.'

Laura's heart sank into her boots as she wondered if that was it? Not wanting to cause any aggravation she tried to say cheerfully, 'Of course not, I'll explain to them that we aren't going out.'

'No, you've got me wrong. I only meant the children. We're still going out. My Grandma wants me to take her to Blackpool for the day, but she does want you to come as well.'

'Oh! I see,' said Laura brightening slightly, but the thought about seeing his grandma made her feel a little bit uneasy. 'Are you sure she wants me along?'

'Of course. If you knew my grandma you'd know she wouldn't ask unless she meant it.'

'Oh, I see,' repeated Laura with her heart dropping even more at the thought of what sounded a difficult day ahead.

'I'll call for you at ten. If you can be ready

we can get straight off. She won't want to wait in the car whilst I come in.'

'Of course, that's fine. I'll be ready, don't worry.' But she couldn't help but think his grandma sounded a formidable old lady. It didn't sound as if it was going to be much of a day of pleasure. She thought it would be a case of smile sweetly and keep the peace.

When he arrived prompt at ten Laura ran out of the house. She was aware of three small faces watching her from the house window. There was already a figure in the front passenger seat of the car so she had no option but to get in the back. A gruff voice asked before Steven had chance to introduce each other. 'Those yours are they?'

Taking it to mean the children she quickly replied, 'Yes, they are.'

It was difficult to see what Steven's grandma looked like from the back, all Laura could see was the back of a head with snowy white hair that was cut in rather a severe style. She knew from Steven that she was in her late seventies but apparently very sprightly. Very little conversation went on the whole journey, Laura just didn't know what to say. It wasn't often she was lost for words, the nature of her job made her very communicative but for once she was.

Although it had become obvious already to

Laura that Steven wasn't a person to make small talk about nothing, nevertheless she had never known him so quiet. He seemed quite tense as she looked at his hands gripping the steering wheel with white knuckles.

Luckily it wasn't the height of the holiday season yet so the traffic was light, but Steven's car was not built to move fast. It was reluctant to go up hills with three in and only did it under protest and at a snail's pace. Laura gave a quiet laugh to herself as she thought of her little old mini which seemed to have more go in it.

But at last the journey was at an end and they were there. A funny feeling came over her as she realized her last visit to Blackpool had been on her honeymoon. Of course Steven wasn't to know this when he had suggested her coming along. A voice from the front of the car asked, 'Have you been here before?'

'Yes, but a number of years ago now.' Laura answered his grandma. She didn't know how to address this old lady. In fact she wasn't sure what her surname was. She knew it was different to Steven's but had never thought to ask him what.

As she climbed out of the car the shock made her exclaim, 'Good grief it's cold.'

Looking at her Steven asked, 'I hope it's a

warm coat you put in?'

'Yes, it is. Had I better help your Grandma out of the car? But before I do, whilst we are out of hearing, what is her surname?'

Steven gave a little laugh. 'I forgot to tell you that didn't I? Sorry, but she never gave me time to introduce her to you and I suppose I just presumed you would know. It's Chapman. You go and help her out of the car. It'll give you chance to get to know each other. Here's her coat.'

'What's this?' she exclaimed nearly dropping the piece of fur she was holding.

'A fur coat, silly, to keep her warm.'

'Oh!' said Laura still in amazement as it looked more like an animal. Then holding it as if it would bite moved to the passenger door of the car. Opening it she said in a friendly voice, 'Here's your coat Mrs. Chapman. Do you need helping on with it?'

'Just give me your hand so I can get out. I'll be all right once I get my legs going.' Laura was amazed to see a very tiny person climb out of the car, who looked nearly as wide as she was tall, dressed in a turquoise dress and jacket. She supposed she had tried to look smart. Laura helped her on with the coat and had to stop herself laughing at the sight. The coat nearly went to the ground and made her look even fatter. She could see the face now and could find no softness of features in it. Instantly she decided she'd better watch her step here or else she could soon be on the wrong side of this lady.

'Ready then, Grandma?' Steven asked.

'Aye, let's go and see if the fish and chip cafe is open for lunch,' she stated without asking the others if this was what they wanted to do.

Somehow she managed to survive the day but felt exhausted when she arrived home just by the mental effort she had to put in to keep on good terms with this lady. She hoped it wasn't going to be a regular occurrence, a Sunday outing like this.

As usual her parents wanted a report on the day but all Laura said was, 'It was rather a strange day. I would much have preferred to be out with the children.' Then she could not help but give a description of Steven's grandma and had both her parents in fits of laughter. Her mother sobered up and asked, 'Are you going to have to watch yourself there? She obviously dotes on her grandson.'

'I know. I've realized that already,' she said reluctantly hoping this wasn't going to spoil any possible future relationship. Already she liked him very much and was possibly falling in love with him, so wanted there to be a future.

20

Now Laura and his grandma had met, Steven no longer kept them apart. He would take her to his home, sometimes for tea. Laura was learning another lesson here, how different people lived and learning to be tactful about this fact. The next time she saw his grandma she was not the tidy lady she had seen at Blackpool. In fact she looked rather dirty, but what stood out more in Laura's mind the most, was the horrible thick stocking she had tied around her neck. The house wasn't particularly clean and was furnished in a very old fashioned way. She could see Steven tried his best to help to keep it clean and tidy but it appeared his grandma thought it was all right. Therefore he had to be tactful how he said or did anything about it in order to keep the peace.

She wouldn't have won a prize for cooking and Laura's first meal was an experience to put her off ever eating there again. The meal she had was rabbit. Never having eaten it before and without appearing rude she didn't know how to eat it? She was nearly sick with the first bite, it was horrible. She just chewed and chewed but it wouldn't go down. Whilst his grandma wasn't looking Steven quickly removed most of it from her plate. As he took her home, later on, he couldn't apologize enough. 'I'm sorry about the rabbit. I'm afraid it wasn't very fresh. Don't be put off it in future by this first experience. It's really delicious if it's cooked properly and is nice and fresh.'

Once was enough for Laura, never again did she eat rabbit. She felt the need to ask, 'Why the stocking around her neck?'

Steven gave a hearty laugh. 'She reckons it keeps her warm and wards off colds. I don't think it makes any difference but I'm afraid she won't be told. You know what these old people are like.'

Not really having known an old person like this before she just said, 'I suppose so.'

Laura soon became aware that his grandma was not making life easy for Steven at home. She'd had him all to herself for a long time and now that she was having to share him with somebody else she resented the fact. But Laura was not letting Steven go. The more she saw of him, the more she realized he was a very nice person indeed and somebody who made her really happy. In fact, he was the exact opposite of Keith and the children by now all thought the world of him. Her parents were impressed and couldn't fault him. She already knew they hoped he was going to be their future son-in-law. He was also full of surprises. He had bought her a gold bracelet for her birthday, then one evening he presented her with a box of chocolates. When she opened the box, inside was a gold charm in place of one of the chocolates. She never did know how he got it there, as the box had still been sealed when she opened it.

Things came to a head one evening when she had been at his grandma's house. Laura knew he'd been having a bad time of it with his grandma for the last few weeks. Sometimes she would refuse to feed him, so after a hard day's work he would go home to no meal prepared. Other times she would go off speaking to him for a week at a time. As soon as Laura stepped through the doorway she could sense an atmosphere. In no time it erupted when the old lady suddenly said to her, 'You're no more than a slut, do you know that?'

Laura's mouth dropped open but before she could answer back the old lady continued, 'Like to think you're posh you do. I know you think my home isn't good enough for you.'

Laura felt her arm being tugged by Steven.

'Come on, let's get out of here.'

With this he dragged her to the door without saying a word to his grandma. Once they were outside he turned to Laura. 'I'm so sorry about that but she's jealous and frightened I'm going to leave her on her own. She doesn't really mean what she says. To be honest I think she's going a bit senile as well. Sometimes she's all right like she always was, then other times she goes in these moods and says all kinds of funny things. She also keeps saying the neighbours are in our loft during the night. That's nonsense, I know that. I mean to say how on earth would they get there and why would they want to, I ask you. Next time you see her, she'll act as if nothing has happened.'

'I don't think I'll be seeing her again after all that she's said to me.' Getting quite cross Laura added, 'How on earth do you expect me to act as if nothing happened? Anyway, you could have stuck up for me instead of just dragging me out.'

'Laura!' Steven exclaimed looking really upset. 'It's not as simple as that. The easiest way is to leave it alone then she'll forget all about it. Anyway what do you mean? You don't mean you don't want to see me again as well do you?'

'Of course not, silly. It's I can't imagine

269

seeing her again after this. I've got to admit all that abuse reminded me too much of Keith and I know he didn't forget and change when I saw him again.'

'I'm sorry Laura, what else can I say? If I'd known she was going to turn like that tonight, there's no way I'd have taken you along. But anyway you'll have to see her again, after all, she'll want to be at our wedding.'

'Our wedding!'

'I know it isn't the best time to propose and it's not very romantic sitting here in the car but I love you so much Laura. You will marry me, won't you?'

'Yes. Oh yes. I love you so much as well.' With this Laura threw caution to the wind and put her arms around him giving him a tender kiss. Then she pulled away and started to say. 'But you do realize I still have to wait for my divorce to be finalized and of course it'll have to be a register office wedding.'

Steven was quick to quell her anxiety, 'Shh, I don't care wherever it is so long as we get married. Now come over here and give me another kiss.'

Laura was glad he had driven along to a quiet country lane in his car. Pulling away from him she asked, 'Have you really thought what you're taking on as well as me? Three children into the bargain. You do realize they'll have to come with me? I couldn't leave them with my parents, they're my children after all.'

Steven gave a laugh. 'What could be better than a ready made family? I love them like my own already and you have to admit they do get on with me as if I'm their Dad. Anyway it cuts two ways, look what you're taking on with me, my Grandma.'

'Well yes, I suppose so, but the children do like you I'll say that. Already they think of you more as if you were their real father than they do of Keith. In fact they already know you better than Keith. Shall we go home now and break the news to Mum and Dad?' Then putting on a serious expression she asked, 'Don't you think you should have asked my Dad for my hand in marriage before you proposed?'

Steven just laughed at this, then added in a more serious voice himself. 'They're building some new houses up the road from my Grandma's. Would you like me to get some details and then maybe we could have a look at them while they're being built. That's if you'd like to look at them.'

Laura looked amazed. 'A new house! Oh, that would be grand. Mind you, all of us would soon fill a house. It'd need to be a decent size whatever we get.'

Looking pleased with himself Steven now added, 'I've quite a bit of money saved for a deposit and furniture. With not going out much I've never had the need to spend all my wages and my Grandfather left me a small amount of money when he died.'

Feeling a bit regretful now Laura said, 'I'm afraid I haven't a great deal saved because as you know I've not been working that long and three children are expensive to keep. They're always growing out of one thing and another. I've managed to save a little each month but it doesn't amount to much yet but I'll willingly put it with yours to help us.'

'Don't worry, I'll take care of everything,' Steven said reassuringly. 'Anyway do you want to go and tell your parents the good news now?'

'Yes, let's go and tell my parents now as I can't wait to see the look of surprise on their faces. I do know they worry about me so maybe at last they can rest easy.'

They were as thrilled as Laura knew they would be. This was how they had wanted it to work out for her all along. She had to stop them getting too carried away at the moment with their plans and remind them she was still legally married to Keith, so they would have to wait for the divorce to come through before all the preparations could start in earnest. As she saw Steven out she could hear her mum already telling to her dad who she wanted to invite to the wedding. Laura smiled to herself, this was typical of her mum.

At times Laura felt frustrated that she and Steven had so little opportunity to be on their own. When they were alone together Steven was affectionate but yet sensitive to her past and how it had affected her. His grandma was back on talking terms just as Steven had predicted, as if nothing had been said. Sometimes she would let them stay on their own in her house whilst she went to visit friends. At other times she would treat them like teenagers who needed watching all the time in case they did something they shouldn't. Laura found it very difficult to show any physical sign of affection to Steven when his grandma was around. Even to touch his hand she felt was frowned upon.

When they were left on their own it was a relief. Laura felt as if she could behave more as herself on one particular Tuesday evening. Barely had his grandma gone out of the door than Steven grabbed hold of Laura. 'I've been waiting all day for this.' With this he instantly gave her a passionate kiss. Laura felt his hands moving around her body with far greater passion than he usually showed. She heard a groan come from him. 'Laura, I love you so. I don't think I can wait any longer to show you how much.'

Laura could only whisper, 'I love you too, but I'm frightened.' Then she realized how silly she must have sounded, more like a schoolgirl than a mature woman. She let herself relax and started joining in as her own feelings got the better of her and ended up groaning herself in the ecstasy. 'Oh, Steven, love me.' Suddenly realizing what she had said she pulled away from him. All the thoughts of what Keith had often called her flooded back into her mind. She began to wonder if they were really true.

Steven looked at her with a puzzled and rather hurt expression. 'What is the matter Laura? You know I would never hurt you. I just love you so. After all we are grown up so surely we don't have to wait until we're married to show each other.'

'I know all that. It's just each time I let Keith have his way I seemed to end up pregnant. Then he started to call me names for being so foolish ending up like that again.' Not really sure whether now was the time to say what she really had on her mind she finally took the bull by the horns. 'Please don't take this the wrong way Steven but I don't want any more children. I don't mean just now, I mean ever again. I know you've none of your own and probably want them but I just can't go through it again, however much I love you.'

Grabbing hold of her and pulling her close to him he said in a soothing voice. 'Oh Laura, Laura! Don't you realize it's you I want? I'm not bothered about any children of my own. After all, yours feel as if they belong to me. Once we're married we'll make them legally mine. You must know better than that Laura that I would take care of you. I'd taken the liberty of making sure I had something for tonight, just in case. But it might be sensible if you went to see the doctor and sorted something better out for birth control. Anyway you'll need to for when we're married so you might as well do it now.'

She'd to agree to this because leaving Keith so soon after the birth of Rachel she'd never got around to being sterilized. There'd seemed to be no need. Now this niggle had been taken care of she could feel her own passion once again mounting inside herself. But then she thought of something else. 'Your Grandma!'

'What about her?'

'What if she comes back?'

'She won't, not once she gets to see Agnes. Those two can't stop chatting for hours. Come on trust me, relax.'

With this she fell into his arms as she felt her longing again mounting in herself. He started kissing her with such vigour that she found herself returning equally as passionate kisses showing her longing. Things seemed to be getting out of hand, she no longer had control of her body — it felt on fire with passion. She wanted him. Suddenly he moved away from her, grabbed her hand and started pulling her towards the stairs. 'Come on, let's go up here before we get too carried away.'

Looking blank for a moment Laura questioned, 'Where?'

'To bed, of course.'

'To bed!'

'Yes, silly. Where do you think we're going to make love, on this lino floor covering.'

Laura burst out laughing at her own silliness. 'No, of course not. What are we waiting for?'

Pulling her up the stairs Steven joined in her laughter. 'You forward hussy you.'

'Just you wait I'll show how forward,' laughed Laura as they arrived in the bedroom. Quickly she grabbed his shirt and started tugging at the buttons. As soon as his chest was revealed she started rubbing her fingers on it. 'I love a man with a hairy chest.'

'Do you now? Come on then, feel more of me,' Steven invited.

With this he pulled her down on the bed with him. Laura was rapidly losing all control of herself. The more she touched him the more she wanted him. 'I need you now please, please,' she begged.

'Just hang on one minute,' Steven said gently.

This startled Laura and for a moment she thought she had shocked him too much but then she realized he was taking care of her as he had promised. Within a few moments he was back to his passionate kisses and caresses. Laura could feel his passion mounting like her own until she could no longer bear it. 'Now, now,' she groaned.

He swiftly pushed her on her back and gently forced his way into her. There was no resistance from Laura, all her body was openly inviting him to enter her. She rose to feelings she had never felt in her life, her body was beyond her control. The whole world exploded and she cried out in ecstasy at the same time gripping Steven to her. Slowly the feeling subsided and she came down to earth to hear a voice in her ear. 'I love you so much, Laura.'

They lay in each other's arms not needing to say much, they could sense what each other felt. Finally Laura said, 'I could stay here all night. How I do wish that we could get married sooner, then it'd all be possible.'

Laughing kindly at her he said gently, 'You are the impatient one.' Then seeing the look of surprise on her face added, 'But I wish the same.'

'We always seem to be doing things to suit other people not ourselves. I know my divorce not being finalized doesn't help but even so we are still waiting so your Grandma gets used to the idea. Then I know we want the children to accept you as their Dad but they already do, you know. No, we seem to be trying to please everybody but ourselves. But I want you now.'

Being serious now Steven sat up and looked at her. 'Laura, I want this as much as you. But it'll come quickly I promise you. We've so much to do you won't know where the time goes. Once we get the house and you start getting it ready it'll bring it all so much nearer. We'll sneak some time like this whenever we can. Do you think after that experience I don't want a repeat soon?'

'It was never like this with Keith, you know.'

'I do, it was easy to tell from your reaction. That's what love does to you.'

'I think we'd better get up now otherwise your Grandma will really catch us here.'

'One last cuddle and kiss and then I'll let you go.'

Laura relaxed, feeling she finally knew the true meaning of love.

21

Somehow the time did go quickly just as Steven had predicted. They managed to grab some time alone though they wished it could be more. Each time they made love it brought a new pleasure for Laura.

But as they anticipated, his grandma didn't accept the fact he was a man now and old enough to leave home to make his own life. She made it unbearable for Laura to go and visit her. She had taken to calling Laura obscene names when they met. So the simplest course of action they both had agreed on was if Laura kept out of the way and met him away from his home. Then Steven suffered. His grandma would either totally ignore him or shout abuse at him.

Luckily their new house was complete and partly furnished by the time things became too much to bear. So although they had both wanted to move into their new home together after their marriage, in the end they decided it would be best for all concerned if Steven moved in before. At least he would be on hand to get more of the jobs done so the house would be totally ready by the time of the wedding.

The girls were excited, they were to be bridesmaids. It seemed odd to Laura that her own daughters were taking this role. Although she had wanted no fuss this time for her wedding, they had begged and pleaded to be bridesmaids as they had never had the chance before. Richard had been totally the opposite. 'Don't expect me to be a page boy,' he said grumpily.

In between all the preparation Laura did have one moment when she realized how much Steven's grandma resented her. It was parents' evening at her school, and the one thing she would never have expected to see was some parents from Steven's neighbourhood, as the school was a fair way from there. But these particular parents were new to the area so their daughter, Joanne, had not been at the school very long. They hadn't been seated two minutes before the mother looked her up and down and said in a snide voice, 'So you're the hussy that Martha Chapman's grandson is marrying, are you?'

Laura was too stunned to answer instantly then summoning all the dignity she could she replied, 'I think we'd better keep on the subject of Joanne's work, don't you?'

Still they just looked at her and finally Joanne's father grabbed hold of his wife's hand. 'Come on Madge, I don't think we want to speak to the likes of her.' With this they both stood up and marched out of the school hall.

Laura was left looking after them with her mouth wide open in amazement. She could feel the tears pricking the back of her eyes and quickly turned to a colleague and whispered, 'Just watch to see no more parents come whilst I nip to the loo, will you please.' As she rushed there she just thanked her lucky stars that it was very noisy in the hall and everybody else had been so busy that nobody had noticed what had gone on.

She'd made a quick exit, shut herself in a toilet cubicle and taken some deep breaths to try to calm herself down. She knew she couldn't stay out of the hall long, the next parents were due anytime. All she could ask herself was, what on earth had his grandma told them about her? She didn't deserve this.

Bracing herself she left the toilets and took her seat again with a fixed smile on her face. How she got through the rest of the evening she didn't know, but somehow she managed to say what she hoped were the right words.

When she told Steven of the incident he tried to reassure her and was full of apologies. 'Look, Laura, it wouldn't matter who I was marrying, she would still say the same things.

She just wants to keep me with her. She would resent any woman in my life other than herself.'

Laura could see the sense in what he said, but it still hurt to be talked to and looked at like that. She didn't let herself be upset for too long, there was so much to look forward to. The girls were so excited and even if it wasn't going to be a church wedding they still wanted to wear proper bridesmaid dresses. Laura herself wanted an outfit that was special. This had to be a day to remember because she was determined this marriage was going to last. She wanted it to work so much this time. She knew it would, because Steven was so different from Keith. He was kind and generous and it was obvious he really did love her.

At last the great day was upon them and just as the first time, it dawned bright and sunny. Getting ready seemed different. She was so excited herself and full of anticipation and hope for her new life that lay ahead. The whole house seemed to ooze happiness as they all rushed around to get ready. This time all her family were to set off together to the Registry Office and they would meet Steven there, who was coming with Pat and Peter. They were to be the witnesses. It seemed appropriate that they should do this duty as they'd had a hand in bringing them together.

Laura felt so contented on the journey to the registrars office. She knew he'd be there waiting for her. He was; and as she climbed out of the car he moved over to her side, his face showing all the love Laura knew he had for her. Gently, he took hold of her hand and looked into her face. 'You look lovely. Thank you for giving me so much pleasure.'

Laura could feel tears come to her eyes as she realized how lucky she was to find such a person as this and be given a second chance at happiness. Looking at him she finally said with a shaky voice, 'It's me who should be thanking you for taking on so much. I do love you, Steven.'

At last managing to tear her eyes away from his face, Laura had a look around and realized that the rest of Steven's family had turned up. His grandma was there, giving her a sour look even on this their special day. Obviously she wasn't going to relent now and forget her ill feeling towards her knowing this should be their day.

She felt a gentle tug at her hand from Steven. 'Come on, Laura, time to go in. No regrets I hope?'

Quickly she turned around. 'Of course not,

none at all. Come on what are you waiting for?' With this she gave him a quick pull to move inside.

No sooner were they outside the door where they had been told to wait, than it was opened and a wedding party came out. A voice called their names from the back of the group. 'Will you all please come this way, the registrar is ready for you now.'

Turning together they made sure all their small party were assembled and the two girls ready to perform their duties as bridesmaids. Laura heard Steven's voice, with a slight tremor in it, give the instruction, 'Come on, folks, this is it.'

It was amazing to Laura how quickly the service went. It didn't seem like a marriage service, just something that this man sitting in front of them performed as his job every day. Laura realized it was indeed just that to him. Before she had digested all that had gone on, the formalities were over and they were on their way out of the building.

She heard Pete shout, 'Come on, you two, let's have you over here and a nice smile for the camera.'

It was no difficulty for Laura to do that, she felt so happy she couldn't stop the smile on her face which came deep from her heart. Each time she looked at Steven she felt her heart give a flip of joy at the thought that finally he was really hers. If ever there was a marriage made in heaven surely this was it. The day passed in a whirl of activity as they had their small reception, then finally they were in the car and on their way to the airport. She'd never had that holiday abroad with Keith as she promised but at least now she was having one with Steven.

The two of them were off to Majorca, much to the protest of the children. She had nearly fallen soft and begged Steven to let them go along but her mother had stepped in and said, 'Come on, Laura, be sensible. This is your honeymoon. After all Steven's kindness the least he deserves is this time on your own. You'll be able to take them with you another year. You do need this time on your own, surely you of all people don't need telling that you never really get to know a person until you live with them. I know within myself that Steven will still be the same person you have got to know but you still need the time on your own. That wouldn't be easy with three children always clambering around you. Now be honest would it?'

Laura could see the sense in what her mother said and besides, if she were truthful, she did want to be selfish and have Steven to herself for a short while. 'No, you're right as usual.'

Being his usual generous self Steven had indeed promised the children a holiday abroad on their next break from school and he'd also told them they'd get plenty of presents brought back from this holiday. Everything he did made Laura's love grow more for him; she couldn't have believed it possible.

She'd confessed to Steven that she was a terrible flyer and even the excitement wouldn't take that feeling away. But she'd have flown to the ends of the earth with him if need be. At last they were on their way. Steven turned to her, 'Thank you Laura, you've made this the best day of my life and I know it'll continue for the rest of our lives together.' Laura felt no need to reply to this but just looked at him with love in her eyes.

By the time they landed at Majorca it was dark so Laura could get no idea what the place looked like. If it had been a desert island she wouldn't have cared, as long as Steven was there. At least she knew the procedure and in no time they had their cases and were looking for the coach to take them to their hotel. There were a few other young couples on the coach. Laura wondered how many others were on their honeymoon.

Looking at them she tried to guess who were, and she wondered if any of the others would realize they were on theirs. They would probably think them too old, or maybe the love in their eyes would give them away.

Knowing Steven hadn't been abroad before, Laura was more interested in watching his reaction to the passing scenery which he could see in the dark than watching it herself. Without realizing it she gave him a quick poke in the ribs and asked, 'It's great isn't it? Just like I told you it would be.'

'You're right there. Oh! Laura I can see this is going to be a time to remember for all my days in more ways than one.'

In no time the coach pulled up and Laura had to nudge him again. 'Come on, this is our hotel, we get off here. You go and get the cases and I'll go to the reception with our passports and get us checked in.'

Laughing at her as she moved away he called after her, 'I always knew you were a woman of experience.'

Laura could feel her cheeks going bright red as she thought what other people, within earshot, were thinking.

Having completed all the formalities, she turned to look for Steven waving the key to their room and called to him, 'Let's see how fit you are. We're in room 303. Do you think you can walk up the stairs with those cases?' Then adding in a condescending voice, 'Or do you need the lift?' She heard no reply but saw a flash of something or someone go by as he moved quickly to the stairs. She ran after him. By the time they had reached the third floor both were panting and laughing. No sooner had he fumbled to open the door with the key, put the cases quickly down, than he grabbed her and they both fell laughing in a heap on the bed. 'Come here Mrs. Watson, at last I've got you to myself.' With this he squeezed her tight and gave her a big kiss. Before they knew where they were they could feel their passion aroused. Pulling herself abruptly away from him. 'We haven't even opened our cases yet.'

'So what, we've two weeks to unpack in. I've waited a long time for this.'

Laura murmured, 'So have I' and with this comment gave up all thoughts of any further protest.

If she had thought their love making perfect before, this time it must have been beyond perfection. Never in her whole life did she think she would have another chance for love like this. Whatever she had felt for Keith in the past, she knew now it wasn't love. She had just mistaken it as that.

Some inner sense made her know that

Steven felt the same way, she didn't need to be told but she did hear a voice in her ear, 'I do love you, Laura. I really do. We'll always be like this, I promise you.'

Laura's only reply was to snuggle up closer.

The whole of the honeymoon carried on like this. On her first visit abroad she had promised herself, that she would have a holiday like this with Keith. That had never happened, but this far exceeded her expectations of that holiday. Maybe she saw everything with love in her eyes, but it all seemed perfect. For the rest of her life she would carry this memory with her.

All too soon it was at an end and she knew they would have to go back home and come down to reality. But that wasn't without its own excitement. She was off to a new home, to start a new life with her little family. What a lovely new home she was going to. The kind she had always dreamt about. Somehow Steven had made it perfect for her, just ready to move in. On much of the journey home, in between snuggling up to Steven and whispering sweet nothings in his ear, she kept trying to picture it. But the journey went quick enough and they were soon driving up outside their new home. Her mum was to keep the children that night to give them a chance to have their first evening alone.

Steven turned to her. 'Welcome home, Laura.'

Her eyes were so transfixed by this delightful place she was seeing that she only managed to mumble, 'Yes.' Then suddenly realizing at last she was really here she jumped out of the car and ran to the house door.

She felt a hand grab her. 'Not so quick. Where do you think you are going?'

Laura turned around looking bewildered at Steven. 'What do you mean?'

Laughing at her puzzled face he questioned, 'Isn't there a tradition?'

Slowly she comprehended what he meant as he bent down to pick her up. Such feelings ran through her at this touch, her body felt as if it were on fire. How she loved him and wanted him to keep holding her close to him for ever. Putting her arm around his neck she clung tight. She heard his voice in her ear. 'That's right, my love, hold on tight to me, I'll always look after you.'

'Don't you fear, I will. I'll never let you go.'

22

Life settled down to a steady pace once the honeymoon was over and the children were back with them. Steven being his usual sensitive self now turned straight into a father figure. He did his best to convince Laura that the way Laura felt about not having any children of his after having her three children at such a young age was not a problem. He fully understood her reasons for not wanting more. He told her he had more than enough to cope with the three he had inherited. Besides that he respected her desire to have a career for herself, and a good job she was making of it. Already she had been promoted and he felt very proud of this clever, new wife of his.

For Laura there was only one fly in the ointment, that was his grandma. She had realized by now it had not been a good thing to get a house so close to her. Even though she was old, his grandma had no difficulty in walking the distance to see them. Also it made it very easy for Steven to call in on her on his way home from work. Being soft natured, if he saw it was one of her lonely days when he called, he would stay a while to keep her company. Then, of course, his tea would usually be ruined as he more often than not did not have the foresight to tell Laura he was calling. This was the only thing that caused arguments between the pair of them.

Laura realized that she was probably being over sensitive after Keith's behaviour but she just couldn't help it. Each time it happened she panicked that he had gone drinking and would come home drunk and hit her. Thinking rationally she knew Steven would never do this, but the fear from the past wouldn't leave her.

The minute he walked through the door she would yell at him like a fish wife. 'Well! What excuse have you this time?'

But what aroused her temper even more was that Steven would stay calm and not rise to the bait but simply say, 'You know how it is once you get talking.' Then Laura would really lose her temper and say hurtful things she didn't mean.

It was the making up that was the best part. Laura would be contrite that she had lost her temper and Steven would promise to tell her the next time he was calling at his grandma's on the way home. Of course he never did, somehow he always forgot, so the argument would erupt again. But if Laura had thought their love making wonderful before, at times like this when they made friends again, it carried her to heights she would have never believed possible.

Then again, she had to suffer his grandma sitting with them evening after evening. For some unknown reason, particularly when the weather was nice, she would take it upon herself to walk up to see them in the evening. Laura had to acknowledge there was nothing wrong in that and it was good that she was still capable of doing so at her age. But she didn't just come one evening every so often, she would come every evening for weeks on end. Laura had never felt such frustration in her life because she wanted to be alone with Steven once the children were in bed. After all, her marriage was still so new she was only really getting to know him fully. Instead, she had this old lady sitting there between them. When it was time for her to go home, each time Steven would fall soft and say he would drive her home. But once he arrived at his grandma's house she would keep him talking or want him to look at this or that in case something was wrong. So what should have been a ten minute job would extend to an hour or more. More often than not Laura was in bed, though not asleep, by the time he came back. Laura would try to stay calm about this but frustration led her to lose her temper every so often. Again they would both say things they didn't mean. Then came the making up.

Laura had to recognize that all the arguments revolved around this old lady. But the arguments turned into upset for Laura as for some unknown reason Steven's grandma once again fell out with them.

Instead of coming in to visit them, she would come to outside their home when she knew Laura was alone with the children and start to shout obscenities, calling her such things as a whore. Richard was old enough to question what this word meant and Laura wracked her brain to try to give him an answer without giving the true meaning. 'She's just being rude to me Richard, that's all. Take no notice just get on with your homework and try to shut her voice out.'

Realizing that enough was enough, Steven at least managed to get his grandma to stop coming outside the house and shouting. Yet she somehow stayed friends with Steven but just totally ignored Laura and the children. In a way, that was a relief as Laura now had peace and quiet to have some time alone with her husband.

But Steven soon started to visit his

grandma again on the way home from work and Laura tried to control her emotions over this so in turn Steven tried to remember to tell her when he was actually calling so she knew to expect him in late for tea. Now at last they had reached a compromise and understanding.

That was why she felt alarm run through her as she heard the outside door opening one particular tea time as Steven had said to expect him late as he would call in on his grandma. What if it was an intruder? Plucking up courage she rushed into the hall and when she saw it was Steven she threw herself into his arms with relief. But then she realized he looked very serious and rather pale. 'What is it?' she questioned in alarm.

'I think something has happened to my Grandma. I've come to phone the police for them to break in. The door is locked from the inside and her neighbour says she hasn't seen her go past for the last three days.'

'Oh, Steven! I'm sorry, but you never know, she might be all right.'

'I don't think so really, do you?'

'No, I suppose not. You'd better call them straight away.'

'Yes, quicker we can get inside, the quicker we'll know.'

As soon as he'd made the call he headed

for the door. 'I'll have to go back and wait for them now.'

'Of course, off you go. Sorry I can't come but I'll have to stay with the children.'

'It doesn't matter. There won't be anything that you could do.'

'Let me know what's going on as soon as you can because I'll be worrying about you.'

'Don't worry, I'll be all right and be back as quick as I can. You see to the children and get their tea. I'll sort something out later.'

As usual, despite his own worries he had to be considerate about somebody else. This was what made Laura love him so much. She couldn't help it, but all the while she had a funny sensation. Part of her felt happy as if she were being released, the other part sad because she could imagine what Steven was going through.

As soon as he arrived back home and she saw his face and she knew it was the worst. Quickly she rushed into his arms. 'I'm so sorry Steven, I really am. I know we didn't get on but I didn't want this.'

'I know, but we have to face facts. She was an old lady although she didn't appear to be. Anyway it was quick, the best way to go rather than suffer. Apparently she had a heart attack and was dead before she hit the floor.'

'Where was she?'

'In the kitchen. It wasn't nasty. She just looked at peace. Oh well, tomorrow I'd better get on and sort all the arrangements out. I'm sure it'll all be up to me.'

'I've just remembered you'd better let the rest of your family know.'

'Aye, you're right although I'm not sure they'll be that concerned.' Giving a cynical laugh he added, 'Maybe in the will but that'll be all.'

She didn't wish to appear as if that was all she was interested in but she felt the need to ask, 'Do you know where her last will is and what was in it?'

'Oh yes, even though she fell out with you, although I have stressed to you it was nothing personal, she did want me to have it all. So the house and the little bit of savings she had will all be mine. That's not going to please the rest of the family. They always thought they were in for a share. I might give them something but that depends how they react to her death and the will being in my favour. They've never really cared for me, so why should I worry about them? Still, if they're okay with me we'll have to see what we do.'

'It's up to you, I want no say in it. As it is, they'll think I influenced you. It's your family after all and I know you'll do what you think best.'

As the days passed before the funeral, Laura could sense the conflict of emotion that was going on within Steven. All she could feel was a sense of release at not having to worry what was going to happen next. She tried her best not to let Steven know of this because she wanted to give him the sympathy and support he needed. She knew he would get none from the rest of his family. At last the day of the funeral arrived and panic set in for Laura. She had never been to a funeral before. Suddenly she felt sad, not really at the loss of this old lady but just the fact that a life had gone. It was to be a cremation which Laura felt at least offered some comfort, as she was sure having to stand by a hole in the ground and watch the coffin lowered into it must be an horrific experience, whoever was in that wooden box.

There again she wasn't sure what happened at a cremation and her mind ran riot thinking about it. In reality it was a very easy process to go through, a few hymns were sung and a nice little obituary was read by the vicar, although Laura did wonder if his words were describing the same person she knew. Finally soft music was played and the curtains parted to let the coffin slide gently away behind them. That was it, the end of another life.

The meal afterwards seemed an anticlimax to the events. Laura wondered how everybody chatted and laughed as if it were a celebration. She knew Steven was deeply affected by it all. She had seen him blow his nose a few times during the service as if he had a cold, but she knew the real cause.

As she looked around, she could see the eager faces of his family as if they were expecting the will to be read out. She knew they were in for a big disappointment. There was no need for them to hear it, as it only applied to Steven. Looking at his sad face she gently touched his arm. 'Are you all right, love?'

'M'm, I suppose so. At least I'm coping. Look at them all, they look like a set of vultures. Well, they're in for a disappointment. They should have cared more when she was alive. They never bothered to visit her. You know that.'

'You've no need to justify it to me, Steven. Remember I'm on your side. Of course you deserve it all. Now stop worrying and let's just get through this then you can go and mourn in private. Chin up, it'll soon be all over.'

'Thanks, Laura.'

'What for?'

'Just being you.'

Laura felt a warm feeling go through her at the realization that not only was she deeply loved but she was appreciated for herself as well.

23

Laura knew Steven was sad about his grandma's death but it seemed to be more than that which had brought the change about him. Not that he was any less kind but he seemed unsettled somehow.

This caused her deep down to worry if it was her, had he gone off her? But he was still as loving as ever so sense took over and she realized it must be something else. She knew she needed to have it out with him, whatever it was, if she was to get any peace of mind again. But how to do this without causing an argument? There again Steven didn't normally get annoyed at her questioning but even so she sensed it was something he felt very deeply about that was making him like this. One thing she knew for certain was the children needed to be well out of earshot when they discussed whatever it was.

Putting her plans together she decided to broach her mother for help, but of course, without telling her the full details why. 'Mum, I want to ask you a big favour.'

'Oh yes! Let me guess, I bet you want me to baby-sit.'

'Nearly there.' Looking a bit sheepish she added, 'A bit more than that really. Will you have the children for a weekend?'

Laughing her mother looked at her. 'Not time for a second honeymoon already, is it?'

'No, of course not. It's just Steven's very upset at the death of his grandma and I thought it would cheer him up and do him good if I booked a surprise week-end away for us both.'

Now she looked at her daughter more keenly, 'That's kind of you. What a good idea. Yes, you book something then just let me know when. You know full well we're usually free at week-ends so it's no problem, no problem at all. Get yourself sorted out as soon as you can.'

Laura gave a sigh of relief. 'Thanks, Mum. Maybe one day I'll be able to repay all these good turns.'

'Be off with you. What are grandparents for? Anyway at least I hand them back after the week-end when I've had enough.'

'I know all that but I never want you to feel I take you for granted and it isn't appreciated, because it is. That's all I meant.'

'I know, lass, and you don't take us for granted. If I thought that do you think I'd be as willing to do all this. No, we like having

303

them and at least they do help to keep us young.'

Now that was settled Laura had to put her next part of the plan into action. Where to take him for this week-end? Somewhere busy and noisy was no good, it needed to be a peaceful and restful place if they were going to talk, really talk. Then it came to mind where she'd heard discussed recently in the staff room, Hawes in Wensleydale, that was where they'd go. She'd heard before about it and it was supposed to be picturesque and a tourist attraction yet offering the restfulness if needed.

Now how to tell him? But first of all she made all the necessary bookings so there could be no excuses why not to go there, at least from him.

Choosing her moment she gently raised the subject. 'I've been thinking Steven.'

'Oh yes. What about this time?' he asked jokingly.

His light hearted attitude gave Laura more confidence to move on. 'With all that's happened I thought a few days rest on our own would do no harm.'

'Maybe not, but still we'll manage without because, after all, there's the children to think of.'

'That's where you're wrong.'

He looked at her with eyebrows raised. 'U'm, what do you mean?'

'Mum and Dad have agreed to have them for the week-end.'

'Honestly, I'm all right. There's no need. I've already told you and we don't want to put on them any more than we need.'

'We're not putting on them. They like the children to stay so we are going away, just the two of us. It's all booked so I want no argument.'

Looking sheepish as if Laura had read his thoughts. 'I wasn't going to argue. Come on then tell, where are we going?'

'To Wensleydale — a market town called Hawes. Have you heard of it or been there before?'

'I've heard of it. Good reports I must say, but I've never been there. Oh well, it'll be a pleasant change I must agree.'

Looking pleased with herself Laura just said, 'Good.'

The organizing hadn't been difficult, it was all the preparation that was the hard task. Working full time and the children to get ready as well as themselves, even though it was only for a week-end Laura thought they would never make it. But they did and as the children and her mum waved them off she sank back into the car seat exhausted.

'Aye, wakey wakey, I thought you were the map reader.'

'I am, but you know your way to start with. Just let me relax a few minutes then I'll be fine.'

'I hope so. I'm sure there's plenty we can do this week-end.'

Laura sank back once more in the seat and let out a weak, 'Yes.'

As they moved away from their home town Laura's interest was taken by the passing scenery and all the sleepiness left her.

Never having visited Hawes before she wasn't disappointed as they drove up the cobble street into the market place and finally to the Fountain Hotel where they were staying. It was a quaint place she had to admit. There was a general store opposite that looked as if it hadn't changed from the year dot. Their accommodation was fine and she felt cheered that she had made a good choice of accommodation from the leaflets that had been available to her.

Having settled in their room Steven asked, 'Do you want to go down for a drink? There's just time before the last orders.'

She was going to say, 'No' but quickly changed her mind as she looked at Steven. 'Why not! After all that's why we've come here to have an enjoyable time.'

She was glad she had agreed to the drink, it was fascinating listening to the locals talk. Steven could barely get a word out of her which was unusual. 'You're quiet tonight.'

In a soft voice she responded, 'I'm fascinated listening and watching the people in here.'

With a twinkle of amusement in his eye Steven looked at her. 'Aye, I know just what you mean.'

Just then a voice shouted, 'Last orders please.'

'Do you want another?'

'No, I think my weariness has overtaken me now. It's time I called it a day.'

It seemed no time after they had gone to bed before Laura opened her eyes and realized Steven was no longer at her side. She lay puzzling where he could be. But not for long, the bedroom door swung open and a cheery voice said, 'Come on sleepy head, are you still in bed? Some of us are up and bursting with energy raring to go.'

'To go where?'

'Look, I've been across to the newsagents and got a small map of the area. The landlord here has also given me some guidance where we can go.'

'Come over here then and show me,' said Laura trying to sound enthusiastic. After all, this was the whole point of the week-end to get him in good humour and talking to her, really talking and telling what was worrying him.

'This is my plan, see what you think.' Laughing he continued, 'I know you'll want to look around the shops, but that shouldn't take us too long and I've got to agree with you this time they are probably worth a look. Then if we take this path, some of it is the Pennine Way, we can go to Hardrow where there's a pub called the Green Dragon and we can have lunch there. Behind the pub is Hardrow Force so we can look at that then walk back this way so we will have gone a full circle. What do you say?'

'Oh yes, if that's what you want to do.'

'Only if you do as well.'

'Of course I'm game.'

'Come on then get ready and let's have a good English breakfast to get our energy all fuelled up.'

Laura was delighted with the perfect day they had. Steven was back to his usual cheerful and chatty self. She began to wonder if she'd imagined his previous change in mood. Maybe it was her misreading the signals he was giving out. But no, she was sure there was something really worrying him and she wanted to get to the bottom of it. It couldn't be money, he would soon have the money his grandmother had left him. She was sure it wasn't herself otherwise how could they have had such a good day. Surely he couldn't just change like that? Then her thoughts went back to Keith, he changed after their marriage. But she gave herself a mental shake and told herself not to be so silly, after all he wasn't Keith. Finally she decided seeing he was in such a good mood one way or another she would broach the subject that evening and get to the bottom of what was worrying him. After all, they were a couple, he should confide in her because maybe that old saying was apt, 'A trouble shared is a trouble halved.'

Laura was pleasantly surprised that Steven had booked for them to go out for a cosy dinner for two. Here was her perfect opportunity handed to her, as you might say, on a plate. Both of them were lively and chatty, probably for different reasons.

Deciding to be tactful and not jump in with both feet Laura waited until the meal was well on its way and Steven was relaxed by a glass or two of wine. 'Steven, I've been wanting to ask you is there something in particular troubling you? Now before you say no there isn't I know there is something. I can tell by your face. Please share it with me then maybe we can work it out.'

Much to her amazement she received a different reply than she'd expected. 'I'm glad you've brought the subject up. I was waiting for what seemed the right time to talk to you.'

Laura's stomach flipped as she wondered what was coming next.

'It's the money I'm getting from my grandma. I know you want a bigger house and better things when we can, but could we put it on hold for a while as I've other plans.'

Not sure what he was really meaning all she could say was, 'Um, well yes, I suppose so, but why?'

'I hate working for some-one else. I've always wanted to be my own boss so this seems to be the golden opportunity to me. I've seen a nice plot of land where I could build a lovely house and make plenty of money. I've worked all my figures out and there'll be a nice profit for us. That's why I said if you'll just wait a bit longer for all you want.'

Looking rather shame-faced he continued, 'I've been to see the bank manager and they're prepared to help with the funding. So you can see it's all organized but I need your agreement as I wouldn't expect you to be any other than a partner in all this.'

Seeing her look of amazement he quickly

added, 'Don't worry Laura, that doesn't mean giving your job up, but I might need a bit of help with the paperwork. I'm not too good at that side of things. Well, what do you think?'

Laura could hardly get the words out, she felt so angry that he'd organized everything without consulting her. 'There doesn't seem a lot I can say despite being given the opportunity to agree, as you seem determined to go ahead whatever. But if I'm to be a partner will you please in future tell me what you are planning. Remember we are partners in marriage too and I thought we had already agreed there would be no secrets between us.'

'I know all that but I'm also aware how much store you set by having possessions, so I found it rather difficult to tell you. But I'll get you a bigger and better house, I promise. Do you know I might even build one for you but you'll just have to be patient.'

'I can have patience if it's going to be worth waiting for.'

Her good humour had returned as she felt she'd at least now said her bit so she laughed, 'It had better be worth waiting for.'

Looking gently at her, he took her hand in his. 'Of course it will. You should know by now how much I love you and I'd do anything for you.'

She knew in her heart she'd done what was the best for Steven by agreeing to his plans when she saw the expression on his face. Once they were back home he went around the house singing and whistling to himself and was full of jollity with the children.

Inside herself Laura fretted about if it would work out all right. There was so much she wanted. She felt she had to have all the good things she could get out of life to make up for the past. They seemed to have changed roles, Laura was now the better one at keeping feelings to herself. Steven had no inkling of what was going on inside her. But to Laura it was burning her up this yearning to possess everything to the best that she could. She wanted a large house, a good car, lots of exotic holidays and anything else she could acquire.

He got his plot of land to build the house and somehow good fortune seemed to be shining on him as he went on from plot to plot. He couldn't seem to build them quick enough for the demand. Being the perfectionist he was, he soon built up a good reputation for his well built homes. People contacted him to find out where he was building next and, many a time, a house would be sold before he started to build it.

He soon had the money to buy the things

he had promised Laura. They worked hard but enjoyed life to the full. She didn't know where the time went with their hectic lifestyle but before she realized it her children were rapidly becoming adults. Each one of them made her proud of their achievements. Not once did she hear them talk about their real father. They accepted Steven totally and all of them idolized him as their hero.

Laura was proud of herself as well, as she achieved what she had wanted in her own career — that of becoming a Head Mistress. So all in all she considered life was good to her. They had plenty of holidays abroad. That first holiday all those years ago had whetted her appetite for more. No longer did she have an old banger of a car, now it was only the best. She knew she was the envy of some of her colleagues as they couldn't believe, even as a headmistress, she could afford all these things. They were right in this assumption, Steven bought them for her. The house he had promised her grew like a phoenix from the ground. Laura knew each brick, each part of it was built with loving care by Steven because he was doing it for her. Everything he did was for Laura and the family. At last she had achieved what she'd always wanted, material wealth and more than she'd expected, being loved into the bargain.

24

Laura came back to the present in the Yorkshire Dales. After all the walking and looking back at her life she was no nearer her decision and she'd have to be soon, time was fast running out. She couldn't stay here much longer, reality had to be faced. Her mind now swung back to the more recent events which had brought all this soul searching about.

She couldn't really pinpoint when things had started to go wrong but one day she woke up to the fact Steven had a drawn, anxious look on his face again. This had made her start to look back and analyze events and realize something had been amiss for quite a while. Of course, when she thought about it, there had been some reluctance at her booking that last holiday for them. But when she said she would pay herself, after some persuasion, he had agreed they could go. The new car he usually bought each year had not materialized. He had given her the excuse that he wouldn't bother because he liked the car he already had and couldn't better it by changing to another one. To Laura that had sounded a plausible enough explanation until

314

she really thought about it now.

The post never arrived until she'd left for work so if he received any reminders for unpaid bills she never knew. Of course, she understood from the news that the country was in a recession. They been there before but somehow or other Steven had always weathered it. She did appreciate that things could be a bit tight at such times. That was why she'd paid for the holiday. She had enough business acumen to realize that Steven would want to use his profits to plough back into the business to help keep it going.

But when she really thought about it, his attitude did seem different. There had definitely been something wrong that she couldn't put her finger on. Even after all the years of knowing him and being happily married, Laura always felt on edge about disturbing the peace, particularly after her first marriage. So she wondered how to deal with the problem and get to the bottom of it. The nature of her job had made her a rather forthright person and she decided a situation like this was best dealt with by taking the bull by the horns. Now her mind was made up, she would simply try and make him talk to her. Once she'd made the decision it did not seem half as daunting a task as she'd first thought.

Eager to know what was going on, no sooner had Steven come through the door than she burst out, 'What's going on Steven? What's the matter?'

Looking as if he'd been punched in the stomach he challenged her. 'I don't know what you mean, nothing's wrong. Why should there be?'

Instantly Laura could feel he was on the defensive. 'It's that look. You have it again like the last time all those years ago. Come on, talk to me, tell me what is really wrong.'

'I've already said nothing is wrong — now don't harp on about it.'

His whole attitude, so alien to him, made Laura even more determined to get to the bottom of things. 'I'm not, but if there is something I want to share it, that's all. Don't forget it's me, Laura, your wife, that you are talking to. I thought that was what our marriage was all about. That's the way we've always worked, you know that.'

Putting his head in his hands he just said, 'Leave it Laura, just leave it.'

Laura remained silent as she could sense she had gone far enough at the moment, but if he thought she was going to leave it there he was sadly mistaken. She was only leaving it for the moment. The more he denied there was anything wrong the more she was convinced there was. Yes, she'd get to the bottom of this and before too long.

Laura never had the opportunity to take the subject up with Steven again herself as events took the control of the situation out of her hands. A few days after she'd been questioning him, whilst they were still having their breakfast, the door bell rang. For some unknown reason, to Laura the sound seemed to have an ominous ring. Without knowing why Laura turned to Steven, 'You answer that. Anyway, it'll no doubt be for you.'

'Maybe, but I can't think who. But stay where you are. It doesn't matter who it's for, I'll go and answer it in any case.'

All the while Laura could feel shivers going through her with a premonition that there was something unpleasant about to happen. Before Steven could get to the door, another impatient knock came. She could hear Steven shout in agitation as he moved towards the door. 'All right, I'm coming.'

Laura carried on with her breakfast yet she could still feel cold shivers running through her body. As Steven came back into the room she looked up and asked, 'Who was that then?'

He looked pale and had a strange expression as he answered, 'You didn't hear what was said then?'

'No, of course not. Why should I have? I'm not in the habit of listening in on your discussions.'

'I didn't mean that. It's the police, we've been arrested.'

Laura felt as if this wasn't herself listening to the conversation. 'Arrested! What do you mean arrested?'

'For possession of stolen goods.'

'But what on earth are you talking about. What stolen goods?'

'I'm sorry Laura, but we've to go with them for questioning.'

'I've never stolen anything in my life. Why should I start now?'

'I've just said, they've arrested us so we've no choice but to go in for questioning. You don't want to get into further trouble by resisting arrest, now do you?'

Suddenly the full impact hit Laura and she let out a scream. 'My job, all we've worked for. It's lost.' In a matter of a few seconds it flashed through her mind how, with a lot of determination and hard work, she'd worked up from her first teaching job, to head of department, deputy headmistress then finally in the last few years headmistress.

Taking her in his arms Steven tried to console her and give her some reassurance.

'No, it isn't. It's me they're more interested in and we are only going in for questioning. It'll be all right, I promise you. Come on, we'll have to go as the police are waiting in the hall for us. They won't wait out there much longer.'

Tentatively Laura walked into the hall and saw that this was no cruel joke, there really were two policemen and in despair she burst out, 'I haven't done anything wrong. Why are you doing this to me?'

'I'm sorry, but we're only doing our job. If you haven't done anything wrong then you've nothing to worry about. Now before we go would either of you like to make a phone call. Also, I'm sorry but we have a warrant to search the house to see if any of the alleged stolen goods are here.'

'Go ahead. I've already told you we've nothing to hide, have we Steven?'

Laura barely heard the very quiet, 'No' that he gave in response to this.

Then realizing a phone call had been mentioned Laura quickly said, 'Can I ring my son? I must tell him what is happening.'

'Of course you can, go ahead. But please don't be on the phone too long. We've to get on our way. Now if we could get on with the search. Mr. Watson do you want to accompany us?'

Steven just nodded his agreement and went out with them. Laura grabbed the phone and quickly dialled Richard's number — she only hoped she caught him in before he set off for the day at work. She heaved a sigh of relief when after only two rings she heard the phone at the other end being picked up. She shouted down the receiver, 'Is that you Richard?'

'Mum, what on earth are you doing ringing at this time? Look I was just on my way out to work. Can I ring you back tonight?'

'No, listen Richard, please,' Laura replied quickly as she became more agitated. 'Steven and I have been arrested.'

She heard an explosive, 'What!' come down the phone line.

'That's what I said. Supposedly for possession of stolen goods.'

'I'll be right over. Just stay calm and I'm sure we'll soon have it all sorted out.'

'I don't think there'll be time for you to get here before they take us to the police station. You'd best meet us there.'

'Okay, which station are they taking you to?'

'The main one in the town centre.'

'I'll go there now. Remember, I love you Mum and try not to worry too much because I'll look after it all for you. All right?'

'What do you think? But yes I'm glad you can help us. Thank goodness you decided to be a solicitor.' Laura had been very proud of all her three children. None of them had been as implusive as her and wanted to leave school at sixteen. She'd had a pleasant surprise when Richard had decided the law was for him but then the two girls each followed with unexpected choices of their own. Katie choose to be a vet and Rachel, following in her mother's footsteps, a teacher.

Once Laura had put the receiver down, the full implication of the situation hit her. She had never felt suicidal in her life, but suddenly she did. It was as if she'd been transported back to her horrific time with Keith and her body could handle no more trauma. All the good times were forgotten as only darkness seemed to surround her now. All her strength of character seemed to dissipate and she knew if only she'd some pills in her hand, she'd do it she was sure. But she hadn't, so somehow she'd to survive this day. How she'd face it she didn't know. She'd never be able to look anybody in the face again. The despair was too much to bear. Maybe her body would do it for her, just give up and die.

Slowly through this haze of despondency she heard voices getting nearer. 'Come on love, we've got to go to the police station now.'

'Did they find anything?'

'No, of course not.'

'Then why have we still to go?'

Here the policeman interrupted to answer instead of Steven. 'There are some questions we need to ask, so I'm afraid you'll have to accompany us to the police station. There you can have a solicitor with you.'

'I've already arranged that. My son's a solicitor so he's going to meet us there.'

'Are you all ready to go? No pills or anything to take during the day that you need with you.'

Laura gave a feeble, 'No' but wished she did have some to help her now.

Neither spoke in the police car on the way to the police station. Never in her life had Laura known such a short journey suddenly seem so long. As soon as they arrived Laura jumped out of the car her eyes scanning quickly around looking for Richard. She let out a sigh of relief as she saw him and she ran quickly up to him to throw herself into his arms. 'Thank goodness you've come.'

'Of course I have. Don't worry, Mum, I'll look after you. Let them do all the formalities then I'll ask if we can have a room of our own to go in to and discuss all this before they interview you.'

Laura could just repeat, 'Formalities?'

'Yes, whatever you are arrested for they go through the same procedure. Come on, we'd best go to the duty officer and let him go through his paperwork.'

Laura was amazed at the size of the form he had to fill in with details about her. When he said, 'A blue dress you have on?' she just looked down at what she was wearing and realized it actually was her clothes he was talking about, as she saw the blue dress. What a silly question! What did it matter what she had on?

At last he finished asking the questions that seemed so time wasting and finally said to her, 'There's an empty interview room over there. You can use it to have a few minutes alone with your solicitor.'

This sounded strange to Laura calling Richard her solicitor, not her son. Feeling her arm being pulled she turned to Richard, 'Come on this way,' he said gently guiding her into the room. Laura turned to move to the room but then gave a bleak look over her shoulder at having to leave Steven on his own to fend for himself.

As soon as they were alone, Laura burst out. 'I don't know what all this is about

Richard, I really don't.'

Trying to calm her he said, 'Let's take it a step at a time. First of all let me tell you a bit more about the procedure here, then you might understand what is happening to you. As your solicitor, my normal first duty is to have a talk with the arresting officer so they can give me the facts they have based the arrest on. Then I'll be allowed to come back to you and we'll go through it all before you have a taped interview with the police. Until I know what evidence they have and what they are questioning you for, I can't say a lot more to help you at the moment. So I'll see if you can stay in here whilst I talk to the police. Also, we need to organize another solicitor for Steven. I don't want to sound funny but it might be better if he had a different one to me then there can be no conflict of interest. The police, in all probability, will want to interview Steven first. Anyway, will you be all right a few minutes if I go and try to get things sorted out a bit and see where we're going from here?'

Still not quite sure of everything that he was telling her, yet at the same time knowing Richard needed to go and talk to the police she quietly agreed, 'Yes' in acknowledgment.

As she sat down now on her own, her mind went around and around asking herself what was going on. Suddenly she realized she hadn't given a thought to Steven. Where was he and why wasn't he with her? She could feel her agitation begin to rise as there was nobody there with her to answer all the questions that were going on in her head. If only she knew what was happening and what it was about she was sure she would feel better. She felt sick with worry. Never had she known that time could go by so slowly. Each time she looked at her watch only a few minutes more had moved on. Then thinking about how she wasn't used to sitting without anything to do, set off the next panic attack. What if Richard had forgotten to ring the school? Her secretary would be ringing all over the place trying to locate her. There again, what if he had rung but not been tactful in how he'd told them why she wasn't in school today? So many thoughts were going on in her mind, yet none of them helped to ease the pain and anxiety of what was happening to her.

At last she heard the click of the door. She quickly looked up to see Richard walk back in and couldn't help the panic in her voice as she asked, 'Where's Steven, isn't he with you?'

'No, Mum, they have put him in a cell.'

Seeing the look of horror on her face he

quickly added, 'It doesn't mean anything. It is simply being used as a room as they have no where else empty to put him. It's part of the procedure to keep you separate. Don't worry, he's all right.'

'Are you sure?'

'Yes, Mum. Now, let's get on with what we've to do. The quicker we get sorted and you both have your interviews then hopefully you'll soon be out of here together.' Suddenly he assumed a different role, that of solicitor not son. 'Now I've talked to the police and they say that Steven has been buying stolen materials cheaply to use on his building sites. They say he was aware that the goods were stolen. As you are a partner in the business, they are saying you are also aware of this fact. What do you have to say about all that?'

'I've no idea what they are talking about. I'm sure Steven has never purchased stolen goods knowingly.'

Quickly Richard interrupted, 'Look, Mum, it's you I'm talking about at the moment and how you'll answer at the interview. Steven will have his own solicitor so they'll talk his side through together just as we're doing. Now the police will have some evidence to show you. Some may point a finger at you or as I said before it may simply be because you're a partner in the business that they also suspect you.'

'I've no idea what's been going on, honestly Richard. As far as I'm aware all things have been purchased legitimately.'

'All right calm down, I believe you. Now you've nothing to worry about in the interview, just tell the truth and take your time about answering. Don't be rushed by them. I'll be there to help you if needs be. Now I've explained it do you think you can manage that? Unfortunately, you'll have to wait a while before they interview you. They want to see Steven first and we're still waiting for his solicitor to come. Then when he does arrive he'll want to talk to Steven so it could be a few hours wait yet for you, I'm afraid.'

'I've never been so restless and worried in my life then on top of that not being able to do anything about it. It's terrible here, it really is.'

'I know but there isn't much I can do about that to help you I'm afraid. You'll just have to be patient. I'll try to keep coming in to see you, but I'd better get back now and see if Steven's solicitor has arrived yet.'

No sooner had he left the room than the policeman who had taken all their details entered. 'Your daughter is on the phone, would you like to speak to her?'

'Oh yes please. Did she say which daughter? I've got two you see.'

'No, sorry. She only said it was your daughter speaking. Anyway, follow me and I'll show you where the phone is but try not to be on too long as it's a busy line.'

'Yes, thanks for letting me speak to her.'

As soon as she picked the receiver up a voice said, 'Hello, Mum, it's Kate.' Then before Laura could say anything this was quickly followed by, 'Are you all right?

'Just, but I'm all at sea with what's going on here.'

'I know. Richard rang and told me, but don't worry I'm sure you'll be all right with Richard to look after you. I wish I could get to be with you, but it's impossible for me today. I'll keep ringing to see what's happening and I'll come to see you as soon as I can whatever.'

'Are you sure you should keep ringing? Look the policeman is signalling for me to come off the phone. I must go now but thanks for ringing me.'

'Whatever they say, I'll keep ringing. Remember, I love you. Bye, Mum.'

As Laura put the receiver down she could feel the tears springing to her eyes, but she didn't want to show herself up. She heard a concerned voice at her side. 'Are you all right?' When she looked it was the policeman again.

'Yes, I suppose so in the circumstances.'

'I'm sorry but the room you were in before is occupied by somebody else. I'll have to put you in here now.'

With this he directed Laura to a cell. She could feel a great fear of being locked in build up inside herself. Quickly she asked, 'You're not going to lock the door are you?'

'No, I'll leave it unlocked and if you need anything just peep out and call me. I'll only be across the hall. Now about lunch, I'll be back in a few minutes with a meal.'

'It doesn't matter, I'm not hungry.'

'It's our duty to make sure you're properly looked after. There is a meal ready for you.' With this the policeman walked out of the door.

As soon as she was back on her own all the fear came back to Laura. What was going on? Why was she here when she hadn't done anything wrong? Then it came to her maybe somebody had set them up. Yes, that must be it. If only Richard were with her and she could talk to him, they would soon have it all cleared up. Looking at her watch she realized another half hour had passed and no food had been brought to her after all. The policeman must have taken her at her word.

Just on this thought the door opened and he appeared with a plate holding a cooked dinner. He looked at her, 'Will you accept this meal from me?'

Not quite comprehending what he was saying Laura looked at him puzzled and answered, 'Of course, but I'm still not hungry. I don't think I can eat much.'

'As I said before I'm only doing my duty in looking after you. Is there anything else you want?'

'Have you anything to help pass the time? I don't think I've ever been so lost with myself in my life.'

'I'll see if I can find any old magazines. They won't be much but I suppose it'll be better than nothing.'

'It will, thanks.' With this Laura was left alone with her thoughts once more. Her mind just couldn't take in what was happening to her. Never a particularly religious person before, she suddenly found comfort in saying a silent prayer for help to get her through the day.

25

Laura let out a sigh of relief as Richard walked through the door. 'Thank goodness you're back. I thought I was never going to see you again. The duty officer has been kind enough to find some magazines for me, but I still feel as if I've been here days not a few hours.'

'Things are moving now. I've talked to the police and Steven is being interviewed at this moment. You and I'll have a chat whilst we've chance and see if we can sort some things out, then before too long, hopefully, it'll be your turn to be interviewed.'

Quickly Laura jumped in. 'After that will we be free to go home again?'

'I hope so. Let's take it step by step and see how things go. Anyway, let's talk things through now ready for your interview.'

'But I've nothing to tell them. I don't really know what they are on about.'

'That's what I've discussed with them and I'll explain it to you now. What they're saying is that the business, yours and Steven's received stolen goods. These goods being building materials such as bricks and blocks etc. and apparently they say this has been going on for quite a while. As a partner in the business they think you're implicated.'

Laura was amazed by all Richard was telling her. 'But we haven't used stolen goods on our sites. I just know we haven't.'

'Maybe that's what you believe to be true but the police have evidence to the contrary. Now when they interview you they'll only be concerned with your answers, in other words, your side of the story. Take your time before you answer and don't be pushed into answering what you don't really mean. I'll be there with you so I'll jump in and help you if needs be. Now before you go in is there anything else you want to ask me?'

'Can't I just tell them I'm innocent then that be the end of it?'

'Afraid not. You'll have to answer the questions and remember these and your answers will be taped. Then the Crown Prosecution Service will decide if they're going to take further action.'

'Further action! What do you mean?'

'Charge you.'

Laura repeated this without fully comprehending what she was saying. 'Charge me, but what for?'

'I've explained to you already, for receiving stolen goods.'

'But I haven't received any stolen goods.'

'Don't worry, Mum. Just answer truthfully and I'm sure there'll be no charges against you.

'But what about Steven?'

'We'll just have to see.'

'But he's innocent, I know he is.'

'Let's leave that and concentrate on you at the moment. We'll see Steven later and hear what he's to say about all this.'

'So what happens now?'

'We've just to wait until they are ready to interview you.'

'Can you stay here with me to keep me company?'

'Sorry no. I've told you before they stick to procedure. They've let me in to discuss what's happening before your interview but now I've done that I've to leave you. I don't like to remind you but you are under arrest and that's how it works. It doesn't matter what you've been arrested for, it is all the same procedure. As soon as they are ready I'll come for you. Anything else before I go?'

'I'm so frightened yet so bored.'

'There's nothing I can do about the boredom, but all I can do to try to set your mind at rest is say don't worry.' Seeing his mother's expression he was quick to add. 'I know that's easy to say but believe me I do have experience in situations like this and I know you'll be all right. I'd better go now otherwise they'll be coming to root me out. I'll come for you as soon as I can.'

The only way Laura felt she could keep any sanity at all was to go into her own dreams. She tried to think of the good things of her life but this was only short lived. She was soon back to reality worrying what was happening to Steven and what would happen to her. She felt so lonely. For many years now Steven had always been at her side if she needed him. But through no fault of his own he couldn't be here at one of the times she needed him the most. She let out a low cynical laugh, it was all down to procedures. That's what she was today, a procedure. When she had reached a point where she felt she could stand it no longer and that at any minute she would start to scream, the door opened and in walked Richard once again.

'Come on, Mum. They're ready to interview you at last.'

'Thank goodness for that. I don't think I could have sat here any longer doing nothing. I was getting to screaming pitch.'

'Are you sure you're all right now to go through with the interview?'

'Of course, let's just get on with it.'

Suddenly her authoritative nature of being

a head mistress returned to her, she held her head high and marched forward.

As soon as she entered the room she saw two plain clothed policeman sat there and immediately she was struck by the thought what a small shabby room to conduct what seemed to be such an important interview.

One of them pointed to a chair and told her to sit down. He then went through the procedure of explaining who he was and what the interview was about. Then he pointed to a tape recorder and explained that the interview would be on tape. Laura had to hold back a giggle when he picked up a pack of tapes, held them up and said, 'You all agree this pack of tapes is sealed.' He looked at each of them waiting for a reply.

Then forms were produced. Laura started thinking they were never going to get on with this interview. These were for the records of the tapes to be used. At last they seemed to be on their way. The tapes were in the machine and switched on.

Looking at her the policeman carrying out the interview gave his full name and rank. Next he turned to his colleague who did the same, then to Richard. He then looked at Laura and said, 'Please say your name and date of birth clearly.'

She was beginning to get annoyed at what

seemed a great fuss about nothing and quickly rattled off, 'Laura Watson,' only to be interrupted by, 'Haven't you a middle name?'

'Yes.'

'Well please say your name again with all names included.'

Laura was really beginning to think this is all rather silly but did as she was requested because she hadn't much alternative.

Once all the formalities were over the questioning began. Laura wasn't quite sure where all the questions were leading, as some seemed so irrelevant to the point in issue.

'How long have you and your husband had the business?'

Here Laura had to do a quick mental calculation and hope she was right in her answer although how that could affect anything she didn't know. What was amazing once she had given her answer the interviewing policeman pointed to a file and said, 'This is my evidence,' with this he opened the file and turned to a page with a copy of the certificate of registration of the business name. 'Yes, that's the year it says here.'

All that Laura could do was give a silent sigh of relief that she'd been correct and now hoped he might believe she was telling the truth.

He carried on and asked a lot of in depth

questions about her involvement in the business and she had to admit it was nil. She pointed out as a headmistress she had enough work of her own to do. He pried a lot into why the business was in joint names. Here Laura had to pause to think about that because she couldn't really say why it was. At the beginning, when Steven first started out on his own it had seemed a good idea but as time went on they didn't bother to change it. Now she wished they had then she wouldn't be here going through this terrible ordeal. At times he came back to some of the questions and tried approaching them a different way in order to trip her up to tell a different answer to the first time. But she was too alert for this and as she had told the truth in the first place it was difficult to alter her answer. He looked rather put out when this tactic didn't work.

It seemed no time before he said, 'We'll have to pause here as the tape is at the end and I'll have to change it.'

Seeing the opportunity Laura quickly asked, 'Whilst you do that can I go to the toilet, please?'

She could see she had put them in a bit of a quandary here but finally he said, 'I don't see why not.'

Laura had to suppress a laugh when the tapes were started again and they went through the same name giving procedure but most of all when the policeman said out aloud on to the tape that she'd been to the toilet during the break. She began to feel as if she'd been set up for somebody's amusement. On the questions went, yet Laura saw no real evidence here pointing a finger at her or Steven as the guilty parties. Suddenly it came to an end as the questions were drawn to a close by the policeman asking if she'd anything else she'd like to add. For one of the few times in her life Laura seemed struck dumb for words. Finally all she could think of to say was, 'I'm not guilty of what you're trying to accuse me of. I've never stolen anything in my life or received stolen goods.'

Quickly seeing an opening here the policeman asked, 'Are you accusing your husband then?'

'Most certainly not.' Laura was quick to respond in defence of Steven.

Then that was the end of the interview, after signing the paperwork for the tapes and given sheets showing the tape numbers the policeman turned to Richard. 'Do you want a few minutes alone with Mrs. Watson?'

'Yes please.'

As soon as they were alone Richard turned to her, 'Well done, Mum. You were excellent. With what you said on tape I'm sure the

Crown Prosecution Service will take it no further.'

'Do you really believe that? I hope you're right. I've had enough with today, I want no more aggravation.'

'I'm sure so. I can only say again you were brilliant how you handled it. At times he pushed you rather hard and overstepped the mark. I was going to step in to help but you kept him in his place.'

Laura let out a giggle. 'I must have thought he was one of my children at school.' Becoming serious again and realizing this was not the time really for jokes she looked keenly at Richard as she questioned, 'What happens now?'

'Follow me and we'll go and see the duty officer.'

As soon as they were with the duty officer Richard looked at him. 'My client has been interviewed now. Are you ready to sort out both Mr. and Mrs. Watson being released?'

'Yes, I'll just get Mr. Watson. If you'll both just go and sit over there then we'll sort the bail out.'

Laura quickly grabbed Richard's arm in panic. 'What does he mean by bail?'

'They'll bail you to come back here in a few weeks when they'll give both of you their decision what further action, if any, they're going to take.'

'But how much will this bail cost?'

Richard gave a little laugh. 'Nothing. Don't worry, all you've got to do is turn up here when they tell you to. Cheer up, you'll soon be seeing Steven again and getting out of here.'

As Steven walked down the corridor he gave a weak smile at her and mouthed, 'Are you all right?'

'Just.'

'These are your bail forms then, here is the date and time you have to return back here. You both understand that you must attend when they've said. This pink copy is yours, one for each of you. Bring that along when you come back on the required date. You're both free to go now.'

As they walked out of the door all Laura could say was, 'I hope the school governors don't find out about this otherwise I'm sure that's the end of my job and career.'

Steven took her arm and said gently, 'Don't worry Laura, you'll be all right. They won't take any further action against you, believe me.'

Laura looked at him keenly and asked him sharply. 'How do you know?'

'I do, just trust me.' He gave a cynical laugh. 'I know that's a bit difficult in the circumstances but we'll talk when we get home and you'll understand it all. No more questions now, just try to relax and calm yourself down.'

Richard quickly jumped in as he could see Laura was ready to blow her top at him here and now. 'He's right, Mum. I'll come back with you now. We need to sort one or two things out.'

Laura instinctively knew they did as she was sure there was a lot more going on than met the eye.

26

'What do you mean you knew the goods were stolen?' shouted Laura as she paced up and down.

Richard was quick to jump in to try to calm her down as he could see the situation could easily get out of hand. 'Don't shout, Mum. Let's talk about this rationally and try to understand it more.' But it was to no avail, Laura just carried on with what she was saying. 'You mean you have jeopardized both of us. What about my career I've worked so hard for? What if I lose all that? Now what can you say about that Mr. not so clever?'

'Laura, please listen and let me explain. I did it for you.'

'For me! What on earth are you talking about? Have you taken leave of your senses? I never asked you to receive stolen goods. Anyway what good would bricks and such like be to me, I ask you.'

'Because those bricks turn into houses, which hopefully in turn sell and make money. That money gets you all the nice things you like. I couldn't keep up with our lifestyle any longer. This house was at risk. You're an intelligent woman, you must know we are going through a recession. I just couldn't sell the houses quick enough to make money to keep up the payments on this. I saw this as a way to help. I never meant to harm you, only to give you what you wanted. I can see now that I've been a fool, but I only meant to do it once thinking I'd never get caught. The first time it all went well so I was persuaded to carry on. Not that I needed a lot of persuading as money was so short.' He sat down and put his head in his hands and said in a sad voice, 'I know it was wrong but I didn't know what else to do. I didn't want to let you down. I know how important your possessions are to you and how Keith let you down.' Giving a low moan of agony he added, 'Now look what I've done to you.'

Still shouting and ignoring his anguish Laura looked at him with disgust. 'So now you're trying to lay the blame on me.'

'Mum, please calm down and listen. Steven's trying to explain to you how it happened and why he did it. What's done is done and shouting at him isn't going to resolve anything.'

Laura looked at her son. 'So come on Mr. Smarty Pants what should he do now? Give all the stuff back and say sorry I've been a naughty boy.'

'Stop it, Mum, that's silly talk. Come back to reality and listen to me. So far they've no real evidence that Steven was involved. They know the materials were delivered to his site but they have no proof he was connected in the theft or knew the goods were stolen. I'm not saying that it's very difficult to pin it on him, after all, who else would benefit from it apart from yourselves? As I said before, I'm certain they'll believe you weren't involved, Mum. What I suggest we do, as Steven hasn't admitted anything, is to see whether the Crown Prosecution Service are taking it further. If charges are to be pressed we'll decide where to go from there. If there are no charges, then all to the good. Now Mum can you stop shouting and calm down then you may understand it all the better. Just remember all this isn't pleasant for Steven either.'

Still feeling shocked and angry Laura had to admit, 'I suppose so.' But she quickly turned to Steven and snapped at him. 'You stupid fool!'

None of them could settle and they went round in circles discussing what had happened until well past midnight when finally Richard said, 'Look, I'll have to go home now.'

The argument went on long after Richard

had gone, neither of them feeling like going to bed because their adrenaline was working over time.

Finally Steven said, 'I don't know what else to say, Laura, other than I'm truly sorry and wouldn't have hurt you for the world. You do believe me?'

All Laura could think of was that first unhappy marriage and none of the happiness she'd had for years now. To her this felt as if this marriage was going the same way. So the only answer she could repeat but with no real depth of feeling was, 'I suppose so. Anyway I'm going to bed now. I can't miss work tomorrow or should I say today. I don't feel like going but I'll have to after missing one day already.'

'Can't you stay off another day? Surely that won't do any harm?'

'You must be joking. I would have thought all that we have gone through today would have made my job even more important. We need one income coming in.' With this she flounced out of the room and up to bed. She could hear Steven moving about downstairs and guessed he was going to follow her. Quickly she put on her nightclothes and once in bed moved as near the edge of the bed, on her side, as she could. She didn't want to speak to him anymore at the moment and certainly couldn't face any physical contact, even him touching her gently. She closed her eyes and tried to breathe evenly hoping he would think exhaustion had finally caught up with her. She felt him get in bed and move up to her but she moved even further away and she heard a sigh as he rolled on his side with his back to her, leaving a distance between them. Was this to be her life from now, a distancing?

She was amazed when she jumped with a start and woke up to look at the clock and find she had been asleep a couple of hours. But sleep wouldn't come to her again. All she kept thinking about was what was going to happen to them. If he went to prison what about the business? Then if the business was lost this house would surely go. Her parents, she would be so humiliated when they found out about all that had gone on. The more she tried to sleep the more horrific it all became in her mind. She felt sick with the worry of it all. She had heard it said that the darkest hours were before dawn and these certainly seemed to be.

Realizing it was now impossible to fall asleep again that night and as she felt fully awake, she finally gave up and went downstairs to make herself a cup of coffee.

It wasn't long before she heard the sound

of footsteps on the stairs. 'Couldn't you sleep, Laura? I couldn't either, it was all going around and around in my head.'

She still felt so angry with him that she retorted back. 'So it should, a fine mess you've got us into.'

'Please, Laura, don't be so hard. I love you so much. I was only trying to do the best for us.'

'Is that what you call it?'

'Yes, it is. Just try to see it from my point of view for a minute. If I'd been on my own, I wouldn't have done it. I was only trying to keep you in the style you like.'

'That's right, blame it all on me. That's all you've been doing all evening.'

'I'm not. I'm only trying to make you understand why I did it.'

'What I understand is you've got us into all this trouble. Now it's up to you to get us out of it.'

'I will, if there's any way I can at all. But first of all we've to wait and see if they do press charges then we'll have to take it from there.'

'Well, what if they do charge us?'

'If they charge anybody it'll be me, Laura. Please believe me in that.'

'Okay, maybe I can see that, but where do we go from there?'

'Can we take it a step at a time and see what the Crown Prosecution Service do. To be honest I can't think straight at the moment with all that has happened.'

'If you ask me you haven't been thinking straight for a long time.'

'Laura, please, can we be friends at least? I need you, I need your support. Doesn't our love count for something?'

Looking keenly at him Laura had to answer, 'I don't know. I really don't.' With these words she saw his shoulders sag in despair and she wanted to put her arms around him and give him the comfort he craved. But she knew she had to be strong and keep this remoteness. He wasn't to be trusted anymore, look what he had done to her.

'Just leave me to rest now. I don't want to hear anymore about it. Soon I'll have to get ready to go to work. That's going to be an ordeal in itself. I'll think they're all pointing the finger at me knowing what's going on. Of course, they won't know and I realize it's silly to feel like that but I just can't help it. That's what all this has brought me to.'

'Okay, I'll let you rest. Do you want me to get you a cup of tea or anything?'

'No, just leave me alone.'

Steven knowing he was beaten left her as she'd asked.

* ★ ★ ★

As soon as she arrived at school and met the other members of staff, they told her how ill she looked. At least this wasn't something she'd to pretend about. She did feel ill, sick inside herself. She just acknowledged their sympathy with a few words. 'It's only a bug. I'll be fighting fit again in a few days. You know how it is, they knock you back at the time.'

All were quick to agree with her about this and told her she should have stayed off longer, they'd have managed. So at least one hurdle was over. Now there was only the time to wait until they went back to the police station to answer the police bail. All she hoped was that she could keep up a front so that nobody would find out what was going on until then. After then she would just have to wait and see where she went with her life and how much became public knowledge. She felt a shiver of fear go through her at this thought.

Somehow she got through the next few weeks, but not without many a strange look and stare. She knew she looked drawn and ill and to make matters worse she kept having sickness bouts with the stress of it all. As old as she was she kept getting a few wondering looks questioning whether she was pregnant even at her age. But there was nothing she could say to contradict her colleagues thoughts without giving the game away about what was really going on.

At home life was very difficult. She could barely look at Steven never mind talk to him. He still kept begging for her to listen to him but she would have none of it. She didn't care or even bother to ask what he was doing now at work. She presumed he was still going to the business each day, but what did it matter to her what he was doing now with his life. She could feel his sadness about him and at times nearly let her reserve slip and give him a love, but then she remembered in the end this would cause her more hurt. She had to be hard and look after herself, because obviously she could no longer rely on Steven.

To Laura, the police seemed to have no consideration that people might have a job of work to go to when they fixed the date and time to answer bail. As they were due to go to the police station at ten o'clock Laura had to take the morning, at the minimum, off work. She just didn't know how long these things took never having gone through it before.

Somehow it hadn't really struck her, over the last few weeks, what answering this bail could really mean. Now, as they sat waiting for somebody to come to them she suddenly realized how nervous she was. Steven tried to get hold of her hand but she just pulled it away. Looking hurt he asked, 'Are you all right Laura? I told you there is no need for you to worry, all will be fine for you.'

She felt her bitterness rise again at where he'd placed her and answered in a sarcastic voice. 'Fine, just fine. I've never felt better.'

They didn't have a long wait when the same policeman who had interviewed them before approached. Straight away Laura saw a difference in his attitude towards them. He actually had a smile on his face and was more polite than before as he said, 'Please come this way with me.'

He took them into a shabby room and straight away apologized for the lack of chairs. 'Sorry we haven't a more comfortable room free at the moment, but just sit on the edge of the desks. This won't take long. Now I'll say what I have to, what has been decided by the Crown Prosecution Service but I want no argument or debate from either of you. Is that understood?'

Laura thought to herself, here we go again but just replied with a submissive, 'Yes.'

He carried on as if she hadn't spoken. 'All the paperwork has been sent to the Crime Prosecution Service and the decision has been made by them how they wish to proceed.' With this he looked at Laura. 'With the evidence I have and your taped interview it has been decided no charges will be made against you.'

With these words Laura felt a tremendous surge of relief go through her body and she felt as if all was well again.

He then turned to Steven. 'With you, Mr. Watson, it has been decided further action will be taken. We feel there is enough evidence to make a case against you.'

All the feeling of well being inside Laura was quickly deflated and panic set in again. She heard a voice carrying on, 'Your solicitor will be supplied with copies of this evidence now.' Suddenly Laura realized the voice was now addressing her. 'We need to take your husband away for about half an hour to go through various formalities. Do you want to wait in the reception area?'

Quickly Laura pulled her thoughts together. 'No thank you. I'll go now if that's all right?'

'Of course, but you can wait if you want to. We won't be that long as I said before.'

'No, I'll go now.'

In reality she wanted to get to a phone and let Richard know what had happened. Now she wished she'd taken him up on his offer to attend with her. As she was moving out of the room Steven turned to her. 'I'd like you to wait for me Laura.'

'I'm sorry but I must get out of here.'

In a resigned voice Steven simply said, 'I understand.'

As soon as she was out she made a rush to the nearest public telephone, keeping her fingers crossed it was empty. She knew that to Richard's secretary she must have sounded as if she had lost her senses, because as soon as the phone was answered she shouted in a voice that didn't seem to belong to a sane person. 'Get me Richard, I must speak to him now.' As soon as the words were out she realized how rude she must have sounded.

She could hear the trained calmness in the secretary's voice as she asked in a patronizing tone. 'Who's speaking please?'

'His Mum of course. Who do you think? Get him quick.'

Again she realized the poor woman wasn't to know this irate voice was that of his mother.

Yet a calm voice came back over the phone to her. 'Yes, of course, just hold the line a minute please and I'll find him for you.'

Laura was aware of muffled sounds as if the secretary was in reality unsure what to do about this phone caller and was asking advice. Finally just as Laura thought she would snap altogether she heard her son's voice. 'Hello, is that really you Mum?'

'Of course.' Then she couldn't help adding sarcastically, 'How many mums have you got?'

'Sorry, but my secretary really didn't think it sounded like you.'

'Never mind that. They've charged Steven.'

'All right, Mum, just calm down. You know we really expected that but what about you?'

'Oh, they've not charged me.' Laura could hear the hysteria in her voice now.

'Look, Mum, calm down. We expected that too, now didn't we?' Not giving her chance to answer he carried on. 'I'll come tonight to see you and we'll see what we can do to try to help Steven. I'll do my best for him, get him a top barrister, don't worry.'

Replying sharply Laura snapped down the phone. 'It's not him I'm worried about. What about me? He's let me down just like your Father.'

Laura heard a roar down the phone. 'Mother.'

'I'm sorry. I suppose that was uncalled for, but to me he has let me down.'

'Just stop for a minute and think how he feels. After all, he did it for you.'

'So he says.'

'Come on, Mum. He's never let you down in all the years you've known each other. He couldn't have been kinder to you and you've been so happy.'

'But he's let me down now.' Sobbing she quickly added, 'I don't know where I go from here, I really don't.'

Realizing that his mother was getting to the end of her tether he gently asked, 'Where are you now?'

'In some public phone box in the town.'

'Is Steven still at the Police Station?'

'Yes, they are back to doing their formalities.'

'Look, Mum, go back to the Police Station and wait for him. Then the pair of you get off home and talk. I mean really talk.'

'I'm not going back to that Police Station. He can make his own way back home. Anyway I've got to get back to work.'

'Forget that for today. Ring in ill and then go home and calm down. You're in no fit state to work. If you won't wait for him now, at least talk to him when he does get home. He'll need your support now more than ever. As soon as all my appointments are finished I'll come and see you both. I've said before we'll sort something out between us. The picture can't be as black as it looks now, honest it can't, Mum.'

He might as well have not spoken for all the notice his mother took, she just carried on with her own thoughts. 'I don't know what your Grandma and Granddad will say, I really don't.' Panic and fear for the future started to come back in her voice. 'My job! Oh, my job and my lovely house!'

Feeling so frustrated that he wasn't there with her, he tried once more to calm her. 'Just go home please, Mum, and do be careful driving yourself. I love you and I'll look after you both.'

Laura gave a sobbed, 'All right,' and put the phone down just as her money was running out. She was barely aware of the curious looks she got as she ran through the town with tears running down her face.

27

Once again Laura came back to the present after thinking long and hard how her life had gone so far. But after all this soul searching and deliberating she was still no nearer coming to a decision about the future. What did she really want from life now? To try to make a new life for herself and still achieve something or to have a companion with her, Steven.

She realized how lonely she'd been this last year. It seemed now, as if the tears that streamed down her face on the day that they were arrested had been symbolic of what the next few months of her life would be like. It had spiralled out of control as everything happened so quickly.

She understood now that she'd probably been too hard on Steven. She'd barely spoken to him in all the months leading up to the trial. It had been Richard who'd been his support, not herself. He'd done his best to help Steven, even though he knew he was guilty of the charges. All along Richard had assured Laura that Steven wouldn't get a custodial sentence. That had been a laugh.

Richard and Steven had decided, after a lot of talking everything through, that it would be best after all if Steven pleaded guilty and with no previous convictions he should, at the worst, get probation or a suspended sentence. But it seemed as if everything was against them. He was given an eighteen months prison sentence. This and the publicity of it all had finally broken Laura. She knew she'd been away from school ill more than she'd been there in the last year. She couldn't help it, she felt as if she was in a bottomless black pit. Her whole life and ambitions had fallen to pieces before her very eyes.

It didn't take long for the vultures to attack once they knew what was happening and that Steven was no longer around to bargain with them. First one debt then another was called in, but there just wasn't the money to pay them. Finally one creditor, who decided Steven hadn't already had enough punishment with his prison sentence made him bankrupt. Somehow, before all the problems Steven had had the foresight to put the house in Laura's name only. Thankfully Laura wasn't made bankrupt, on top of everything else. But it did leave her to keep up the luxurious home on her own income only. She sighed as she thought back to the impossibility of it all. She'd pleaded with the Building

Society to come to some arrangement with her but all her pleas had fallen on stony ground. As far as they were concerned Steven was finished, he would never again make anything of himself once he was released from prison and they knew that despite her good job it wasn't enough to make the payments required. So they called the loan in on the house. Laura decided they had been some of the worst days of her life. Far worse than living with Keith, that seemed nothing in comparison.

Thinking back it seemed as if it was some television black comedy she'd been living through. No sooner had she finished for the summer holidays than she was in front of a judge herself for him to give the Building Society possession of her lovely home. She pleaded and begged but two days, just two days all she was given to pack up all her possessions. How she would have done it, without the help of her family, she just didn't know. Not only did they help with the packing but they gave her the moral support she so desperately needed. But they did it for her and it was amazing how many people came forward with the loan of a room or their garage to store things in.

But it was the stepping over the threshold that made it all seem so unreal. She thought her eyes were deceiving her when she saw all the cars lined up outside on the road just before the deadline of twelve o'clock. It was like a wake. But on the dot they all walked up the drive. She couldn't believe her ears when they were told to step over the threshold. Then one of the men looked at her and asked if she'd any pets inside. At first she thought she'd misheard what he'd said but when he repeated the question and before she knew it the words were out. 'Yes, a dog. Do you want her to step over the threshold as well?'

Everything seemed to have come back full circle. Once more she went back home to her parent's house. Her friend Jackie, who she'd got to know so long ago at college had come forward with an offer for Laura to go and live with her and her family. Instinctively Laura knew it would have hurt her parents deeply if she'd refused their offer. But this time it did really take some getting used to, she wasn't sure if it was old age that had made them worse to live with or maybe she was just less tolerant and more independent. But then they hadn't refused their home to her but welcomed her with open arms. It now worked as a two way process. They needed her help as much as she needed a home, as neither of them were in good health.

Laura gave a cynical laugh thinking this

was it then. This was what her life had come to. She knew her children had been good to her, they couldn't have been more supportive. All of them had offered her a home, but somehow it didn't seem right, her children having to take her in. No, she had done what was right by going back to live with her parents.

But where did that leave her now? Steven was due out of prison at the end of the week. What was she to do? Surprisingly her parents had been more understanding about everything that had happened than she'd imagined they would be. They'd even understood Steven's actions and not condemned him for what he'd done. Even though he had admitted to being guilty and been sentenced for the charges, they seemed to hold no direct blame against him. They only offered sympathy for what had come about. At times it infuriated Laura how defensive they were of him. It surprised her even more as she was the innocent one, yet it felt as if they were telling her she was the selfish one and should see Steven's point of view. They seemed to have forgotten or were ignoring all the hurt it had done to her. Her father even went as far as to say, 'You've got a good one there, hang on to him.' Now Laura decided her father had really gone senile.

Then to make things worse she heard rumours that Keith had done well for himself. Maybe, just maybe, she should have hung in there. But then the full remembrance took over of the horrific beatings she'd suffered at his hands and there was no way she could have carried on being so abused, however well he'd done for himself. After all, a leopard never changes it's spots.

Luckily the school governors and her colleagues had been very supportive and held no blame against her, so she still had a job. They had even accepted her frequent absences and could understand her breakdown in health.

Gradually her mind turned to all the good times she'd had with Steven before all this trouble. How many of the things he'd provided that she'd always yearned for. Was she selfish? If she was really honest she did miss him so. It wasn't the same living with her parents as a husband. Those small intimate things that they'd talked about when they were alone in bed. Were those things worth more than possessions? He still loved her, she knew that. He had sent that message back each time some member of the family had visited him. She was surprised he did when she thought about it. Laura felt really selfish now, that she had never been able to face visiting him in prison despite him putting his name on the visiting permits. All his letters he had been allowed to send had been love letters to her begging her forgiveness and asking if she could find it in herself to have some compassion and forgiveness so they could start afresh when he had been released. She'd not answered any, just torn them into pieces in disgust.

It suddenly hit her how hard it must have been for Steven stuck in prison. The children had visited him when allowed, three times in twenty eight days and had held no details back from her what it was really like in there. At first he'd been held in custody at a top security jail. He'd shared a cell with a young lad convicted of possession of drugs. He was locked up for as long as twenty three hours a day. They had what was known as association time some days, where they were allowed out for two hours to mix with other prisoners or make any phone calls. But to make the phone calls they had to be able to purchase a phone card from the prison. It had been the children who had even had to send him his weekly allowance of money, as she couldn't bring herself to do it. Laura had made sure she wasn't around to receive any of these calls. She knew he'd tried because he'd spoken with her parents. But she felt she'd nothing to say to him, she'd said it all before the trial.

Finally he was moved to an open prison where life became a little easier for him or so the children said. There he'd had to work in the gardens. At least he'd been outside some of the time and Laura knew how much he hated been hemmed inside. Although he'd more freedom there with the key to his room, rather than being locked in a cell, he was still kept confined by the fencing. The children had reported back how frustrated he was at times, all he wanted was to be out. He couldn't say back home because he didn't think he had a home. But she also knew from them that he'd been very sad not knowing what the future held for him. At times he'd been in despair thinking he had no future. Yes, she'd to admit it had been hard on him. He'd certainly more than paid for his crime one way or another.

Suddenly it all became crystal clear. That was it, her mind was made up at last, now it had to be all action to do what she planned. Once the decision had been made she was impatient to get everything sorted out and ready. She threw her few things into her bag, paid the hotel bill and was on her way.

For the first time in her whole life she knew what she truly wanted out of life. She actually knew what she was doing and where she was going. This gave her a deep inner contentment that she had never felt before.

★ ★ ★

She was glad it was a bright sunny day as she stood outside the prison gates. She felt sick inside. What if he didn't want her after she'd been so hard and ignored him all this time? He might have finally gone off her, realized what she really was. If only he'd give her another chance, he'd see she'd changed. She now knew where she wanted to go and what was the most important thing in life. How she wished the gates would hurry up and open and he would appear. Then she would know for once and all and this uncertainty would be gone.

At last she saw the gate moving, she only hoped it would be Steven who would appear. A figure came out who looked much like Steven but older, he had grey hair and was slightly hunched over. He was clutching a black dustbin bag with all his worldly possessions.

Laura let out a gasp as she realized this figure was really Steven. She felt a pain of anguish inside herself wondering if this was what she'd done to him. Slowly he took a few tentative steps towards her. A few feet away from her he stopped and looked around hesitantly, not sure what to do next. Looking at him Laura quietly murmured, 'Hello Steven.'

Still looking at her intently as if not really believing it was her he was seeing, he questioned, 'What are you doing here, Laura? You're the last person I expected to see.'

Feeling more confident now she said in a firm voice. 'I'm here to take you home.'

Uncertain what she really meant he carried on looking at her in a puzzled way. 'Home! Home where? I don't have a home.'

Wanting to wipe away the look of desolation in his face she reassured him. 'Yes, you do. I'm taking you to our home.'

Still not sure what she was saying he said in a dazed voice. 'But you don't want me anymore. You've made that more than obvious.'

She couldn't hold herself back any longer. Suddenly she ran forward and threw herself at Steven crying with anguish in her voice. 'I do. Can you ever forgive me? I realize how selfish I've been. At last I understand. I love you Steven, I always have and always will. I really love you and want to spend the rest of my days with you. We've a new home now to start again. I found a nice flat to rent and I've got it all ready for us. Can we make a fresh start?'

'You really mean that, this isn't some cruel joke?'

Laura looked really hurt by this comment. 'You don't really believe I could do that to you?' Not waiting for him to reply she carried on, 'I know I probably deserve that but come on I'll prove it to you.'

Still not sure what was really happening he carried on questioning her, 'But what about your fancy house and all your ambitions?'

'What do they count for in comparison to people? I told you I've come to my senses and realized when there's somebody who really loves me.' Then looking rather sheepish she continued, 'Like you love me, that's what really counts in life. It's worth far more than money and possessions.'

Quietly she went on to ask, 'You still do love me don't you?'

Suddenly she felt as if her ribs were going to be broken as he grabbed hold of her and gave her a hug. 'Of course I do. I've never stopped loving you for one moment.'

'Well then, what are we waiting for, are you coming to look at this flat or not?'

'Lead me on. I'll just follow wherever you go.'

As she drove along, at the same time as

concentrating on the road, she was full of relief that he still wanted her. This was it, this was what life was really about. People and caring, not the amount of possessions she'd collected. She realized what a rich person she really was in having such a loving and caring family. Now there was only one way forward for Laura, to a full life with this wonderful man beside her.

Tentatively she put her hand out into his and felt him give it a squeeze, which seemed to say everything. There were no need for any words to be spoken between them. They at last understood each other totally and were in perfect harmony.